THE CRY OF THE GO-AWAY BIRD

Andrea Eames

WINDSOR
PARAGON

First published 2011
by Harvill Secker
This Large Print edition published 2011
by AudioGO Ltd
by arrangement with
The Random House Group Ltd

Hardcover   ISBN: 978 1 445 85814 2
Softcover   ISBN: 978 1 445 85815 9

British Library Cataloguing in Publication Data available

Printed and bound in Great Britain by
MPG Books Group Limited

THE CRY OF THE GO-AWAY BIRD

PROLOGUE

'Where is it?'

'How should I know?'

'You said you knew.'

'I said I thought it would be a good place to find one.'

The place at the bottom of the garden, over a small hill, where almost nothing grew—only a straggly acacia tree with white thorns, and a few tufts of khaki grass. An old, rusted tap dripped red water into a small pool fringed with weed and dotted with water-boatmen, insects with long, oar-like legs that rowed in jerky strides across the surface. Away from human eyes; quiet; near water. The perfect place for a *tokoloshe*.

'Maybe we have to wait till night-time.' I flopped down in the one scraggy patch of shade that had escaped the glaring sun. It was a hot, humming afternoon, alive with bees and flies, scented with honey and grass seeds.

My cousin Hennie sat on the ground next to me. He looked a bit like a *tokoloshe* himself—small and brown, with white hair like a dandelion clock and feet that were even harder and dirtier than my own. We had competitions where we compared bruises, cuts, blisters and calluses, and Hennie nearly always won.

'I'm not waiting here all day,' he said.

'It'll only be a couple of hours.'

'Where's the food?'

I had liberated five Marie biscuits from the pantry, a little soggy, but still edible, as well as a torch, a map and an apple for the *tokoloshe*. I did not know what they ate—although I had an uncomfortable feeling that it might be children—but I thought an apple might serve as good bait or a helpful distraction.

My nanny, Beauty, had often told me the story of the *tokoloshe* she saw when she was a little girl. One day, when she went to the pump to get water for washing, as she did every day, there was a child-like figure standing there. When it turned around, she saw that it had the face of an old, old man. No eyes; just sockets, scarred and burnt as if someone had gouged them out.

'I was very afraid,' said Beauty. 'But I needed water. It stood there watching me. I thought that perhaps it wanted to drink but did not know how to work the pump. It stepped back and let me pump some water into my bucket, and when I had finished it grabbed my bucket with its monkey hands and took a drink. Then it ran away.'

I had caught glimpses of what could be *tokoloshes* now and then, but never close enough to tell for sure. I wanted to see one for myself, up close.

My cat Archie materialised as soon as he heard the packet of biscuits crinkling. I pulled one out and divided it carefully into three. Archie swallowed his piece in one gulp. Hennie also finished his quickly. I had a special method that involved eating all around the edge again and again until it was gone, and so mine took longer. By the time I had finished, my two followers were drooping again.

'I want some juice.'

'I didn't bring any juice.'

'I'm going back to the kitchen.' Hennie stood up.

I grabbed his hand to stop him. 'You can't.'

Archie strolled over to the kitchen and collapsed on the cool concrete steps outside. A startled lizard shot off the steps and up the wall.

Hennie seemed to resign himself. 'Okay. What do we do now?'

I was not really sure. I had a vague plan of using a stick as a spear and creeping through the undergrowth, but the only sticks were thorny ones and there was no real undergrowth; only a few patches of brittle grass. It was the sneaky kind, that drew its blade along the back of your knees and left red welts.

'We wait,' I said with finality. Hennie looked unimpressed.

'Can we eat the rest of the biscuits?'

I thought about it. 'I suppose so.'

We divided up the biscuits and ate. Then we sat looking at the acacia tree and listening to the slow plonk, plonk of the rusty tap dripping into the puddle.

Hennie started to get grumpy. He got up. 'I'm going home.'

'You can't go home! We haven't found the *tokoloshe* yet.'

But my older cousin authority had lost its power for the day. Hennie stomped off, and I settled down to wait alone.

The sun cooked the top of my head and turned my saliva into thick peanut butter. After what felt like several hours, I wondered if I could go back to the house and get some juice. That felt like cheating, though, and so I stayed, making a little rock garden out of pebbles and twigs. And then I sat for a bit longer.

Mum came to check on me, wearing a stained apron and flip-flops and shielding her eyes from the glare. 'Are you okay? Do you want to come in for some tea?'

She had not heard about the expedition, but was used to my games.

'I can't come in, I'm waiting.'

Mum disappeared, then reappeared with a sandwich and a green plastic cup full of juice. She also brought a hat, which she wedged firmly on to my head. 'What have I told you about wearing a hat?'

'Agh, Mum.'

'It's important. Are you sure you don't want to come inside?'

'Ja.'

'All right then. Don't take the hat off.'

I ate my tea. Time passed. The tap dripped. A persistent fly tried to land on my face. A beetle climbed over my toe. The swift African sunset came: the shadows grew longer, the air cooled and the first mosquito of the evening whined in my ear, followed by an ominous silence when it found a spot of skin on which to feed. I heard the clinking of plates from the kitchen—Mum making dinner— and saw a silhouette at the kitchen window. I sniffled a little, feeling sorry for myself. It was a luxurious sniffle, because I knew that, if I wanted, I could go inside where it was safe and cosy, but I had chosen to stay and fulfil my quest. There was a strange satisfaction in it.

The sun fell away, and it was dark. I clicked on my torch, shone it into the sky and wondered if people in Space could see me. The light made a dusty, pale cone for a few metres and then vanished.

Night-time was noisy in Zimbabwe. Crickets ululated and the mosquitoes droned like faraway aeroplanes. The grass rustled and snapped. As the night grew darker, hunting a *tokoloshe* no longer seemed like a game. I turned off my torch and sat in the dark. A feeling like fear, but not quite, spread from my chest down both of my arms.

Something moved in the acacia tree. I bit my lip, and tasted blood. I stayed very still. Too late, I remembered the apple, still in the bag, that I had saved for the *tokoloshe*. Hennie might as well have eaten it, because I was paralysed and could not get it out.

A pair of round, pale eyes appeared in the tree, watching with ancient cunning. I stared back. I did not know what to do. Was I planning to catch the *tokoloshe*, like Pooh and Piglet setting a trap for the Heffalump? No chance of that. The air seemed to thicken and concentrate itself around that glowing paleness, and I knew that I had made a mistake, that you could not go looking for something if you did not want to find it.

I forced my eyes downwards, away from those of the *tokoloshe*. I heard a low chittering, and then nothing.

I ran to the house. My limbs felt like thick sap, bendy and unreliable. The kitchen light and the moths fizzing and dying around it were the most comforting things I had ever seen.

When I burst into the kitchen, sobbing, Mum asked me if I was all right. I could not explain.

*   *   *

Later, Mum told me that it must have been a bushbaby. 'It's unusual, though,' she said. 'You hardly ever see them up here.'

I had seen bushbabies on the farm before. They had round, yellow eyes that blinked down from trees. But I knew what I had seen. And I knew what I found the next day, under the tree where I saw the *tokoloshe*: a small bundle of herbs, a crow feather and a porcupine quill, tied together. A talisman to ward off evil spirits.

CHAPTER ONE

Beauty's skin was smooth and many-coloured, like the patina on old copper. When I was a baby, I sat with my nose buried in the sweet, meaty smell of her armpit, where it curved to meet her breast. Now, at twelve years old, I sat beside her, legs outstretched, back against the sun-warmed wall. The proper way for a woman to sit.

I listened to a stream of Shona, a language that lingered on long vowels. Each sentence was met by a chorus of women's voices, in agreement or mild horror or quiet amusement.

'Eh-eh.'

'Oh-oh.'

Comfortable, lazy sounds. They had settled in for a long gossip. I could understand most of what they said, but some words stood out like bright pebbles in muddy water. *Amai*: mother, or a term of respect for an older woman. *Mangwanani*: good morning. *Maiwe!*—variously, oh my goodness, you don't say, I can't believe it.

The earth was red and baking, the sun almost invisible in a white-hot sky. I stared at the ground, an endless source of amusement, covered in ants, worms, *chongololos* and beetles. I watched red ants swarm over the body of a rhino beetle stranded on his back, who rocked back and forth in dumb bewilderment until Beauty reached out a hand and flicked him over on to his front. I was torn between happiness at the beetle's redemption and faint disappointment that I could not watch him die.

The women sat around the cooking fire,

1

drinking greasy tea from enamel mugs. Occasionally a man passed by the coven; tall or short, fat or thin, he always wore overalls of thick, scratchy fabric over a bare chest, and usually had no shoes. The women became more subdued when a man passed, only a few daring to laugh at him or call a remark. I knew that black men (apart from the gardener, and other men the family knew personally) were something to be feared, like strange dogs, and I stayed silent. They flicked me quick glances—who was this white kid sitting with the women? I was the whitest of whites, I knew, with freckles and pale eyes that blinked and burned in the sun, but I did not feel white.

I loved to sit with the women in the *khaya*, even though Mum did not approve of me spending too much time there.

'It's dirty,' she said. She was proven right when I came home sick one day after drinking water from the pump, and she made me promise not to go back. I did not feel guilty for breaking that promise, however, because the Elise who sat quietly and did her homework in the white house at the top of the hill was very different from the Elise who played with the workers' children, threw stones at pigeons and helped pluck the chickens for supper.

'You are going back to school soon?' one of the women said in English. Her hair was glistening and oily under her *dhuku*, a brightly coloured tangle of cloth tied over her head.

'She starts Grade Seven next week,' said Beauty, also speaking in English.

'Just one more year, and then to high school!'

She smiled at me. I looked away. I did not want

2

to think about high school just yet.

'Oh-oh.' The other woman said something in Shona that I could not catch.

'We must go now.' Beauty stood up with a great deal of exclaiming and brushing away of dirt and ants.

'Do we have to?' I asked.

'Your *Amai* will be wondering where you are.'

We made our way up the road, passing women who carried their babies in slings on their backs. Little round macadamia-nut faces peeped over their shoulders.

'*Mangwanani*!' the women said as they passed. I imagined the word like a *chongololo*, a black and yellow centipede, unfurling.

The road on the farm was red dust and tyre tracks. Eventually it led to the houses of the farm managers, and huts gave way to whitewashed walls and green lawns. All the other grass, especially in the Bush, was golden brown like baked bread, but the grass by the houses was broad-leaved and squeaky to walk on. Sprinklers sput-sputted along the side of the road, unwinding and spinning backwards with a hiss.

Our house was at the top of the *kopje*, just in front of the Bush, a prickly, dry tangle of thorns, branches and grasses full of buzzing things that bit. Ever since I was little, Beauty had told me that the Bush was also full of spirits. You must not insult the spirits. If you did, they would make you get lost for ever.

When I was small, my uncle had taken me walking in the Bush. He put a red cloth down where we stood. 'We'll see the red cloth and know that this is where we started,' he said. He shook the

3

compass a little and started the needle swinging. 'And the compass makes sure that we know how to get back.'

We walked away from the red cloth, carrying our rucksacks. After a while, I grew hot and tired. There was nowhere to sit. A fly buzzed around me, trying to land on my eyeball.

'Bluddy flies,' said Uncle Pieter. I wondered if this counted as insulting the Bush. 'We'll go back now.'

We turned around and followed the compass. After a few minutes Uncle Pieter began to look worried. We could not be very far from the house, but it was impossible to tell—every part of the Bush looked exactly the same.

I asked if we were lost.

'No, no,' said my uncle.

The spirits were mischievous and quick to take offence. I did not know how to appease them. The Bush suddenly looked malicious, and the light was fading. I blinked, and through the film of tears saw a sharp face winking from a tree. I looked again, and it was gone. I did not know if I had imagined it.

'Ah, here it is,' said Uncle Pieter. He reached up and took the red handkerchief down from a branch. 'I wonder how it got up there.'

I knew how, but did not say anything in case the *tokoloshes* were listening.

I had lived on the farm all my life, in the little house on top of the *kopje*, and I knew all the best ways to spend my time. Spotting an antlion's tiny burrow in the red soil, and mimicking the footsteps of an ant with a slender twig. Watching the antlion emerge in an avalanche of dust, pounce on the

4

stick, then disappear beneath the surface, disappointed.

Finding a chameleon on a branch and letting it walk along your hand, feeling its scaly feet loop and scrape along your fingers like Velcro. Spending half an hour with a sharp rock and a concrete slab, trying to break open a macadamia nut. Catching black beetles and keeping them in an old ice-cream tub with some grass and a bottle-cap of water.

'Be careful,' Mum always said.

I knew that we were not welcome here. Too many things could kill us: snakes, leopards, hippos, hyenas, charging elephants, spiders. Potential death or pain in every step. Even the plants were out to get us. Walking barefoot, I grew hard and crusty soles on my feet to protect against acacia thorns lurking on the ground. Every expedition outside was accompanied by insect repellent, sunscreen, a hat and calamine lotion, and Mum eternally dabbed things on me, pulled out splinters or bee stings and slapped on plasters. A day did not pass without a cut or bruise.

My mother, however, was someone I saw in the mornings and at night, and for some parts of the weekends: it was Beauty who made me breakfast, Beauty who walked with me to school every day, Beauty who was waiting for me at the gates when the final bell rang. Beauty heard all my stories about the teachers and the other kids. Beauty put plasters on my knees when I grazed them, and promised not to tell Mum that I had not eaten my apple again.

Beauty had come to live with us when my dad died, which was before I can remember. Dad had

5

worked with Uncle Pieter on the farm, and when he died, we stayed there.

'Shall we go and get a Penny Cool?' asked Beauty.

Penny Cools were little tubes of flavoured ice in a plastic bag. I liked to bite a hole in the top, squish them in my hands until the ice warmed up and melted a little, and then squeeze the slush out through the hole.

The village shop was full of colourful things: Freddo Frog bars; white Milko chocolate; Mazoe orange juice; cream soda; fake cigarettes made from sugar and food colouring; real cigarettes; Coke; a lost chicken chased out by a broom. The man behind the counter wore blue overalls and was missing a tooth.

'Would you like a wem?' he asked.

'A wem?'

'A jelly wem,' he explained.

'Oh, a worm!' I said, over-pronouncing the word. 'Yes please.'

The man did not seem to mind my arrogance. He opened a jar and pulled out a long, multicoloured strand of gelatine. 'Here is your wem.'

'Thank you,' I said.

'No, no.' The man cupped his hands together and clapped them with a hollow clock clock sound. 'You must say *mazvita tatenda*.'

I copied his movement. '*Mazvita tatenda*.' Two words both meaning 'thank you'.

'Why don't you just say one word?' I had often wondered this.

'Because you are very grateful for the free wem.'

When we got home, there were visitors on the

stoep. There were always visitors.

Chinhoyi was a small town where everybody knew everybody. People were always coming up to me and pinching my cheek, or patting me on the head, because they knew my parents. They had names like Hennie and Nicky and Marie, but I had to call them all 'Auntie' or 'Uncle', even though they were not related to me at all. The men wore shorts and long socks like Uncle Pieter, and they had hairy legs. The women had sunglasses pushed back on the top of their heads.

There was always some new gossip. When people came over they drank gin and tonics in short glasses and complained about their servants, who always seemed to be stealing or doing something stupid.

'Did you hear about Hendrik?'

'*Ja*, his houseboy took off with their safe, hey.'

'Typical bluddy *munt*.'

'He had worked for them for years, apparently. It just goes to show . . .'

'You can't trust them.' Someone stubbed out a cigarette. Everyone was smoking, and the ashtray overflowed.

'It's his own fault for putting temptation in their way.'

'*Ja*, no, hey.'

'*Ja*, no, hey' was a long way of saying 'yes' or 'no'. If you meant 'yes' you nodded your head and raised your eyebrows. If you meant 'no' you said the 'no' part louder and shook your head.

Everyone agreed that Hendrik was too soft with his servants. If you were too soft and sweet, you were snapped up like a fat buck by a crocodile.

'Those bluddy *munts*. If we hadn't come here

7

they would still be killing each other.'

They were always saying things like this. Or they said that the blacks would still be slashing and burning, there would be no land for farming, there would be no water, hospitals, roads, schools. But all this didn't matter. You could not win.

'They should be bluddy grateful.'

I knew from listening to the adults that black people were like children, but also that they were cunning and not to be trusted. I knew that they did all the jobs like packing bags at the supermarket and driving buses. There were lots of them, like busy worker ants scurrying about around spilled juice on the kitchen floor. Adults said that it was hard to tell them apart unless you knew them personally. Women were always 'girls' and men were always 'boys', no matter how old they were. White men and women were 'Baas' and 'Medem'.

The whites were special, somehow. They did the important jobs; had nicer clothes and bigger houses. You never saw a poor white person. I thought that we must have done something to earn all these nice things. It made sense.

CHAPTER TWO

Beauty smelled like Vaseline and Sunlight Soap in the mornings, and, as the day went on, she started to smell of fresh sweat and cooking fires as well. She had taught me a song about five green frogs many years ago, and we sang it together as she did the washing up or polished silver on newspaper sheets laid out on the lawn.

8

'Five green frogs
Five green frogs
(The word 'frogs' must be shouted)
Where can they be?
Where can they be?
(Here you shaded your eyes with one hand and
looked around)
Hiding away
Hiding away
Hiding away
From me!'

Beauty had also taught me how to count to ten
in Shona. I said the numbers over and over until I
could recite them without thinking. *'Poshi piri tatu
china shanu tanatu nomwe sere pfumbamwe gumi.'*
Years later, I still said the words to myself just for
the pleasure of their sounds and the way they felt
in my mouth. I learned a strange mixture of
English and Shona words that had the farm
workers cackling with delight when I visited them.

Beauty told me about totems. *'Mitupo* are the
animal spirits that protect the family,' she said. She
was polishing the floors, which always put her in a
contemplative mood. I sat on a rag, legs crossed, so
as not to spoil her work with footprints. 'My totem
is the buffalo. Like the buffalo, I am strong.'

'Does it also mean you are fat like a buffalo?'

Beauty took a swipe at me with the duster.
'Don't be cheeky.'

'What's my animal?'

Beauty sat back on her haunches. 'I do not know
if you have one.'

'A cat?'

9

'Why not?' She clicked her tongue and got back to her work. 'Remember, it is unlucky to kill your totem animal.'

'I'm not going to kill a cat.' I remembered a dead kitten I had found on the farm—one of the wild ones. There were farm cats that lived in the barns and gave birth to endless litters of tiny tabby kittens. This one had not survived. When I found it, it was partly eaten away by maggots, its body falling apart into sandy crumbs when I poked it with a stick. It exerted a horrible fascination over me and I went back to visit it every day until it disappeared—either removed by one of the farm workers or carried off by some animal.

'Still, you remember,' said Beauty, and I nodded. It felt like a solemn vow.

On the weekends, Beauty dressed in white robes and went to meetings. She did not talk about where she went, but I knew it was to some kind of church. When we were driving to our church on Sundays, I saw big groups of people, all in white, standing under trees and singing. It looked a lot more exciting than our church, where we had to stand up, sit down and kneel as if we were playing a big game of Simon Says. I asked Beauty if her church was like that. She pursed her lips.

'It is not exactly like yours.'

'What do you do?'

'We sing, and we praise God.'

'Why?'

'Because we are grateful.'

'What for?'

'Everything.'

Beauty wore a cross around her neck. Sometimes I thought it was strange that she wore a cross and carried a talisman at the same time. I asked her about it and Beauty explained that, although she worshipped God and Jesus, she also had to be careful of the spirits and make sure to keep her ancestors happy. When I told this to Mum, she shook her head and smiled, but did not say anything.

Mum had been behaving oddly lately. She had changed her perfume from something light and flowery, like the pot-pourri in our bathroom, to something smokier. It smelled good, but dangerous.

She had also started cooking in the evenings. Usually Beauty made one of the five things we ate during the week: meatloaf, roast chicken, spaghetti Bolognese, sausage and mash, and, on glorious Fridays, *sadza*, white and stodgy as mashed potatoes, and relish which I could eat with my hands.

Now, however, Mum started to make curries—yellow ones, with swollen raisins floating in them.

'What's this?' I asked, pushing at it with my fork. The raisins wobbled.

'Chicken tikka masala,' said Mum.

I gave Archie my plate to lick after dinner, but he did not like it either.

'Elise,' said Mum. I looked up. Mum only used my name when I was in trouble—otherwise it was Treasure or Darling or nothing at all.

'*Ja?*'

'Do you miss your dad?'

I thought about it. He had been dead for so long and I was so young when he died that his death was really only a way to garner sympathy. I felt guilty for not being sadder. 'No, not really.'

11

Mum touched my hair. 'I thought so,' she said.

*   *   *

Soon after that, I went with Beauty to consult the *N'anga*, the witch doctor. Someone in her family was very sick and she thought they had been cursed. I was sworn to secrecy.

'Why is your aunt cursed?' I asked with great interest.

'Shush.'

'Did she do something bad?'

'*Kwete.*' No.

'But why would someone . . .'

'Shush! It is not lucky for you to speak of these things.'

A worrying thought occurred to me. 'Could I be cursed? If I go to visit him?'

'I do not think so.'

'Why not?'

'I do not think our curses work on white people.'

'Oh.' I thought about this. 'What if a white person cursed me?'

'White people do not have magic like this.'

I felt insulted. 'We might have.'

'No.' Firmly. 'Now we have to go. Stay quiet, hey?'

I followed Beauty to a part of the workers' compound to which I had never ventured before. No grass or flowers here, just red dirt. People stood in front of their houses sweeping the ground until all the grass had gone and it was all red and dusty. Uncle Pieter called these people Sweepers.

'Now there is a Red-breasted Sweeper,' he would say, pointing out of the car window to a man

12

in a red shirt. 'It is a shy and retiring specimen.'

In this part of the farm, there were more Sweepers than I could count. There were also thin dogs with their ribs showing and their tails down, and *piccanins* in shorts and colourful shirts. They looked at me curiously as I walked beside Beauty.

'Hello! Hello! How are you?' they shouted, showing off their English. I glanced at them, secure in my position as a Baas's daughter, and said nothing.

We passed a shebeen, a drinking hall. There were a few men outside, sitting on the edge of the stoep and drinking Chibuku Scud—a sweet beer that came in big plastic tubs. I had persuaded the gardener to let me have a sip once, and it tasted like milky sweetcorn and batteries.

Beyond the tin-roofed houses I could see huts. The walls were made of earth, and the roofs were thatched.

'The *N'anga* lives here,' said Beauty. She looked nervous. 'You must be quiet, you hear?'

I nodded. There was a sign outside, written in blue paint on a white-washed stone. Two words, and a number.

'What does it say, Beauty?'

Beauty had her High School Certificate and liked to show off her learning.

'NGANGA. WITCH DOCTOR. 122.'

'What does the number mean?'

'It is his address.'

Of course. I followed Beauty as she walked up to the hut door and knocked.

'*Gogogoi.*' Meaning 'knock, knock,' like the jokes.

The *N'anga* was a younger man than I had

13

expected. From a distance he had always looked stooped and old, but up close his face was only slightly lined. He wore a mangy, feathered headdress, one feather sticking out at a rakish angle over his ear, and a leopard skin was draped across his shoulders. It was smelly and looked dusty, but I knew that to wear a leopard skin was a sign of great power; the leopard was an important animal that produced potent *muti*, and this particular leopard had been an old man-eater that had killed a three-year-old boy. When the hunters caught and killed it, they brought it to the *N'anga*, who cut its heart out and ate it in front of the whole village. It imbued him with power.

'Come, come, come.' The *N'anga*'s speech was fast. 'Come inside, sister.' He saw me and said something in Shona that I did not catch. Beauty replied, and started to usher me outside to wait for her, but the witch doctor grabbed my arm.

'No, no, she must come in.' He grinned, showing a gold tooth. His hand felt dry and scaly and his palm was bright pink.

Beauty looked worried, but did not contradict him. 'You stay with me,' she hissed.

I was delighted. The opportunity to see inside a *N'anga*'s hut was too good to pass up.

It was very clean. The floor was swept and there was a small pit for a cooking fire. There was a tidy pile of bones in one corner of the room, and I positioned myself with my back to it.

'Now, how can I help?' The witch doctor spoke in English rather than Shona, giving me a sidelong glance from one yellow eye. Showing off.

Beauty told him the story of her aunt: how she had suddenly become sick, was coughing and

14

covered in sweat, getting thinner and thinner.

The *N'anga* nodded gravely. 'She has indeed been cursed,' he said. 'It is because of something your ancestors did. But I can help.'

He picked up a handful of stones and chips of bone, muttered something and threw them on the ground. He spent a while staring at them while we waited. Then he heaved himself to his feet, straightened his loincloth and wandered over to the shelves. He selected a jar of something orange and powdered. 'You must give this to her to mix in water and drink,' he said. 'I will also make spells for you tonight and tomorrow night, asking for the curse to be lifted.'

'Thank you, *N'anga*,' said Beauty respectfully. She clapped her cupped hands together in the traditional gesture of a woman receiving something from a man. I watched as she gave him a bundle of crumpled notes. I could see it was a lot of money.

'And you,' he said, ruffling my hair with his scaly hand. 'You are well behaved?'

'Yes,' I said. 'Sir,' I added.

'Good, good.' He brought down a little plastic bag of brown powder.

'This is for you.'

'For me?' I glanced at Beauty uncertainly.

'You must drink this. Will make you grow up strong.' He passed it to Beauty, who hesitated and then took it.

'What is it?' I asked.

The witch doctor bent down until his face was only inches from mine. I could feel his spit land on my nose, but didn't dare move. 'You have misfortune following you,' he whispered. 'I can see

15

the eyes of your ancestors behind you, and they have told me.'

My eyes were dry. I realised I had not blinked. 'Why?' I asked.

Beauty put her hand on my shoulder. 'We must go, *N'anga.*'

'Something has happened to you,' the *N'anga* said, still staring at me. 'You have been marked.'

'Elise.' Beauty looked worried. 'It is time to go home.'

The witch doctor seemed taller, his eyeballs like egg yolks in his dark-leather face. He was grinning. The relentless hum of the crickets outside sawed and screeched at my ears. I blinked, and when I opened my eyes again the room seemed lighter and I could hear the birds above the crickets' song.

'Drink the powder,' said the *N'anga*. He patted me on the head. 'It will make you strong.'

Beauty tugged at my arm. 'Come along.'

We left the *N'anga*'s hut with both our little packets.

'*Fambai zvakanaka*,' he said as we walked away. 'Go well.' It was what you said to someone going on a journey.

'Beauty,' I said as we walked away, 'Can I carry my medicine?'

'No,' she said curtly.

'Why not?'

'I told you. Black people's medicine does not work for white people.'

'But it's mine!'

'Shush.'

'He said I was cursed.'

'He did not say that. He said he saw misfortune behind you.'

16

'Same thing.' I reached for the packet, but Beauty held it out of reach.

'The *N'anga* is old. He does not know what he is saying.'

'Okay.' I stuck my hands in my pockets and kicked at a stone. I would persuade Beauty to give it to me later, I thought.

Before I could form a plan, however, Beauty took out the packet of powder and opened it. She shook it out. A fine brown film floated down to the red dust of the road and was lost.

'Beauty!'

'This medicine is not good for whites,' said Beauty. Her mouth was set in a straight line. 'Come along.'

'But what about the evil spirits?' I asked.

Beauty reached into the pocket of her uniform and pulled out a little bundle. I could see feathers, twigs and leaves, tied together with twine. A talisman. 'This keeps you safe from *tokoloshes*. Or *ngozi*.'

I had never heard of *ngozi*. 'What are those?'

'Ghosts who are looking for revenge.' Beauty put the bundle back into her pocket.

'Can I have one too?'

'I will make you one.'

I thought about the visit to the witch doctor. He was nothing like the white people's doctor, who was a very old man with a white coat and a jar of sweets on his desk. The white doctor did not believe in spirits.

'They're dropping like flies,' he said, 'and they blame it on spirits, or curses, and go to the bluddy witch doctor. All they need is a packet of condoms.'

17

I had seen condoms before, on the side of the road. Beauty always tutted and turned her head away when we saw one.

I asked Beauty if her aunt was getting better.

'I think she will, when we give her the *muti*.'

For a while I wondered who was better, the doctor or the *N'anga*. The *N'anga* was undoubtedly much more interesting to visit, but in the end I decided that maybe the doctor and the *N'anga* were both right. When I had an earache or a runny nose, the doctor fixed it, but as far as I knew he could not do anything about the evil spirits. And I knew they existed. Even Mum believed in them.

*   *   *

When we got home, Mum was fizzing with excitement.

'Beauty, where have you been? It's getting late.'

'Sorry Medem.'

'Never mind, it doesn't matter. Come on, Elise.' She hurried me into a bath and clean clothes.

'Where are we going?'

'We're going to visit a friend.'

'Who?'

'Just someone I want you to meet.'

Mum drove us to a neighbouring farm. I had not been there before, but I knew it belonged to one of Uncle Pieter's friends. Hennie went there sometimes to shoot pigeons.

'Where are we going?'

'I told you, we're nearly there.'

'Why won't you tell me?'

'It's a surprise.' Mum turned to smile at me. 'Just be patient.'

18

I slumped in my seat and watched the sky change colour.

'Here we are.' Mum pulled up outside a house. A man was waiting on the stoep.

'Who's that?'

'Steve,' said Mum. 'One of the farm managers. Come on.'

We got out of the car, and the man started towards us. I recognised him—he had been to our house before. He was blond and tall, with red skin on his face and a beard like all the men had.

'This is Steve,' said Mum.

I had never called an adult by his first name before. Everyone was Mr and Mrs This or Auntie and Uncle That. I decided to avoid calling him anything. 'Hello.'

'Hello, Elise,' he said. His accent was thick, with clipped and flattened vowels. He reached out a hand, and I shook it. 'Come in.'

His house was small and brown, with brown furniture and brown curtains and black-and-white pictures on the wall.

'So,' said Steve. 'Elise.'

I sat.

'How are you getting on at school?

The maid brought out tea. I cupped mine in both hands. 'Good,' I said. I saw Mum glaring at me and added, 'Thanks.'

'Do you have any plans for high school yet?'

Why did adults always ask this? School was something I endured for six hours before I escaped back to the farm and Beauty. I knew that I might have to go to boarding school next year, but I tried not to think about it.

'Not really,' I said. I swallowed a mouthful of

tea. It was hot, and too sweet. Mum and Steve talked for a while. I sat, letting my mind drift, and watched the way Mum put a hand on Steve's arm when she laughed.

There was a head above the television—a little buck with big eyes. 'What's that?' I asked, interrupting.

Mum sighed, but Steve leaned forward. 'A Blue Duiker.'

The duiker looked at me with melting plastic eyes. 'Did you kill it?'

'No, a fella gave it to me when I was working on a game farm,' he said.

I touched the duiker's head. I had expected its fur to be soft, but it was bristly and hard like the brush Beauty used for scrubbing floors.

'Don't . . .' said Steve, but Mum shushed him. I drew my hand away.

'Sorry.'

We drank our tea. Mum and Steve sat close together. Their arms were resting on the couch, side by side, but not quite touching.

'Steve might be visiting us more often now,' said Mum.

She and Steve were both staring at me as I drank. It made it hard to swallow.

'All right,' I said, and I watched them exchange glances. The Blue Duiker on the wall gazed at me mournfully, as if it knew a secret that I was yet to find out.

CHAPTER THREE

This is what happened the day we found a snake in the garden.

I was playing with Archie next to the compost heap when I saw leaves and grass start to slip and move, as if someone were moving the garden hose, but the hose was not there. I screamed 'Snake!' and Mum came running to grab me by the arm and Archie by the scruff. Maxwell the gardener ran up with a big spade. Inside, behind the big French doors, Mum had her arms around me as we watched the gardener circle the snake, holding his spade. There was a sharp movement. Maxwell darted forward and crunched the metal edge into the ground. Then the snake reared up, high as Maxwell's waist. Its head was gone, leaving a big red hole ringed with white. It stayed there for a minute and then dropped down.

Dreaming of snakes was a sign of trouble ahead, Beauty said. That night I saw snakes as tall as buildings, and ran through them trying to reach something on the other side. I did not tell Beauty about my dream, afraid of what she might say.

The day after the snake was killed, we drove to Uncle Pieter's farmstead, down a long dirt road that made the car hop from wheel to wheel. Sometimes I was allowed to sit in the back of the *bakkie* and watch the wake of sand kicked up by the wheels. More often, however, I sat inside, to keep my clothes from getting dusty. On hot days my legs stuck to the leather seats and felt like raw chicken getting slowly cooked. We could not wind the windows down because of the sand and the bugs, and the *bakkie* did not have air-conditioning.

On this day, however, I was allowed to sit in the back. I watched the groups of farm workers walking along the road. They had been strolling in the middle, but moved to the side with good-natured smiles and shouts when the *bakkie* caught up to them.

Hennie and I had invented a game called 'Sweet and Sour' that we played in the back of the truck: we waved at someone, and if they waved back they were sweet, and if they did not they were sour. I waved at a worker now, and he chased the *bakkie* for a while, grinning, before falling behind.

The farmstead was down a long driveway, lined with thin, whispery gums, sharp-scented like medicine. On the other side of the driveway was a row of long, low chicken sheds. They smelled of feathers and must and they made a racket.

The house was right at the end of the driveway, behind tall gates that were kept closed for the dogs. There were three dogs—two big and one small. Phineas ran to the gate when we arrived, waved and grinned as we drove through, then ran after the dogs, who always escaped when the gate was opened.

Auntie Mary was waiting in the doorway. 'The weary travellers!' she said. She always said this when we arrived, even though we only lived down the road. Auntie Mary joked about everything, even Phineas. He was the garden boy, and he stole from the farm all the time. She called him the Trinepon Man. Trinepon was something sticky Uncle Pieter used to fix things in his workshop, and Phineas's hands were so sticky that things

22

stuck to them and would not come off—things like tools, small change and food.

She hugged Mum. Mum's shoulders looked bony and small. 'How are you?'

Mum replied with something, but I could not hear her. I walked into the kitchen, flanked by dogs.

'Hi Hennie.' He was hovering in the doorway, carrying his BB gun over one shoulder—he had probably been out shooting pigeons on the farm. He was already taller than me, although he was a year younger. He wandered in, dragging his feet on the floor.

'Walk properly,' said Auntie Mary. His white-blond hair was standing on end, and she patted it down.

'Mum!'

'Shush, stand still.'

Hennie rolled his eyes at me as his hair was flattened. She finished and pushed him away. 'Put that gun down. Do you two want to ride the horses?'

There was something artificial about the way she said this. Mum slid her eyes away.

'*Ja*, okay,' said Hennie.

'I'm happy here,' I said.

'No, no,' said Mum. 'It's a lovely day, you don't want to waste it inside. Go with Hennie.'

'But the worker hasn't brought the horses round yet.'

'I know,' said Auntie Mary with that same brittle tone. 'Why don't you help your uncle feed the chickens while you're waiting? He's over at the hen house.'

'Agh, *nie*, Mum,' said Hennie. 'The hen house

23

stinks.'

Auntie Mary clapped him across the back of the head. 'So do you. Go on.'

Mum and Auntie Mary had their heads close together, talking. I looked over my shoulder at them as we left the room.

Uncle Pieter was a big beard in the sky, on top of a pair of hairy legs in *vellies*, sturdy boots made from rawhide. His voice was so loud that we heard him long before we arrived at the hen house.

'Why are you two coming to *shuper* me?' he asked when we arrived. 'Haven't you got anything better to do?'

'Mum asked us to help you feed the chickens.'

'Agh, all right then.' Uncle Pieter winked at me with one leathery eyelid. I knew he was deliberately gruff with us—it was his way of joking—but I was still a little nervous of him. A piece of biltong hung permanently from his mouth, and he chewed on it all day. As far as I knew, it was always the same piece of biltong.

The workers tipped out trays of tiny, incubated chicks on to the shed floor. They were sweet and fluffy, but there were hundreds of them running around, and the cheeps echoed off the corrugated iron roof and hurt my ears.

'Shit!' said Uncle Pieter when he opened the door to the chicken run. He called over one of the workers.

He told us to stay where we were. I did not move forwards, but I could see what he was pointing at— a mess of feathers, gloopy chicken poo and blood, right against the wall of the run.

'*Nyoka, nyoka, nyoka,*' the worker said, over and over. Snake.

24

It was probably still in the hut somewhere, or just outside the wall. Snakes do not run away after they have fed; they sit with their eyes half-closed and rest until they get hungry again.

The chickens clustered in the far corner. They seemed quite unconcerned, slapping about on their scaly feet and pecking at the ground. Uncle Pieter took us out of the building. Looking back, I saw that chicks were already pecking at the remains of the dead one.

'We'll just ride the horses today, *ja*?' said Uncle Pieter. 'Don't worry about the snake. We'll get it.'

His hand was heavy when he rested it on my shoulder. It was not comfortable, but I did not want to move away because I knew he was being kind.

The horses had arrived—or, rather, one of them had. 'The only one I could catch, Baas,' said the worker.

Uncle Pieter helped me into the saddle. I could feel the hot metal of the stirrup through the thin rubber and the horse's hair on my bare legs was hot and gritty. I patted its neck and watched a little cloud of dust rise.

I wanted to ride by myself, but Uncle Pieter hefted Hennie up in front of me. He was warm and heavy, and his hair tickled my chin.

'Move back,' he complained, wriggling his bottom on the saddle.

'I can't move back.' I pushed him forwards slightly. We jostled until we reached something approaching comfort. Uncle Pieter slapped the horse's rump and said something in Shona to the worker, and we started to amble around the garden.

'Can we go out on to the farm?' I asked.

The worker grinned. 'All right, Medem.'

He led us out of the gate and on to the white road, thick with creamy dust. We passed fields of cows, flicking their tails lazily to keep off the permanent cloud of flies.

I had been thinking. 'Do you think something's up, Hennie?'

'Like what?' Hennie was not someone who picked up on nuances.

'I thought Mum wanted to talk to Auntie about something.'

'Probably.' Hennie shrugged. 'Probably woman stuff.'

'I'm a woman.'

He snorted. '*Ja*, sure.'

'Mum says I'm a young woman.'

'Nah. Although you do have boobies.'

'I do not.'

'You do too.'

My boobies were the bane of my existence, two little nubs that made it uncomfortable to sleep on my front and stopped me from running around without a shirt on in the hot weather. It was very unfair. Hennie made a move as if to grab them and tweak the nipples. He had done that before, and it hurt. As there was clearly no point asking Hennie any more questions, I pinched him instead.

When we got back to the house, Mum and Auntie Mary were sitting on the verandah.

Mum's napkin was in tatters in her lap and she was twisting a little piece around her finger.

'Did you have a good ride?' she asked as we ran up. 'I have some exciting news.'

I glanced at my aunt, but all I could see was a

26

fixed smile.

'We are moving to Harare.'

I blinked. 'Harare?' The capital. I had never been there. 'Why?'

'I've got a job there,' said Mum.

'In Harare?'

'It's a wonderful opportunity,' said Auntie Mary. 'You'll like it there, Elise.'

My face felt hot and fat, as if it had been stung by bees. It took some effort to move my tongue. 'When did you get the job?'

'Well, Steve got a job first,' said Mum. 'You remember Steve.'

I stared at her.

'On a farm.' Mum was smiling. 'And he wants us to go with him. There's a house ready and waiting for us. It's very exciting.'

Hennie was standing on one leg beside me, saying nothing.

'Sit down and eat your lunch,' said Auntie Mary.

I could not talk to Mum during lunch. When she spoke to me, I felt my face numbing into a mask as I mumbled back. My hands seemed twice as big as normal, as if I were wearing big, fleshy oven gloves. I could not touch her at all without feeling my body straining away in the opposite direction, and when I asked her a question I had to remember to raise my voice at the end and not speak the whole thing in a monotone.

As soon as we got into the car, I started screaming. 'You can't just change everything without telling me!'

'Well, things have changed,' said Mum.

'What things? What am I supposed to do in Harare?'

Mum snorted a laugh. 'The same things you do here. Go to school, play with your friends.' She had a glow about her, like someone with a secret.

'What about Beauty? She has a family here! You can't just ask her to leave everything behind.'

'Beauty is staying.'

On car trips, Mum and I played a game where Mum drove over bumps at high speed so that we could get that floating, empty feeling in our stomachs. I felt that now.

'We can't leave Beauty behind.'

'This is her home, Elise,' said Mum. 'She is happy here.'

'She wouldn't be happy here without me,' I said, and I truly believed it.

'Elise.' Mum took a hand off the wheel and held it out as if to clasp mine, but I hung back. 'You can't be selfish about this. We can't ask Beauty to pack up everything and move to Harare.'

'Why not? She would like Harare.'

'Elise.' That was her No Arguments voice.

There was a short silence.

'When are we going?'

'This weekend.'

I felt as if I had swallowed a lump of something hard and bitter that stuck in my throat. I leaned my head against the hot glass of the car window, wanting it to hurt and burn.

'I hate you,' I said.

'You don't mean that.' Mum leaned over me, and I shrank back. I inhaled her familiar, flowery perfume for a second, and heard a click.

'Seatbelt,' said Mum, who had buckled me in. The seatbelt was too tight across my chest, but I could not loosen it.

I clung to Beauty for the next few days as if I were a baby again. If I could, I would have climbed up on her back and sat there as I used to do. I followed her around as she did all her chores and did not help Mum pack any boxes. Mum did it all herself, kneeling and lifting and sweating in the heat that wrapped around us all like clingfilm, while the cat slunk anxiously through the clouds of newspaper and sellotape.

'Everything that happens, happens because it is meant to,' said Beauty. I shook my head and rested it against her warm shoulder. I could not believe that this was happening for a reason. What possible good could come of it?

On the final evening, Beauty came round to collect her last pay cheque, and to say her goodbyes. I launched myself towards her.

'Elise.' Mum's cold hand closed on my arm, then released me. I buried my nose in the meat of Beauty's arm and inhaled her smell. Vaseline, cooking fires, fresh sweat, something pungent and herbal. Her skin was as familiar to me as my own.

'*Fambai zvakanaka*,' Beauty said.

'I will write,' I said.

'I will write too,' said Beauty. I had seen her labouring over letters before, painstakingly forming the words in blue biro on sheets torn out of an exercise book.

'Elise.' Mum stood in the doorway. 'Beauty has to get home. It's getting dark.'

Beauty tied her *dhuku* over her head. It was white and crisp, fresh every day and smelled of

29

ironing. It flattened the wiry hair on her head and made her look nondescript, like every other maid and nanny walking home. I could see them outside, coming out of the farm managers' houses, starting their walk down the *kopje* to the farm village. Their voices floated up to me in strings of long, rounded vowels and shrieks of laughter.

'*Chisarai*, Beauty,' I said.

'*Chisarai*,' she said, and 'Goodbye, Medem' to Mum. She reached into the pocket of her uniform and pulled out a little bundle of herbs and feathers. 'I said I would make you one,' she said. 'It will protect you from the evil spirits. Better than *muti*.'

I took the bundle, still warm from her hands.

'*Fambai zvakanaka*,' she said again. And she was gone.

'Now we have to start looking again,' said Mum when the door was shut. 'Bluddy nuisance. And in Harare! God knows what servants are like up there.'

'Is that all you care about?' I said.

'Elise, try and see this from my point of view, won't you? You need to be grown-up about this.'

'No, I don't.'

'She was a good servant, Elise, but she couldn't have stayed with us forever.'

'Beauty is my real Mum,' I said. I watched Mum's face melt and dissolve, and I felt nothing but fierce joy that I had hurt her. She was in her dressing gown. The sleeves were too short for her and her bony elbows poked out. I pushed her out of the way, feeling soft flannel and skin under my hands, and ran out of the back door.

'Elise!' I heard her calling.

I sat in the long grass, crouched down so low that I could barely see over the top, and watched the sun going down. The smell of the earth changed from freshly baked bread to something darker, more mineral. A fine spray of dew settled around my shoulders. When the final ray of the sun flared once, briefly, like a match being lit, darkness drenched the hills and I said goodbye. Only in my head—there was no need to be soft.

'Elise!' Mum called again. I unfolded my limbs with difficulty and walked back to the house. I came inside, still smelling of night, and buried my face in Mum's dressing gown, smearing it with snot and tears. It smelled of fresh laundry and the remnants of her perfume, like dying flowers. It felt like a betrayal.

CHAPTER FOUR

The removal men jumped down from their van.

'Morning Baas, Medem.'

Mum and Steve had laid most of the furniture out on the lawn, to make it easier.

Archie sat in one of the armchairs, washing, as if he had not even noticed that the walls and ceiling were gone.

The removal men carried the pieces of furniture into the van one by one. Mum winced when they banged the edge of the sofa against the van door, but they were cheerful and laughing. There was also much hilarity when they almost dropped one of the beds.

'I can't watch.' Mum went inside.

I stood in the driveway. It seemed obscene that all the pieces of our lives could fit into one van. I knew better. We were taking all the best bits, and leaving behind a rubbish tip of stuff, things we could not take to Harare. All the toys I had lost in the garden over the years. The hair clips I had dropped behind the dressing table. Cat hair in the carpet. The tiny body of a pet bird buried in a shoebox at the bottom of the garden. Carved initials on the trees, fingerprints on the walls and footprints on the wooden floor. The endless memorabilia and detritus of two lives lived in one house.

Steve loaded some of the smaller boxes into Mum's car. It was a grey, very old *bakkie*, called Grandpa Elephant by the farm workers, and the doors had a habit of falling off.

'Do you want to ride with us?' asked Mum. She had crammed Archie into his cat cage and a supplicating paw poked its way through the mesh.

'You can go with the removal men if you like,' said Steve. He stretched his teeth over his lips in what was meant to be a grin. He was trying to make friends.

I did not answer, but went to the van and jumped up next to the driver in the front cab of the truck. The seat was disembowelled leather, leaking stuffing, and it was hot and sticky. The top of the gearstick was rubbed smooth by years of sweaty hands. 'Is there a seatbelt?' I asked the driver.

'Ah-ah, no,' he said cheerfully. 'She does not work. Do this.' He showed me how to hold the broken middle seatbelt so that it looked like it was fastened ('in case we are stopped by *mapurisa*'). The other removal man slammed shut the van's sliding door, then jumped in the cabin. The whole truck shook.

'Okay,' said the driver, and started the van. It was hot and noisy, and juddered like an old washing machine. I looked in the rear-view mirror and saw Mum and Steve getting into the car to follow. I slumped in my seat.

'Is it far?' I asked.

'*Ja*, about two hours,' said the driver. He negotiated the gate with hardly any room to spare. A branch squeaked and scraped against the roof.

The other man turned on the radio. Crackling static, and then Shona music, sunshiny and jangling with mbiras and drums. They started to sing along. I stared out of the window at my secret places. The corner where I had hunted the *tokoloshe*. The macadamia tree, a favourite home of chameleons. We passed my aunt and uncle's house.

Hennie was standing at the gate with the dogs, waving.

The removal man in the passenger seat waved back with enthusiasm.

'Is that your friend?'

I nodded.

'Aren't you going to wave at him?'

By now we had passed the gate. I craned my neck to look in the rear-view mirror. I could see Hennie mouthing 'Sour!' and smiling.

The yellow grass and bush of the farm was almost white in the early-morning light, and the sun was a red *naartjie* in the sky.

Farm gave way to long dirt road, then smooth tarmac again and town. The Farmers Co-op, where Uncle Pieter bought his flour and seed. The corner shop where I had bought Freddo Frogs and jelly

33

wems. My school.

Every time we turned a corner, the whole van lurched sideways. I could hear furniture sliding about in the back, and an occasional bang.

'Is everything okay?' I asked.

'She is fine,' said the driver. He was still singing lustily.

I closed my eyes and leaned back in my seat, falling into an uneasy doze. In a half-dream, I saw the hut of the *N'anga*. He was standing outside, watching the road, and raised a hand.

I awoke from my sleep. We were passing through the dykes now—round, brown hills studded with dark green scrub and acacia trees. The removal van juddered over the bumps, then followed a winding trail downhill. My stomach developed a hollow, furry feeling that I recognised.

'*Pamusoroi.*'

The driver was humming, and his companion was asleep.

'*Pamusoroi*! Excuse me!'

I poked the driver with a finger.

'What?'

'I feel sick.'

He pulled over to the side of the road, and parked on the long, dry grass. More bangs from the back of the van. Mum and Steve pulled over behind.

'What's wrong?' Mum asked the driver.

'Ah, this one she is sick.'

Mum made me sit in the open doorway of the car with my head down.

'Take deep breaths,' said Steve.

I turned my body away from him and crossed my arms. I watched bugs crawl around the toes of my

34

flip-flops, and inhaled the rusty smell of the ground. The air sizzled above the car bonnet.

'Feel better?' asked Mum. I nodded.

'*Ja.*'

'Right. Come and ride with me.'

'Got a bit of a dodgy tummy, hey?' said Steve when he got into the car. I ignored him.

'It's that crazy driver, taking corners like he's trying to win a bluddy race,' said Mum.

I felt the car-sickness start up again as soon as we drove off, but did not say anything. I just rolled the window down and leaned my head against the frame. Anything to keep the car moving and avoid talking. Through half-closed eyes I could see Mum and Steve holding hands on the gearstick.

I must have slept again, because when I looked up we were on a big main road next to a yellow bus bulging with people. The roof of the bus strained under suitcases and crates, strapped down by rope, and chickens squawked and fussed in a cage.

'Where are we?' I asked Mum. My mouth felt sticky.

'The outskirts of Harare,' she said.

I saw brown blobs ahead that I thought were huts in a village. When they came closer, however, I saw they were rows and rows of shacks made from cardboard and corrugated iron. Scraps of washing fluttered from makeshift lines. One shack had a television aerial.

'Shantytown,' said Mum.

I sank my chin on to my chest and crossed my arms. Harare means 'he does not sleep'. It was much bigger than Chinhoyi, and there was no sign of the Bush anywhere.

We drove through the centre of town, down

Samora Machel Avenue. The street was wide enough for six lanes of cars, lined with purple jacarandas and red flamboyant trees—and beggars. There had been a few in Chinhoyi, but I had never seen so many all in one place before. Every pavement we passed was divided into two invisible lanes: one for the pedestrians and one for the people sitting against the walls with cups held out. People in suits—black people and white people—marched past the beggars without looking at them. Whenever we stopped at a traffic light, half a dozen street kids clamoured around the car.

'Money for bread! Money for bread!' one of them yelled. He was about nine years old and skinny. The whites of his eyes were milky and mottled.

Mum wound up the window right in his face, and we sat in the hot, smelly air of the car watching the street kids mouth silently outside.

'Can't we give him some money, Mum?' I asked.

'No.'

'But he wants to buy food.'

'No, he doesn't.'

'What does he want to buy, then?'

'Glue,' said Mum, and put her sunglasses on. I saw her reflection in the window; bland and faceless behind the glasses. It floated like a pale ghost in front of the crowd of street kids.

The lights went green and Mum sped up. I looked back and saw the kid shaking his fist at us.

The sound of a siren spiralled from behind us. Mum pulled over, and the car bumped up on to the grass verge.

'It's Bob and the Wailers,' said Steve.

Three motorbikes with sirens went past, then a

36

big black car with dark windows.

And another. And another. There were nine in all, with little flags on the bonnets.

'Who is Bob?' I asked Steve, after a few moments of silence. I suspected him of enticing me into talking, but I was too curious not to ask.

'President Mugabe.'

'Was he in that car?'

'*Ja.*' Steve looked grim.

I could not believe it. I had just seen the president drive past. Something this exciting would never have happened in Chinhoyi.

'What happens if you don't get out of the way?'

'Everyone gets out of the way.'

'But what happens if you don't?'

'Everyone does.'

'Can I wave at them?'

'No!' Mum grabbed my hand before I could move it. 'Never do that.'

I rubbed my wrist. I was only going to play the 'Sweet and Sour' game. Even the guards at the farm had found it funny. 'Why not?'

'Just don't.'

Harare seemed to leave many questions unanswered. Mum switched the indicator on, and we pulled out into the traffic again.

City gave way to suburbs. Everything was very green. Gardeners moved on the verges, mowing lawns or watering.

We had been driving for so long that my stomach felt hollow and I did not know whether I felt hungry or sick, or both. I could still smell the sandwiches and bananas that Mum had brought for lunch. The odour had soaked into all the upholstery and it infected the scent of hot leather with a cloying ripeness.

Suburbs gave way to countryside. White buildings became smaller and smaller, then vanished entirely. The grass grew from short and green to long and yellow. The sky widened and deepened. Soon we were in a deep bowl of a valley, yellow studded with brown bushes and the occasional flat-top acacia. Aeroplanes winked white in the sun and cut a sluice through the high, brushed-out clouds.

'Airport is nearby,' said Steve, twisting around slightly in his seat. I had been staring at the back of his neck for most of the drive and it was disconcerting to suddenly see his face again. I looked out of the window and did not reply.

We passed under a white arch with a tail like a fish's. 'Independence Day April 1980' was carved at the top.

'Nearly there,' said Mum.

Pools of sweat had collected under my bare legs, but I almost enjoyed feeling uncomfortable. After all, if I was never going to be happy again, what would be the point of shifting position or putting my head out of the window to catch a breeze? If this was going to be hell on earth, I might as well start hating it now.

The car skipped over stones and rutted tyre tracks. After about ten minutes, we pulled up at an iron gate and a black man in uniform came out. He and Steve had a short, jovial conversation, and the gate was opened. The man in uniform gave the car a playful smack with his truncheon as it went through.

'We're here,' said Mum.

I looked over my shoulder. There was a sign on

38

the gate: 'Cooper Farms.'

Someone had scrawled a Shona phrase over it in red paint. I did not know what it meant.

The earth was a different colour from Chinhoyi—white and powdery rather than sandy, as if someone had emptied a vat of talcum powder. I had never thought that even the soil would be unfamiliar. I rested my forehead against the window. Sky, yellow grass and electric fences streamed past; three ribbons of colour above the road. A dead, furry something that I did not look at too closely. A small group of women walking in slow, stately steps with bags of mealie-meal and flour piled high on their heads. A herd of cattle, and a skinny *piccanin* flicking a switch at their flanks and kicking at stones.

I saw dark green fields and rolled down the window. The air smelled almost like cigarettes, but fresher, sweeter, a heady smell. The plants were waxy and poisonous-looking, and men in overalls waded in slow motion between the rows.

'What's that?'

'Tobacco. It's a tobacco farm,' said Mum.

There was something menacing about the blade-like leaves. I saw a white man standing in the fields, knee-deep in tobacco. He shaded his eyes as we passed, watching the car, and I felt a flicker of foreboding.

The car came to a halt. 'Out you hop,' said Mum. I peeled myself off the seat. Now that there was no longer a breeze from the car's movement, it was like stepping out into an oven.

'Your new home,' said Steve, shading his eyes from the sun. He put a hand on my shoulder, and I twitched my skin like a horse ridding itself of a fly.

39

'Elise,' said Mum.

I ignored her, and turned to look at the new house. It was whitewashed, sitting low to the ground, with that blank, bare expression that empty houses have. The lawn was green and lush, scattered with tiny thorn plants. The farm belonged to the Cooper family—a father and his teenage son.

'You'll like them,' said Mum.

I shrugged. I was helping to carry boxes from the car, but still refusing to speak unless absolutely necessary.

'You will. The boy is only three years older than you.'

'Okay.' That would make him sixteen, intimidating, and not a potential playmate. 'What's Mr Cooper's wife like?'

'His wife?'

'*Ja.*'

'He doesn't have a wife.'

'But . . .'

'Oh, he did, but she died,' said Mum. 'A while ago. It's just him and the boy now.'

'Do you know what . . .'

'No.' She gave me a sharp look. 'And don't ask.'

'I wouldn't ask!'

'Okay, just don't, all right?'

I lifted Archie's cat box out of the car. It was almost impossible to see him, a black cat in a dark box, but if I squinted I could see two panicked eyes peering at me.

'Don't let him out just yet,' said Mum. 'He'll run away.'

I opened the door. Archie crept out, his belly almost touching the ground. His paws touched the strange soil and he sniffed in disgust.

'Fine, it's your own bluddy fault if he goes missing,' said Mum.

Archie turned right around and scooted back into his box. I did not blame him.

'You going to sit there all evening?' said Mum. I did not reply, and after a moment she turned and went into the house. I crouched down next to Archie, and inhaled the unfamiliar air. I heard the loerie, the Go-Away Bird, calling from a tree. I could hear Mum and Steve laughing inside, and although the sun had not yet set, I felt cold.

CHAPTER FIVE

Mum and Steve started work the next day. Steve was going to manage a section of the farm and Mum was going to do the accounts. Mum took me to the office with her on the first day.

'Can't I stay here?'

'And do what? Sulk in your room?'

I had not even been out into the garden.

'I don't want to come.'

'Tough *takkies*.'

We had toast for breakfast. I remembered the porridge Beauty used to make for me every morning, and the remembering was like an ache.

We drove to the farm offices after breakfast, Mum talking brightly all the time. 'You can help me with the filing or something. Be a good way to earn some extra pocket money, hey?'

I made a noise that could mean yes or no.

'Here we are.' Mum turned into a dirt road. It

41

was wide and rutted with lorry and tractor tracks. A buck stood at the edge, giving us a bright, accusing stare before disappearing into the yellow-brown scrub. We drove past one of the workers' compounds. A Sweeper was busy outside and a crowd of children in red and brown T-shirts jumped up and down and waved.

'How are you? How are you?' they shouted and collapsed in giggles.

'They don't know my car yet,' said Mum. 'They think I'm a visitor. They'll get to know us soon, hey?'

In the rear-view mirror, I could see the black kids dancing in the dust from the wheels.

Mum pulled up to a row of low, whitewashed buildings. 'These are the offices,' she said as she turned off the engine. Her cheeks were pink.

There were long runs covered in chicken wire next to the office. 'What are those?'

'The baby ostriches,' said Mum. 'Mr Cooper keeps ostriches as well as the tobacco.'

I got out to investigate the ostrich pens.

'I'll be inside when you're done,' said Mum. She took a big keyring out of her bag and opened the door.

The ostriches were divided into age groups: a row of incubators, a pen of fluffy chicks, a pen of slightly less fluffy and taller chicks, and then the gangly, moulting teenagers. They smelled of feathers and greasy excrement. I sat with my back against the wall and watched them watching me through the chicken wire.

Mum came out with a Coke. 'Don't you want to take a look around?' she asked.

'No.'

42

'You'll have to eventually.'

'No I won't.'

Mum rolled her eyes and disappeared inside again.

Since it was the school holidays, Mum took me to work with her every day that week to help with filing and addressing envelopes. I did not mind as much as I pretended to. It was something to do, at least, and it took my mind off Beauty and Chinhoyi—and school, which I would be starting soon.

'Could you get me a Diet Coke from the fridge, treasure?' Mum asked when we took a break.

I went to the fridge. 'Mum?' A bloody heap of feathers. And a pot of yoghurt. 'Mum!'

Mum came over. 'Bluddy yell.'

'What are those?' I saw more details; bits of skin, scaly feet, veined eyelids stretched over bulging eyes.

'Baby ostriches,' said Mum. 'They died in the pens. Jeans said he was going to get rid of them . . .'

'I suppose he needs to keep them cool,' I said, 'until he moves them.'

'I suppose so.'

We stared at the fridge in silence for a while.

'Shut the door,' she said eventually. 'No, wait, grab us a couple of Cokes first.'

I lifted out two cans.

'Cheers.' Mum flicked the can open. It made a sound like kissing. We drank.

*   *   *

The next day I came to the farm office, I noticed a complicated contraption of ropes and pulleys, on a

43

little platform.

'When did they put that up?' I asked Mum.

'Just this morning.'

We watched. A group of men approached, dragging a cart behind them.

Something big and brown was slumped on it. I watched in interest as they lifted it off at the little platform. Then in horror as they started to hook it up.

'Mum!'

'What?' Mum came over to the window and watched.

'Well, that explains that,' she said.

The men had big cleavers. We turned away from the window, but could not stop the hot, metallic smell of blood from creeping in. The cow's head lolled from its shoulders, its eyeballs dusty and unseeing.

'Maybe I'll ask if my office can be moved,' said Mum.

I felt sick, but strangely thrilled. I remembered the time Uncle Pieter had killed a kudu and brought it back to hang in the room next to the workshop. Hennie and I sat watching the blood drip from its neck for hours, fascinated, as it bubbled pink and pulsing from the vein to flush itself down a drain in the middle of the floor. The doors were shut to keep the dogs out and the light was dim and eerie.

We stayed there all afternoon. I could still see the red- ness of it, like bright flowers blooming on the concrete floor, or the juice from a pomegranate squeezed too hard in a fist.

The new farm smelled all wrong. There was the same sharp, medicinal scent of eucalyptus trees

44

and the warm stench of manure, but mingled with those were the foreign, feathery smell of ostriches, the sweet nicotine scent of the tobacco and something else that I could not identify, but which was clearly Not Home.

Mum and Steve were different here, too. Sometimes I heard Mum giggling, and I saw Steve's hand creep down Mum's back. Sometimes they shut their door in the middle of the afternoon to take a nap, and no matter how much I knocked on it or how much noise I made they would not open it. Mum stopped wearing pyjamas to bed and started wearing silky things with lace around the hem.

I missed Beauty. It felt like hunger pangs in my stomach. We did not have any servants yet, and it felt strange. The house was too quiet. There was no Beauty, no Maxwell, no Hennie, no aunt and uncle and no workers to sit with. Just me.

Archie was my ally in this. For the first week he stayed indoors, under the bed, with only an angry tail-tip emerging.

*   *   *

I put up with Steve for a while, because I secretly thought we would go back to Chinhoyi. After a few weeks, though, I realised we were not going anywhere and that Steve was going to be living with us for ever. I started to be less polite to him. I did not like the way he was always touching Mum, and the way she ignored me when he was whispering into her ear.

'Elise,' he said one day, 'You need to snap out of it, man. This sulking isn't fair on your mother.'

45

'I'm not sulking.'

'*Ja,* you are. And it's time to stop it.'

I flew into a rage. 'You can't tell me what to do! You're not my dad! You're not anyone!'

Steve flushed. 'Shut up!'

'No! I hate you both!'

'You don't mean that.'

'I want to go home!'

He grabbed my wrist to hold me still and smacked me hard, as if I were a little kid. He missed my bottom on the first try because I was wriggling, and caught me on the back and the arm before finally landing a hit. Three of those, and then he let me go and I ran out of the front door. I heard him yelling at me to come back.

We did not talk about it, and I did not tell Mum. I did try to run away, however.

I had a vague idea of hitchhiking a lift back to Chinhoyi somehow. Not with a white, obviously, because they would bring me straight home, but I thought I could bum a lift off an emergency taxi driver if I pretended I had money. I knew even as I set off, carrying a backpack, that it was a stupid idea, but I had to prove to myself that Chinhoyi was still there—that it had not disappeared when we had left, that Beauty and Hennie and the house still existed.

I made it to the outer fences of the farm, just before the airport road. The security guard was not at his post at the farm gate, but a group of black men were sitting on the storm drains, holding their tubs of Chibuku between their knees. They started to laugh as I approached. One said something in Shona, too quickly for me to catch.

'Come and sit on my knee,' said another, and

46

sniggered. I hesitated in the gateway.

'*Voertsek*,' I said. It was one of the rudest ways to tell someone to get lost—the word used for shooing dogs and chasing kids off your property.

'*Iwe*! What was that?' The smile dropped off the man's face. 'You think you clever, white girl?'

I shoved my hands in my pockets. I was suddenly very aware of my pink *takkies* and the flower embroidery on my jeans. I looked like a little girl. A little rich white girl.

'Hey, come here,' said the man.

I backed away and bumped into something warm.

'*Maiwe*!' The guard had come up behind me. He was zipping up the fly of his trousers, and smelled suspiciously of something sharp.

'What's going on here?'

The men laughed and turned back to their Chibuku. One waved his hand in a dismissive gesture.

'What are you doing out here?' he asked again. He was carrying a paperback book with a pirate and a girl with long hair on the cover. I did not reply, but he saw my rucksack. 'It is not a good idea to go wandering by yourself.'

He had a round, open face and a bushbaby's unblinking eyes. It was difficult to imagine him being a guard or intimidating anyone.

'I'm going for a walk,' I lied. I moved back inside the gates, and he followed.

He stuck out a hand. 'I am Cephas.'

I took it. He had the usual Shona handshake, a gentle brush with the palm.

'Elise.'

'You are going back home now?'

47

I shrugged.

He swayed back and forth on his heels, looking down at me. Then he asked, 'Would you like to hear some of my book?'

I blinked.

'It is a good one.' Cephas was painfully eager. He pulled his chair out from the guard hut and sat down.

'All right.'

He unfolded it so that I could see the cover more clearly. The man I thought was a pirate was actually just a bare-chested man with a sword and long hair tied in a ponytail. He held the woman in his arms and the pair stood on the deck of a ship in a stormy sea. They did not seem too worried about the storm, however, because they were kissing.

The book smelled a bit funny, as if it had been wet and then dried out. He moved his hand across the page and I noticed he was missing a finger.

'What happened to your finger?' I asked.

He blew air out through his mouth. 'I got in a fight.'

'With who?'

'I do not remember. It was at the shebeen.' He acted out the story. 'I have drunk a lot of Chibuku and I am saying things. Then this man, he come up to me and say, stop talking all this rubbish. I say no, and he take me outside and hit me with a *bhadza*.'

I could see how the skin of his finger stub had puckered. It looked like a little pursed mouth.

Cephas laughed at the memory. 'It came off . . .' he made a popping sound with one finger in his cheek, 'and I go back into the shebeen and my friend says, what are you doing? You are bleeding

48

all over the floor. Then I remember and I go to the hospital.'

'What did the hospital do?'

'They put a bandage on for me. I had lost the finger, so they could not sew it back on.'

I imagined a finger lying on the ground outside the shebeen, where anyone could pick it up.

'Do you want to hear this story?' Cephas asked. He opened to the bookmark that marked his place. I sat cross-legged in the dust, shading my eyes from the sun.

Cephas ran a finger along the lines as he read, and read slowly. His accent was very strong and I started to feel sleepy in the sun. I leaned my head back against the creosoted wood of the guard hut, inhaling its petrol scent. His voice was soothing.

I heard the familiar rumble of Steve's car and opened my eyes. Cephas jumped up to open the gate.

'What are you doing here?' asked Steve.

'I came to talk to . . .' I hesitated.

'Cephas,' the guard supplied.

'Well, come on,' said Steve. He leaned over the back seats and unlocked a door.

'You come and talk to me anytime,' said Cephas. 'I have lots of books.'

CHAPTER SIX

The new farm seduced me, despite my efforts. I was not stupid or rebellious enough to go behind the electric fences into the game farm portion of the property, but there was plenty to explore on this side. There were the ostrich pens, where the birds stood like enormous feather dusters, swaying their long, soft necks down to blink at me with ridiculous lashes.

There were the tobacco fields, lush and wickedly green, where I would pull off a leaf or two to chew as I walked. There were the workers' villages, swept to dustbowls by the industrious Sweepers, where I could join in with a game of football that quickly became impossible in the dustcloud and heat haze.

I only tried joining the adults' circle once. I saw some people sitting in a little open space between the huts, around a cooking fire, and I went to join them. I recognised a skinny old woman who worked in the farm clinic, the gardener who did all the common areas, and the fat woman who worked next door.

They were talking, but they stopped when they saw me. 'Eh-eh!' said one in surprise. 'What is that one doing here?'

I stopped and stood on one leg, uncertain.

'*Voertsek*!' one of the maids shouted, and shooed me with her hands.

I was acutely aware of my whiteness. I backed away. 'Sorry, sorry.' I had a feeling that Beauty would be disappointed in me. Why, I was not sure.

I still had not met Mr Cooper. I heard stories about him, though, from the farm workers, and from Cephas.

'He has eyes in the back of his head,' said Cephas. 'He always knows what is going on.'

I asked Mum about him.

'He's a nice man,' she said. 'Busy, though, always on the move.'

A couple of weeks after we moved in, however, Mum told me that Mr Cooper wanted to meet me.

'He's invited us for lunch.'

'Do I have to go?'

'*Ja*. Mr Cooper's given us jobs and a place to live. You're coming to meet him. No arguments.'

'He won't care if I come or not.'

'I said, no arguments.'

*   *   *

We pulled up outside a heavy iron gate with spikes, set in a big wall with broken glass on the top. Mum stopped the car a little too far away, which forced her to open her door and lean right out to press the intercom. A red light flashed, and the gate began to rumble open along little tracks.

The car crunched up the gravel driveway and parked. The house was enormous, with elaborate Dutch gables on the roof and a wide sweep of verandah running its whitewashed length.

'There he is,' said Mum.

Mr Cooper. I did not know why all farmers stood like that, but they did—legs apart, hands in their pockets or on their hips, thrusting their pelvises slightly forwards. He had a baseball cap on, so I could not see his face at first. This was unusual. Most farmers wore broad-brimmed golf hats gone floppy at the edges with age and hard wear. He was also wearing a leather jacket rubbed thin and fibrous at the elbows, despite the heat. I recognised him—he was the figure I had seen in the tobacco fields when we arrived.

'Oh, hi!' said Mum in an artificial voice. She wiggled her fingers at Mr Cooper as if she had

51

spotted a friend across a crowded café, rather than her new boss. She had her phone voice on, which is how I knew straight away that Mr Cooper must be good-looking. She was wearing her nice sandals, the ones with the gold braid, and her hair was done. She ducked her head as she got out of the car so as not to squish the curls.

'Howzit,' said Mr Cooper. He was a tall, spare man, with dark hair greying in silver spiders at the temples, wearing a collared shirt. I knew that under his socks he would have a farmer's tan—pale shins giving way to red-brown knees the colour of soil. He kissed Mum on the cheek. 'Good to see you. And this must be Elise?'

We shook hands. His was covered in interesting calluses. He asked all the usual questions adults ask. What's your name? How old are you? *Ja*? Good, good.

The maid opened the front door for us.

'Come in, come in,' said Mr Cooper. 'Tea?'

I wiped my feet carefully and climbed the steps to the front door.

'You have a beautiful house,' Mum said. This was an understatement. The floors were polished wood, so smooth and shining that they looked like pools of dark water. Ceiling fans turned lazily, stirring the hot, soupy air.

There was a stop-and-start flurry of polite conversation. Hello, hello hello, long drive, hot, tea? Yes, please. And juice for me. I did not know how anyone could drink tea when it was so hot outside. The white walls grew brighter and more dazzling and spots danced in front of my face. A maid appeared, yes Baas yes Baas. Disappeared. My head felt full of liquid, sloshing about behind my eyes.

'Are you all right?' said Mum.

I told her about the sloshing head, and they both burst out in relieved concern. Sit down, have a drink, put your head between your knees. Hot day, too hot.

They nodded. I had broken the ice, which was all very well but my head hurt. After a few minutes we were sitting down, I had finished my juice and my head was starting to feel better. When I looked up, the walls did not seem as bright.

The maid came in with a tray, which she put down on the coffee table. It was silver, bright and polished, and so was the teapot and milk jug. She gave me a smile. She had sad eyes, but a sweet face.

'Thank you, Mercy,' said Mr Cooper.

Mercy bobbed her head and went back to the kitchen, where I could hear her clinking dishes and running taps. I wanted to go with her and sit on the cool tiles and watch her legs moving about. I wondered if Mercy had any children. I heard her call to someone out the window, and the familiar musical sounds reminded me of Beauty. I realised that Mum was trying to get my attention.

'I'm going to the powder-room,' said Mum, who had never called a bathroom a powder-room in her life. 'You stay here with Mr Cooper.'

Mr Cooper and I sat for a moment in sudden, loud silence. I stared at the bobbles on the carpet. He leaned forwards in his chair and rested his elbows on his knees.

He sucked some air into his cheeks and blew it out. After a moment, he spoke. 'I was in the army with your father.'

'My father?' I sat up.

'*Ja*. Your mother and I talked about it. He was a bluddy good guy.'

There were guns and swords all over the walls and on a table there was a black stone bust of a man wearing an army uniform.

'That's me. A fellah who sold sculptures on the side of the road did it for me. From a photograph.'

Mr Cooper lit a cigarette and its smell filled the room. Something like manure, a sweet, brown smell. I sniffed.

'It's good for you,' he said. The cigarette scooted to the corner of his mouth when he talked and wagged up and down. 'Stops you getting colds.'

I looked around the room. There were rows of animal heads on the wall, looking down at us with frozen expressions of surprise. There was also a long, carved stick balanced on two hooks.

'What's that?' I asked.

'That?' Mr Cooper followed my gaze. 'Oh.' He stood and lifted it down.

'Here, take a look.'

I traced the carving on the stick—a monster that looked like a snake, curling around and around the stick and baring its fangs on the top. It was surrounded by tiny people carrying food on their heads.

'That is the Nyaminyami.'

'Nyaminyami.' The word stuck my tongue and the roof of my mouth together.

'What's that?'

'The River God of Lake Kariba.'

'What does the Nyaminyami do?'

'He protects the river.' Mr Cooper settled back in his chair. 'When the whites came to the Zambezi

River they decided to build a dam on it, so that they could use the water to make electricity. Nyaminyami, so the people say, didn't approve of the dam because it harnessed his power. When the whites had almost finished building the dam, Nyaminyami struck with terrible floods. The waters washed away the partly built dam and killed many of the workers.'

I touched my finger to the tiny wooden fangs.

'Some of the dead workers were white people and their bodies disappeared into the river. The whites called the local tribesmen to help them search for the bodies. The *N'anga* of the tribe explained that Nyaminyami was keeping them until a sacrifice was made.'

This seemed only fair. I was familiar with the eye-for-an-eye philosophy of most of the local gods.

'The whites brought a calf to the river bank, slaughtered it and pushed it out into the river. Three days later, the bodies of the missing white men appeared where the calf had been sacrificed.'

'Did they ever finish building the dam?'

'They did, but only after years of flooding and destruction.'

'So we've beaten Nyaminyami.'

Mr Cooper paused. 'The whites like to think they have tamed Nyaminyami. They fought with him for ten years to build the dam. But I do not think he is tamed. I think he is waiting.'

'Waiting for what?'

'For his opportunity.'

Mum came back into the room, smiling brightly. Mr Cooper heaved himself to his feet.

'Would you both like to see the garden?'

The garden was full of trees. Mr Cooper listed them as we walked: banana, avocado, macadamia and pecan nut, Australian cherry, lemon, acacia and flamboyant. All whites had nice gardens, but this one was different. The colours clashed. Spiky, aggressive plants were flanked by low mists of ground cover and frills of flowers. The air smelled sweet, like decay, and the hum of insects was almost deafening. I strained to hear Mr Cooper's voice over it.

'I like it,' said Mum. I was not sure. It scared me a little.

'All the gardener's work,' said Mr Cooper. 'He worked for my father, too—been here longer than I have. The man's a genius when it comes to planting. He's never had any proper teaching, it's all instinct.'

Mr Cooper had chickens in a pen at the end of the garden. They were fat, with dusty feathers and comfortable broad backs.

'Can I pick them up?' I asked. Mum gave me a look, but I ignored it.

'If you can catch them.'

I reached out for one of the chickens. It flounced away, but slowly, and I managed to catch hold of it. Once I had it firmly under one arm it did not struggle, but swivelled its old-lady neck to blink at me.

'Now what are you planning to do with it?' said Mr Cooper. He and Mum chuckled. I felt my face grow hot. I put the hen back down, and it fluffed itself out before rejoining its friends.

'Help me collect the eggs,' said Mr Cooper.

There were beds of straw at the back of the hen house, and there was a special roof on hinges that

56

lifted up. When Mr Cooper lifted it, I saw one egg in each bed, two in some. They were warm and round, with little bits of feather sticking to them. I held one on my palm, and it felt like a stone that had been warmed in the sun.

The door to the chicken run creaked, and something moved to block the light. A tall black man with hollow cheeks and wide, staring eyes. He looked like a picture of a prophet from the Bible. I stepped back involuntarily.

'Ah, Jonah.' Mr Cooper continued, unhurriedly collecting the eggs. 'This is my gardener, the one I was telling you about.'

'Baas,' he said and I saw he was carrying a bucket of chicken feed. It clonked against the gate frame as he moved through.

'That's Jonah,' said Mr Cooper as we left carrying the eggs. 'Married to Mercy. They live in the *khaya*.'

I could see it, beyond the vegetable garden; a little, grubby building surrounded by a fence. We started back to the house.

'Jonah has been with the family for years,' said Mr Cooper. 'Started work as a houseboy, and then when he grew up my father made him the gardener. Bluddy good guy, for an Aff.'

I looked over my shoulder. Jonah was standing perfectly still, watching us. I turned back quickly.

'Quiet,' said Mr Cooper. 'A good man, though. Very loyal.'

I was looking around at the garden and so did not see what I was walking into until it was too late. There was a sickening crunch, and a feeling of softness under my foot. Something hard pierced the rubber of my flip-flops.

'Damn.' Mr Cooper leaned down to look at what I had stepped in. It was a crow—a very dead one. Under my foot, its chest caved in and leaked sluggish blood.

Ants were already marching to its dusty eyeballs.

'Are you all right?' Mr Cooper asked. He examined my shoe. The bird's beak had pierced the sole of the flip-flop. 'Don't worry—it doesn't bite,' he said, laughing at his own joke. He pulled out the beak and held the shoe at the ends of his fingers. 'We'll take this to Mercy and get it cleaned up. You'll just have to hop to the kitchen. Think you can manage that?'

I nodded.

'Jonah!'

The gardener came over.

'Bird fell down again.'

There was a rope attached to both the scaly feet of the crow. Jonah picked up the end of the rope and it revolved slowly, its toes curled and tangled together as if it were turning an upside-down pirouette.

'Put it back up, will you?' asked Mr Cooper. Jonah nodded and started towards the shed.

'Why?' I asked. I felt a bit sick.

'Why what? Oh, the crow? Well, those things are a damned nuisance.' Mr Cooper looked up into the branches of the pecan nut tree. Half a dozen crows had settled there, looking down with blank yellow eyes. 'They punch a hole in the nut with their beaks . . . look, here's one.' Mr Cooper stooped and picked up a pecan nut. It had a neat round hole in its side. Some of the meat was missing, but there was still a great deal left.

As I watched, an ant popped its head out of the

58

hole and then disappeared again.

'They don't even eat the whole thing.' Mr Cooper shook his head. 'So, every so often, Jonah will shoot one and hang it in the tree.'

Looking over my shoulder, I could see Jonah up a stepladder, reattaching the bird to the branches. It fixed me with a dead glare.

'Kill one, and the others will go away,' said Mr Cooper.

CHAPTER SEVEN

By the end of the week, I was very bored. No Hennie, no Beauty. Just me.

'Jonah's girls are back from school for the weekend,' said Mr Cooper. 'She might like to go and play with them.'

Mum nodded, but Steve looked uncertain. 'I'm not sure it would be appropriate . . .'

'Nonsense.' Mr Cooper was brisk.

And so I met the two girls. Their names were Jane and Susan.

'When Mercy first fell pregnant,' said Mr Cooper, 'Jonah was going to name the baby after me. Unfortunately, when it popped out, it turned out to be a girl. He asked me to suggest a name and I told him the most English name I could think of. Susan. Same thing happened with the second one.'

When I found the girls, they were playing Tag around the vegetable garden. They were pretty, with long hands and feet, and small, neatly shaped heads with close-cropped hair.

I felt colourless next to them.

They stopped their game and waited for me to say something.

'Hello.'

We stood for a minute. I felt a fly land on my arm, then take off again.

'Would you like to see our house?' asked Susan.

'Yes.'

*   *   *

The *khaya* smelled like cooking fires. 'Is this it?'

'*Ja.*'

I could stand at the front door and see the whole house. There was only one bedroom, with a big bed and a mattress on the floor. Some cut-out pictures from magazines were taped to the walls. Next to it was a small bathroom with a concrete floor, a toilet, and a showerhead sticking out of the wall. The only other room was a kitchen with a big stone sink, a stove, a table and some chairs.

'It's so small,' I said.

Susan was surprised. 'This is a nice house. You should see some others.'

'They are very bad,' said Jane.

'Oh.' Nice houses to me had pools and big gardens.

I could see a Barbie doll on the mattress. Its hair was fuzzy. 'Do you all sleep in one room?' I asked.

'Yes.' Susan looked a bit uncomfortable.

'What about when you want to get dressed?'

'We get dressed in the bedroom.'

'But . . .' I saw that Susan did not want to answer any more questions. 'All right.'

There was a small noise from behind me. Susan

spun round, looking guilty.

Jonah was in the doorway, his skin blue-black in the dim light. 'She should not be here.'

'But *Baba* . . .'

'She should not be here.'

He looked straight at me.'Go home.'

Later, I realised I could have argued that, technically, he did not own his house. Mr Cooper did. And I was allowed to play anywhere I liked. But Jonah's staring eyes scared me, and so I ran.

'Will you come again?' whispered Susan before I left.

'I think so.'

*   *   *

We started looking for new servants. Somehow the word got out before we officially announced it—'Jungle drums,' said Steve—and applicants came to our door.

We liked Saru at once. She was a round, cosy woman with a big smile and a wide repertoire of recipes. Our new gardener was a young man from the Eastern Highlands who had come to Harare to make his fortune. His name was Tatenda, and he was a goatherd.

'You realise we don't have any goats,' said Steve.

'Yes, Baas.'

He was bright-eyed and smiling, and very new to city life. He told us about the nice man he'd met who said he would get him a driver's licence without the need to take the test. Tatenda gave the man money and his identification, and the man disappeared, 'to get the licence'. Tatenda waited for hours, but the man did not return. 'He must have got lost,' he said.

Steve and Mum exchanged glances.

After we hired both Saru and Tatenda, Steve hung a sign on the gate: '*Hapana Basa*'. No work. Signs we saw all around town those days.

I still had a couple of weeks of freedom before school started.

'Mr Cooper asked if you wanted to do him a favour and earn a bit of pocket money,' Mum said.

I paused. 'All right. What is it?'

'He wants someone to walk the dogs during the day.'

'How many dogs?'

'Three. Five dollars per walk.'

'All right.'

'*Ja*? So you might as well start today. You know how to get to the Big House?

Mr Cooper's grass was thick-bladed and felt like plastic, clean and squeaky. I felt as if I would have to take off my shoes before I walked on it. There was a kidney-shaped pool in front of the verandah that shone blue, with glitterstone tiles that winked up through the water. A servant stood at the edge, dragging a net through the water to gather all the leaves, insects and scorpions. He was an old man with a beard and hooded eyes, and he stared beyond the pool into the far distance as he swept the water. I wondered what he was thinking about.

'What are you doing here?'

I jumped. It was Jonah, standing behind me, leaning on a spade.

'Medem,' he said, touching an imaginary cap.

'I've come to walk the dogs,' I said. 'Where are they?'

Jonah said nothing, but turned and led me

around the back of the house. The dogs were delighted to see me, leaping up so much that it was almost impossible to attach their leads to their collars.

'Thank you,' I said to Jonah when I left. He did not even turn around.

The Coopers had three dogs—a big Labrador called Shumba, a schnauzer called Sergeant and a Rhodesian Ridgeback called Ian, after Ian Smith.

Mum told me that Mr Cooper's parents were Afrikaners who left after Independence. Mr Cooper stayed on to work in the new Zimbabwe. There were different kinds of whites: the Afrikaans, the British whites, and the Rhodies. Most Afrikaans lived in South Africa and spoke their own language, but some of them had moved to Zimbabwe, hoping that it might treat them better. We were British whites, originally. When I saw my first map of Zimbabwe, I realised that it was shaped like a teapot and I imagined it filling up with all the cups of tea the British whites drink every day. Rhodies were white people who lived in Rhodesia before it became Zimbabwe and wanted to go back to the Old Days. They knew the words to 'Rhodesians Never Die' and they leaned back in chairs and talked about the Bluddy Banana Republic and drank big glasses of gin and tonic. Poor whites were something else again. They had straggly hair and strange clothes. It was strange seeing white people begging for money or offering to wash your car windscreen. We kept our eyes turned away from them.

It was more fun than I imagined, walking the three dogs. They did not need to be on leashes, really—they knew the farm far better than I did.

The farm kids kept their distance from me when I was with the dogs, but followed in a fascinated and giggling crowd. The soft slap of their soles on the dirt road and muffled, half-fearful laughter was always in the background of our walks.

In the second week of my dog-walking duties, Jonah let me in the gates of the farmstead. I avoided his eye, as usual, and concentrated on patting the dogs.

'They *shuper* me too much,' he said.

The dogs jumped all over me, more excited than usual. 'What's wrong with them?' I asked.

'The Small Baas is back from school,' said Jonah.

'Mr Cooper's son?'

'*Hongu.*'

I was eager to get away. I did not want to bump into the farmer's son.

'Come on, boys.'

Shumba dropped a ball at my feet. It was caked in grass clippings and old saliva—the traditional start to a never-ending game of fetch.

We set off along the dirt roads. As usual, I collected a few followers at each worker compound I passed—black kids in shorts and bare feet, who clapped their hands at the dogs and grinned at me. By the time I reached Mum's offices, I had a parade of about twenty kids following me, and an impromptu soccer game had started up on the dusty road.

'Good grief,' said Mum, looking past me. 'Do you want a drink?'

'Yes please, and for the dogs.'

We poured cloudy tap water into bowls for the dogs, and they lapped it up with loose, lolling tongues.

I was bending over, filling up the water bowls, when I heard the gulping roar of a motorbike behind me. Mr Cooper? I turned around and shaded my eyes.

'Howzit,' said a voice.

'Hi.'

'I'm Sean.'

I squinted. Once he had taken off his helmet, I could see that he had brown skin and yellow-grass hair that flopped in front of his eyes. He seemed adult-sized, but I knew from Mum that he was only sixteen.

'Mr Cooper's son?'

'*Ja*. Who are you?'

'Elise. My mum works here.'

'The new accountant?'

'*Ja*.'

'How long have you been here?'

'Just a few weeks.'

'I like to know what's going on around here,' said Sean, and grinned. He stepped off the bike and propped it up. It seems incongruous, a bright and plastic red against the lion-coloured bush. The dogs stopped their drinking and swarmed around him, a mass of wagging tails and happy panting. Shumba lifted up a corner of his black lip in a grin. Sean was offhand with them, giving them absent-minded pats and scrunching their ears, but paying little attention.

'Want to come for a ride?'

'On that thing?'

'What do you think?'

I eyed the machine. 'Is it safe?'

'Of course.' Sean leaned a hand on it.

65

'I'll have to ask my mum,' I said, and inwardly cringed for being so childish.

'Well, go and ask.'

I ran inside. 'Mum, can I go on the back of Sean's motorbike?'

Mum looked dubious.

'Please, Mum.'

'Has he got a spare helmet?'

I had no idea. '*Ja.*'

'Well, okay. But you be careful, all right?'

'I will!'

Outside, Sean was facing away, as if any second he would jump back on the bike and disappear. When I appeared, he smiled. '*Lekker*. Hop on.'

The seat was hot and smelled like melting plastic.

'Hold on around my waist,' he said, turning around. He was impatient. 'Look.'

He grabbed both my hands and pulled them around to his front. 'Like this.'

I felt the rough cotton of his shirt scratching the whorls and bumps on my fingers. He smelled of sweat and Persil. I could see the backs of his ears, curved and glowing from the sun, and the tiny yellow hairs that ran down the back of his neck.

'You holding tight?' he asked.

I nodded. My cheek scraped his shoulder.

'Okay.' He started the bike. *Mhudhudhudhu* is the Shona word for motorbike, and that was exactly the noise that this one made. Mhu-dhu-dhu-dhu-dhu-dhu-dhu, shuddering and juddering. I felt that if I opened my mouth my teeth would fall right out of my head.

Sean accelerated and we started to move. The world dissolved into stripes of colour. I could not

66

look ahead because my eyes watered and insects zipped into my face with a puzzled buzz—where is this human coming from so fast? All I could do was lean my head against Sean's back and concentrate on the weave of his shirt.

He shouted something over the engine. I did not know what. I shouted something back and he seemed satisfied.

The bike coughed to a halt. Sean had seen a group of farm workers walking back from the tobacco fields. They were young men, for the most part, anywhere from sixteen to thirty, and they threw laughing remarks at the Baas's son.

'Who's your little girlfriend, hey?' (This one made me hide my face.)

'Playing with the toy bike again?'

He answered them right back in fluent Shona with an impressive range of slang and swear words, to their delight. White teeth flashed in their faces as they replied, and as Sean kicked the bike back into life they waved us off.

'Where are we going?' I shouted in Sean's ear.

'Huh?'

'Where are we going?'

'Home.'

'Where?'

'Home!'

'Your house?'

'*Ja*!'

'But I have to get back . . .'

I had no idea where I was. Did he expect me to walk back? We were miles away from the offices. We had passed the tobacco fields, the greenhouses and the ostrich pens.

It would take me over an hour to walk back to

the offices and collect the dogs, and it would be dark by the time I brought them home. I felt like an idiot.

We sped through the gate and into the lush garden, where we came to a halt. Jonah gave me a look, and winked. I looked away, my ears burning. Stupid.

'Just going inside to grab something,' said Sean, taking off his helmet. He swung his leg over the bike and got off. I stayed where I was.

'Coming?'

'No, I'll wait here.' I ignored the cramp in my legs.

'Come on. I'll get you a drink.'

I climbed down. My legs felt like jelly, as if I had been running all this way instead of riding.

'Come on.'

I followed Sean into the Big House. He did not go in through the front door, as I had on my first visit, but opened French windows into a sun-room.

I hung around on the verandah, looking at the buck heads displayed along the length of the house. It was cool there, with deep wells of shade and a clean, rich smell of expensive floor polish.

'Come on!' Sean appeared in the windows again. 'What are you waiting for?'

'I'm fine out here.'

'What, you're afraid you're going to break something? Come in.' He turned, and I followed. The first thing I saw was a buffalo head, hanging above the fireplace. It was easily bigger than my entire body.

'We call him Buffy,' said Sean. He had poured two Cokes. They were in tall glasses, with ice. I sipped mine and felt the fizz like little pins pressing into my tongue.

'You have a nice house,' I said, as Mum had said to Mr Cooper before.

'*Ja*, it's all right, eh.' Sean threw himself into a chair, legs and arms hanging off at strange angles.

'You live on the farm?'

'*Ja.*'

'Brothers and sisters?'

I shook my head.

'Like me.' He gulped more of his Coke. I sat holding my glass until he had finished. I dared not have too much to drink in case I burped from the fizz, which would be so embarrassing that I would never be able to look at him again.

'Well, I suppose I'd better take you back, eh?'

'*Ja.*' Thank goodness. 'What was it you needed to get?'

'Oh, *ja*, thanks for reminding me.' He disappeared for a second, then returned, slipping something into his pocket. 'Okay, let's go.'

But we did not go to the bike. Instead we went around the side of the house.

'Where are we going?'

'The generator shed.'

'The what?'

Sean opened a corrugated iron door. 'The generator shed. We only use it when we have power cuts, it's perfectly safe. Come on.'

The shed was hot and thrumming with electricity. Sean leaned against the wall and opened the packet of cigarettes in his pocket.

'Why are we in here?' I eyed the machinery uncertainly.

'So Jonah doesn't see us and tell Dad. How old are you?' he asked.

69

'Nearly thirteen.' I watched him. The cigarettes were slim and elegant in their white-and-gold casing—adult and impossibly glamorous. Sean mumbled the cigarette from one corner of his mouth to another and lit the end, cupping his hand over the flame as if he was keeping it a secret. When he took his first breath, he dragged it in with a sigh, leaned back and looked at me through half-closed eyes. I knew he was showing off, but that did not make it any less impressive.

'Want one?' he asked.

Of course I wanted one. I took one of the cigarettes he offered and held it between my fingers.

'Like this.' He took my hand and corrected me. His fingers were warm and slightly sweaty.

'Oh, *ja*.'

He glanced at me, amused. 'Want a light?'

I watched the flame come close to my face, flapping in the breeze. It looked like something alive sitting on the end of his lighter, like a moth with orange wings. I leaned back and inhaled. For a moment it tasted like the tobacco fields and I felt proud, but then it scorched a woodsmoke taste down my throat and started me coughing and spluttering.

By the time the tears cleared from my eyes, he had lit his second cigarette.

'You can't own a tobacco farm and not smoke,' he said. 'Although Dad doesn't want me to. Fat chance. And he smokes.'

Cigarettes, motorbike. I could smell petrol and nicotine. It would be easy to be carried away by Sean's air of glamorous adulthood.

'The workers call me Mini Cooper,' he said.

70

'Oh.'

'I'm going to be running the farm one day.'

'All right.' I was getting tired of all these studied poses, the way he let the cigarette dangle from one hand as if he was too tired to hold it properly. I watched it burn down.

'I want to go now.'

'In a sec.'

'Fine.' I walked out of the shed, into the bright world.

'*Iwe!*' he chased after me, stubbing out the cigarette with his foot. 'Hold up.'

'I need to get back.'

'Fine, I'll take you now.' He grinned. 'See, all your *shupering* paid off.'

I said nothing as I climbed on the bike behind him, and I said nothing on the way back to the offices. When he dropped me off, he gave me a distant grin, as if in his head he was already on to the next thing.

'See you later.'

I was in love.

CHAPTER EIGHT

I felt hot and overdressed in my school uniform, with its heavy blazer and woollen socks. It was designed for a different country.

'Such a smart blazer,' said Mum as she straightened it. 'How are you feeling?'

'Fine.'

My new teacher was called Mrs Starling. She had dyed blonde hair that hung straight down, dry and chemical-smelling, a husky voice and a squawky laugh that coughed out cigarette smoke with every 'Ha'. As soon as I arrived at school, I knew she did not like me. Instead, she liked the pretty girls who crowded around her desk at lunchtime and talked about boys. Their names were Cheydene, Lamese, Tasha, Kerry and Dallas—girls with breasts and periods and older brothers and mascara.

Dallas was assigned to me as a buddy on my first day. She had white-blonde hair and a hedge of dark eyelashes. She showed me around the school and introduced me to the harem of pretty girls. I knew already that I would never be friends with any of them.

On my third day at school I realised that my new girl status had disappeared and I had become a target. A black boy called Simba took a dislike to me. He was one of the leaders of the class, lounging in his seat during lessons and making smart remarks. Bored and looking to cause some trouble, he told Mrs Starling that I had called him a black pig.

I was called to the front of the class.

'Is this true?'

'No!'

'It is,' said someone from the rows of desks. 'I heard her.' A girl I had not even spoken to.

'I didn't,' I insisted.

Mrs Starling sighed. 'There are witnesses.'

'They're making it up. I . . .' My voice was getting gulpy and I could feel tears rising in my throat. I swallowed them back. No need to be soft in front of everyone.

'We have to take this seriously,' the teacher said.

'You can't speak to people like that.'

I had never been so aware of blacks and whites at school before. I did not know if it was just because I was older, or because things were different in Harare, but there was a very clear division between us. And, after Simba had called me a racist, I was unwelcome in both camps. There was no way to defend myself against it, so I kept out of everyone's way and stared at my desk during lessons.

This was how I first noticed Kurai—from the corner of my eye as I was hunched over the desk. She was a tall and beautiful black girl, truly black, her skin dusky and shining blue in the light. I heard from others in the class that she had been battling it for years with lightening creams and moisturisers, but they never worked. Her hair was short or long, in braids or close-bound to the side of her head, black or red or brown, hers or someone else's, depending on her mood, and it seemed to change every few days.

Whenever I walked near her, she pulled out a ruler and brandished it at me.

'What is she doing?' I asked Dallas, my supposed buddy.

'It's because you're a racist,' said Dallas, flipping her hair. 'She doesn't want you to come too close.'

'Thirty centimetres,' someone else chimed in. 'That's why she uses the ruler.'

Mum picked me up after school every day. 'So, how's it going?' she asked.

'It's fine.'

After a few weeks the racism incident seemed to blow over. Kurai stopped carrying a ruler and the class stopped hissing the word at me between lessons.

Only one person kept tormenting me. Stuart was a handsome, overgrown boy, too old for our class. For the last few weeks he had been pushing me against walls and casually grabbing my (almost non-existent) breasts, spitting in my face while he talked and trying to flip up my skirt in the corridors. When I would not let him, he told everyone that I was half-boy, half-girl.

One break-time, Stuart trapped me in a corner with the teacher's wheeled chair and he and the other boys shouted and jeered at me. My eyes started to swim and I felt like I was going to fall over, but I heard Kurai yelling at them. I was suddenly outside, with a brand-new bruise on my wrist where she had grabbed me.

'*Bhenzi*,' she called me, 'idiot'. 'Don't you know any better?'

'No,' I said, rubbing my arm.

'They'll tear you apart,' she said. 'Come sit with me. You shouldn't be wandering about on your own, you're certifiable.'

I followed, minus my hat, which I had left behind in the classroom. The sun tore at my hair and bit my scalp. We were not allowed outside without hats, even in the winter.

'Shit,' said Kurai, 'I'll go get it. You don't want to go back there.'

She disappeared, and I scratched my legs and swatted flies until she returned triumphant. She crammed it on my head. 'There. Come on.'

We walked around during lunch, talking. I realised that, although tall and blindingly confident, Kurai was a natural defender of the weak.

74

'You have to stand up for yourself, sha.'

We became friends.

That is when we discovered the secret place behind the classrooms. We needed somewhere away from the others—or, at least, I did. We picked our way over weeds and dead earth to get there.

'*Maiwe*, this place doesn't smell so good,' said Kurai.

'I think something died here.'

'Yes, those beans.' They flopped depressingly over the fence.

'It's disgusting.'

It was behind a classroom block, invisible from the rest of the playground, a patch of dusty red earth that coughed up a slimy weed now and then. Chicken wire separated it from the black caretaker's vegetable garden; limp carrots and tomatoes that ate up the sun and guzzled the thick, solid raindrops of the big storms, but never actually grew any bigger or lost their yellow, frayed edges. The air was a warm facecloth pressed over our noses and mouths; our schoolgirl legs, bare under ugly summer dresses, itched from the bites of invisible creatures with too many legs. It was worth it, though, to be hidden from everything but the tiny green eyes of beans.

'This is great,' I said.

'Are you kidding?'

'No one will be able to see us here.'

Kurai sighed and sat down. She stood up again, pulled off her school jersey and sat on it. I knew I had won, and we sat there every break-time.

Being friends with Kurai raised my cool factor. I listened with awe as she told stories of six hours

75

spent in the hairdresser's, wearing relaxing creams that burned her scalp and pulled out her hair in angry tufts. Mine took half an hour at the most. I felt cheated.

We created catchphrases, in-jokes, secret words. We talked about our futures.

'I want to be an executive,' Kurai said. Her hair was braided close to her head that day, and had a greasy shine in the bright sun.

'An executive who does what?'

'I don't know. I don't care. I want a corner office with a view. I want my secretary to have a secretary.'

Her mother taught at a prestigious girls' college; her father owned five companies. She had an older brother and sister who were both impossibly cool, like her. I was especially lost in admiration of her older brother, with his baggy clothes and heavy gold jewellery. He listened to loud rap and called himself T-Zone, although his real name was Tafadzwa.

No one ever bothered Kurai or me again after Tafadzwa visited the school. Simba had called Kurai's mother a whore. Kurai tore furiously at tufts of grass in our secret place and announced that she would tell Tafadzwa. The next day he came in with two of his friends, black men in heavy jackets, with heavy rings on each finger and a heavy stride.

Tafadzwa held Simba by his collar and crunched him against the wall. I could not hear what he was saying, but I could see Simba's eyes: white and round, spinning in his anxious face. I could not help laughing.

'That sorted him out,' Kurai said with

satisfaction. 'No one talks about my *Amai* like that.'

*   *   *

There was a school play at the end of term. We lined up on the polished floor of the hall to find out what parts we had been assigned. I was hopeful. I did not want to be the main character, but I would not mind being one of the princesses.

It was a very short process. All the girls with long hair (the Lameses, Dallases, Laras and Kerrys) were princesses. All the girls with short hair (me and two others) were going to be rocks, dressed in all black. The black girls got to be the front and back ends of the pantomime horses. Worst of all, the boys and girls had to pair up at the end for a dance number.

'Great,' said Kurai, picking the polish off her nails.

I was assigned to partner Gary, a blond boy who was Evil Stuart's best friend, and shorter than me. He tried his hardest not to touch me at all, but it was a waltz and required us to clasp hands. He kept his head turned, and I could feel his fingers straining to get as far away as possible. If an extra millimetre of skin happened to touch, he flinched as if I had given him an electric shock.

We were both terrible at the dance. The partners were meant to practise on their own, but I knew that we would not. As we walked away from the hall, I overheard Gary talking to Stuart.

'That dance is gay, man.'

'*Ja.*'

'But at least you have someone decent.'

77

I laughed it off to Kurai later. 'He's a pathetic excuse for a human being,' she says.

But I worried about it at home.

Kurai taught me about music. She taped the Top Ten hits from the radio and brought them to school in her Walkman. She liked rap and hip-hop. She especially liked Tupac Shakur, and did a school project on him.

'He didn't die,' she said. 'He left clues in his lyrics. If you play the songs backwards they tell you where he's hiding.'

She taught me how to rollerblade. I wore her brother's skates, which were too big for me. Eventually I became good enough to follow in her wake, skating around the block with a practised swish and clip. We stopped only to press an electric gate bell and run away when someone answered.

She told me about the time her maid took her to visit her boyfriend.

'I was only about three,' she said. 'I remember her taking me to this scummy *khaya* somewhere down the road, and putting me in a chair. She told me to sit there and face the wall. The chair was in the bedroom and I could hear them behind me, grunting and gasping away. It was disgusting.'

'Did you tell your parents?'

'No. The maid told me not to or she would kidnap me and take me away.'

'That's horrible!'

'*Ja*, well, I was just stupid.' Kurai stuck out her tongue and crossed her eyes.

Her house was exotic, smelling of strange cooking and a body odour different to my own.

Her family spoke Shona and English indiscriminately, and ate *sadza* at almost every

78

meal. They found me exotic too, Kurai's white friend with the fair hair, who sat quietly at their table being small and pale while white teeth flashed around her, hands gestured, and voices rich as molasses talked in two languages.

Kurai was at once fiercely loyal to and contemptuous of her family. Every month she, her parents and her siblings travelled into the rural areas to visit their extended family, the country cousins.

'We're going to the *gwash* this weekend,' she would tell me when I invited her over. 'Sorry.'

She sounded bored, but these visits were important to her. She returned with dusty skin and stories of cooking freshly killed chickens, pounding peanut butter, hoeing gardens to plant sorghum or maize. She had a mysterious air after these visits. Even though she told me long stories about what this cousin said to that cousin, what the witch doctor said to her aunt and what her aunt did to her grandmother afterwards, she knew I could never quite understand. I felt whiter than snow and boring. But then she was suddenly the Kurai I knew again, talking about chart music, clothes and cars. I never knew how to deal with the air of black magic and tribal secrets that hung about her after her visits to the country.

*   *   *

For the first time, I had formal Shona lessons. Our Shona teacher was called VaChihambakwe. He had little round glasses and his hair grew down the sides of his head in a neat beard. None of the other male teachers wore a suit and tie, but he did. His

79

accent was not Shona at all—he sounded just like a white, except when he read aloud from our textbook.

Everyone hated Shona lessons.

'They're pointless,' said Dallas.

'It's a waste of time,' said someone else.

Even some of the mums and dads did not like the Shona lessons. 'It's hard enough to get them to do their English reading,' I heard one say to the teacher. 'Why do they have to learn all this Shona rubbish as well?'

'All they need is a bit of Kitchen Kaffir to use with the servants,' said one man, who was quickly shushed by his wife.

I loved Shona. It reminded me of the farm, and of Chinhoyi. When we were first asked to speak some words aloud, VaChihambakwe was impressed by my accent. No one else was, though. I quickly learned that the white kids were meant to read Shona in their normal voices, without bothering to pronounce things properly.

He must have been lonely, being the only black teacher at the school. All the other blacks who worked there were gardeners, cleaners and groundsmen. I watched VaChihambakwe sometimes through the glass window of the staffroom—as the only dark shape in the room, he was easy to see. While the other teachers chatted at lunchtime, he read his book and ate *sadza* with a fork.

Once I waved to him through the window. He seemed to catch the movement out of the corner of his eye, and looked up. '*Mangwanani!*' I mouthed at him, and he smiled and raised one hand. I felt like we had a secret, and I ran back to my classroom, giddy with my own daring.

80

Learning Shona properly for the first time, I saw that everything had two names, an English and a Shona one, side by side. This had not occurred to me before. Bread in Shona was *chingwa*. I had always thought that bread was something white and sliced that came in plastic packets sealed with a clip, while *chingwa* was brown and thicker and spread with peanut butter. *Mombes* were skinny animals with mbira ribs that lived on the bald, scrubbed lands in the rural areas. Cows were fat, glossy things in paddocks. It seemed strange that the two words really did mean exactly the same thing.

When you learned an English word it stayed learned and it looked the same no matter where it was. Shona words were more complicated. You learned a good, solid word and then discovered that all sorts of extra bits got tacked on the end or at the beginning, to tell you whether the word was singular or plural, big or small, respected or not respected. English words stood upright in a straight line, not touching one another. Shona words blended in together and you could not have one without having a whole family of others.

The kids at school had a language of their own, too. *Lekker* meant good. *Mushi* also meant good. The boys called other boys *oens* or *oeks*, and we were all called lighties by the older kids. When someone got into trouble, the whole class would shake their right hands as if they had just burned them on a hot stove, and say 'Ee-ee, ee-ee, ee-ee!'

I settled into the rhythm of classes, assemblies and break times. We sang the national anthem every day. The tune was meant to be grand, but somehow it was sad.

'Simudzai mureza wedu weZimbabwe
Yakazvarwa nemoto weChimurenga;
Neropa zhinji ramagamba
Tiidzivirire kumhandu dzose;
Ngaikomborerwe nyika yeZimbabwe.'

In English, it meant: 'Oh lift high the banner, the flag of Zimbabwe. The symbol of freedom, proclaiming victory. We praise our heroes' sacrifice, and vow to keep our land from foes. Oh God bless our country—the land of Zimbabwe.'

I did not know what sacrifice they were talking about, but it probably had something to do with the War that no one mentioned. I did not know who our foes were either, but I assumed that they were comfortably Out There, far away, and unlikely to come any closer.

I received a letter from Beauty that year. It was written on a lined piece of paper torn from an exercise book, in blue biro.

Dear Elise

How are you? I hope you are well. I am very well. I have found new job working for a nice family in Chinhoyi since the Madam has moved away. Everything is good here but we miss you very much. I hope you are happy in Harare.

Love from Beauty

I replied to that one with a long letter full of news about school and the farm and how much I missed her. Beauty sent a reply. I kept the second letter on my wall for weeks and always meant to answer it. But when it fell off the wall and down the back of my desk, I did not even notice.

CHAPTER NINE

Mum and Steve went to a party at the Coopers' house one night. I begged to come too, but they said it was for adults only. When they got home I came through in my pyjamas. They had bright eyes and flushed cheeks. Mum was still holding a glass.

'Mum, is that one of the Coopers' glasses?'

'Oh.' Mum glanced down. 'Yes.' She seemed surprised.

'Great evening,' said Steve.

'What's in the glass?' An unappetising brown slush clung to the bottom.

'Hooligan juice.' They exchanged glances and giggled. 'Brandy and ice-cream.'

They collapsed into the sofas. Steve got up again. 'Shee-yit, I'm going to put the tea on.' He meandered through into the kitchen.

'So, Mum, what did you do?' I was agog for details of the glamorous party at the big white house.

'Agh, we had a *braai*, we had some drinks . . .' Mum thought. 'The farm managers played a game.'

'What sort of game?'

'They jab a toothpick into their foreheads and set fire to the end.'

'Wouldn't that hurt?'

'*Ja*. The winner is the person who lets it burn the longest.'

'Oh.'

Steve came back and tickled Mum. She started giggling again, and I thought it was probably time to go to bed.

*   *   *

Mum was in charge of calculating and giving out the wages to all the farm workers. This happened once a month, when a long line of black men in bright orange, blue or green overalls snaked from Mum's office. There was a festive atmosphere, as people laughed and joked and planned their trip to the shebeen after work, to spend some of their pay packet.

Some of the workers had Shona names, but others were in English: names like Jeans, Lettuce, Hatred, Oblivious, Killer, Murder, Doesn't-Matter, Enough, Lovemore, Loveness, Gift, and a thousand others. I liked the Shona way of naming a child after a particular meaning.

I helped Mum by slipping the money into named envelopes and holding them out to the workers.

'Here you go.'

'Thank you.'

'Thank you, Medem.'

'*Mazvita tatenda.*'

A parade of faces, each one different. Steve sometimes said that all blacks looked alike, but he could not look into each face, as I was doing, and say the same. I finished handing out the envelopes and sat on the front steps of the office, tilting my closed eyes up to the sunshine to see the red

84

patterns inside my eyelids.

'Howzit.'

The voice was familiar. I looked up. A pair of strong brown legs ending in dusty feet in flip-flops. A Zimbabwe cricket team shirt. Blue eyes.

'Sean.' I wondered whether to jump up or not. I decided not to, because I had a small hole in the back of my pants that had not mattered when it was just me and Mum and the workers. I tried to remember what colour underwear I was wearing. 'Hi.'

'*Ja*, hi.' Sean stepped over me and inside, to see Mum. He gave her a message from his father.

'Phew, hot day,' he said when he was finished, making a point of drawing the back of his hand across his wet forehead.

'Could you get us some Cokes?' Mum asked me.

The Coke fizzed in the glasses and shone red in the sunlight. 'Here you go.'

'Thanks.'

I was not sure whether to stay. I hovered in the doorway. If I went out, I could not come back in. It would look like I was coming back to see him. I made the decision and went outside, to sit under the trees behind the office and trace patterns in the dust.

Sean stayed for a few minutes, sipping his Coke. When he left, Mum made me come back inside to say goodbye.

'Agh, no, Mum.' I was whispering, hoping our voices didn't carry.

'Come on, don't be rude.'

'I'm not being rude. I just don't want to come and say goodbye.'

'What are you getting so worked up about?'

85

'Nothing.'

'You like him, is that it?'

'No way!'

'Well fine, then, come and say bye.'

I was dragged inside. 'Bye, Sean.'

'*Ja*, bye.' He looked amused.

As soon as he was gone, I wriggled free from Mum's grasp and back outside. I could hear her laughing, and I wanted to kill her.

*   *   *

The next time I went with Mum to the office, I made sure to wear my nicest denim shorts. No holes. I hung around on the front steps, filing invoices.

'Why don't you come inside?' Mum called.

'I don't want to.'

'But it's hot out there.'

'I don't mind.'

The terracotta steps were cool under my bare legs, and most of me was in the shade. And my waiting paid off.

'Howzit.'

'Hi.'

Sean was standing in front of me. 'Do you want to come for a ride?'

'I'd have to ask Mum.' I could not believe I had to say this again, but Mum would kill me if I went off without telling her.

'*Ja.*' Sean was impatient. 'There's an elephant on the game farm.'

'An elephant? I thought there were just buck and zebra.'

'That's why I want to go look at it, *domkop.*'

'Is it a good idea? I thought they were dangerous.'

Sean was losing interest. 'It's fine. Do you want to come or not?'

'I'll come.' I scrambled to my feet. I was wearing flip-flops. 'Are these okay for riding the bike?'

'*Ja*, you can ride in anything.'

Mum had told me to wear proper shoes when I was on the bike, but hopefully she would not notice. I went inside, but Mum had gone. She must have walked down to the other office to deliver something. I wrote her a note and stuck it on the computer screen, where she couldn't miss it.

'It's fine,' I said when I came out.

'Good. Hop on.'

I was more familiar with the bike by then, but the noise always surprised me. It filled up my ears so tightly that no other sound could creep in.

The sand on the road stung my feet and rattled inside the bike frame. There were two dark patches of sweat under Sean's arms, and I worried that I might be sweating as well.

A tuft of hair stuck out of the back of his baseball cap, shiny and almost white in the sun, and I could see Shumba running behind us if I turned my head away from the burning wind. Two long lines of saliva streamed from each side of his grinning mouth like the strings of a kite. Eventually he tired and fell behind, panting.

'Where's the elephant?' I yelled.

'What?'

'The elephant!'

'Jonah saw it by the waterhole.'

'What was he doing there?'

'Drinking.'

'No, what was Jonah doing there?'

'What?'

'Jonah!'

'I don't know.'

'Has anyone else seen it?'

'Nah. I wanted to find it first.'

'All right.' I was quiet for a while. The only other time an elephant had wandered on to the game farm, it was a rogue male who charged one of the workers and had to be shot. I knew we were not meant to go on to the game farm without taking one of the workers with us—someone good at tracking who would know if there was a leopard nearby.

My hat was whipped off my head. 'Hey!' I nudged Sean. 'Stop.'

'What?'

'My hat.'

'Huh?'

'Hat!' I jabbed him with my finger. His shirt was damp with sweat. 'Stop.'

He pulled over, and the world became miraculously silent and still. The hot air fell on to us like a blanket, and my body started to sweat all over.

'My hat.'

'What about it?'

'It's not on my head.'

'Were you wearing a hat?'

Showed how closely he looked at me.

'*Ja.*'

'How far back?'

I gestured vaguely.

'Well, shee-yit, man, we'll never find it. It could have blown off anywhere.'

I supposed this was true.

'Look, I'll grab you one of my old hats when we get back, hey?'

'All right.'

We roared off again. I did not even know what part of the farm we were in. And Sean had not brought a radio with him.

We stopped by a big waterhole. I could see mosquitoes hovering above the flat, metallic surface.

'It was round here,' said Sean. He jumped off the bike and waded through the long grass to sit on a rock next to the pool. I followed him, shading my eyes with my hand. I wished we had gone back for my hat. I could feel the sun like an itch on my scalp—it would turn pink, and Mum would be furious.

We sat there for a long time, waiting.

'I think Jonah was lying,' I said.

'Why would he lie?'

'Well, why would he be down here looking at elephants? When does he ever come on to the game farm?'

Sean shrugged. 'It'll come.'

'Sure.'

We sat in silence for a while.

'What happened to your Mum?' I asked.

He picked at the dry grass at our feet.

'She died,' he said. 'Cancer.'

'Oh.' Sean had built up quite a pile of grass by now. He could not seem to sit still. Even when he tired of pulling up the grass, his knee jiggled and he hummed under his breath.

'My dad died,' I volunteered.

'Really?'

'*Ja*, car accident.'

'Do you miss him?'

'No, not really.'

'I don't either,' he said. 'With my mum.'

'All right.'

'I mean, I did. But these things happen, hey.'

'*Ja*.'

We sat for a minute.

'You're good to talk to,' he said.

'Oh.' I could not swallow. My heart travelled up my throat and stopped right up under my chin.

'You're almost like a boy,' he said.

'Oh,' I said again. I flicked a fly off my knee. 'Well, people have always said I look like a boy.'

'*Ja*, you do a bit.'

'*Ja*.'

We sit.

'Maybe I should have been born a boy,' I said. I was still hoping for some sort of contradiction.

'*Ja*!' He was enthusiastic. 'We could have gone camping.'

'Well, we can still do that.'

'Not overnight, though.'

'No, not overnight.'

We sat for half an hour, slapping insects on our arms and legs. I could feel the sun sizzling deeper into my skin.

'I don't think it's going to come,' I said.

Sean took a breath, and let it out. '*Ja*, no, hey. All right, I'll take you back.'

'Thanks.'

He did not help me to my feet. We headed back to the bike. Before we got there, however, there was a cough from the Bush, and a sound like tearing fabric.

'Shush, man,' said Sean. I did not even realise that I had made a noise.

'It's the elephant!'

'*Ja*, shush.'

Sean crouched down next to the bike, and I did too. The grass raised red welts on my bare legs, and it was almost unbearably itchy. An ant crawled over my big toe.

There was a crunch from the scrub, and a deep, heartfelt sigh. An ancient, blinking eye emerged from the Bush, followed by wrinkled, tortoise-like skin. The elephant moved softly, lifting each foot and putting it down with care. A fly buzzed around its velvety eyeball, and a great fringe of lash blinked it away.

'Eesh, man,' whispered Sean. 'Look at the size of that thing.'

'Shut up!' I was sure the elephant had noticed us—no matter how quiet humans try to be, they are no match for an animal's ears—but so far did not see us as a threat.

'It's a girl,' said Sean.

The skin on the elephant's knees was creased into folds like the skin on my knuckles. The wind dropped. Even the ant on my toe paused in its senseless exploration of my feet and looked up, as if it were worshipping the elephant too.

The elephant used her nose to investigate a bush, running it over the leaves like a loving finger, then looping her trunk around them, like a grey, wrinkled bride holding a ragged bouquet. She stuffed the leaves into her mouth and chewed with a great sloshing, grinding noise that echoed off the *kopjes*.

It could have been five minutes or forty-five

91

before the elephant left. I did not know. I did not see her go. I was amazed that something so large could just disappear into grey-brown scrub without a trace.

We did not move straight away. We waited until the spell had broken, the birds had started singing again and the wind had started humming through the tall grasses.

'That was *lekker*,' said Sean. 'Glad you came?'

'*Ja*.' My legs tingled with pins-and-needles, and my skin itched from the grass. 'We should go back.'

'Come on then, let's get moving.' Sean climbed on the bike and tried to start it.

It coughed once, then was silent.

'Shit,' he said.

'What?'

'Bike won't start.'

I thought he was joking. 'What?'

'Bike. Won't start.'

I realised he was serious. I was suddenly very aware of the noises of the Bush around us—twigs cracking, an eerie bird call, something sliding through the long grass.

'What are we going to do? Did you bring a radio?'

'Nah.' Sean stood like his father did, legs wide apart, hands on hips. He looked tough and capable. I could tell he was worried, though.

'So what are we going to do?'

'It'll start.'

He tried the bike again. Nothing at all this time. 'Shit,' he said.

'What can we do?'

The sun dipped towards the horizon, and the shadows were splayed across the ground like

92

lizards flat on a wall.

Sean sat down. 'We can't do anything.'

'We could walk.'

'It's miles. And I don't want to leave the bike here. And I don't want to walk through the Bush, it's not safe.'

'Sitting in the Bush isn't safe either. At least if we walked we'd be getting somewhere.'

'I said no,' said Sean, drawing himself up to his full sixteen-year-old height.

'We'll wait here.'

We sat in silence, watching the shadows move and lengthen. When the first cricket started to shrill, I felt my bare legs getting chilly.

'What if no one finds us?'

'They will,' said Sean.

'What if we have to stay the night?'

'What if, what if.'

'But what if we do?'

'We'll be fine. I know all about camping. And how to make fires.'

Jackals roamed the farm at night, and worse.

We sat there for hours. The sunset was an orange flare before the darkness. The crickets were deafening. Every noise was magnified. The cold pinpricks of stars were no comfort, and made me feel dizzy. I dropped my head on to my knees.

'Hey, what's that?' Sean's voice was unexpected and flimsy in the dark world.

'What?'

'Campfire.' He pointed. There was a small yellow fire in front of us. I had lost all sense of distance, so was not sure whether it was a campfire a few kilometres away, or a candle flame hovering in front of my face.

Sean stood up with a crackle of undergrowth and a scatter of small stones. 'I'm going to talk to them.'

'Who?'

'Whoever that is.'

'You don't know it's a campfire.'

'Yes I do.' I knew he was looking down at me, because his voice was closer and clearer. 'You don't have to come. In fact, it's better if you stay here.'

'I'm not bluddy staying here.'

I followed him, hoping like hell that we would find our way back to the bike again.

'Must be workers having a *braai*,' said Sean.

'On the game farm?'

'*Ja*, well, they're not meant to come out here, but they probably do. I do.'

The campfire dipped and swayed in my vision as I walked. It was all I could see—the rest was blackness. We crunched over leaves and twigs, walking in a cloud of curious mosquitoes who had gathered to see what we were doing.

We came into the clearing. Three men were sitting around the fire, roasting meat on a stick. There was a crate of beer beside them.

'*Manheru*,' said Sean, and held his palms open and upwards in a supplicating gesture. The men stood up.

People! I was so relieved to see another human being that I wanted to hug all three of them. Then I saw how they were standing, and I saw their smiles, and I was afraid. I noticed other things: a stack of rifles. An animal pelt, recently skinned. A net.

Poachers.

'I'm the Baas's son,' said Sean. I willed him to shut up.

'The Baas?' said one of the men. He had an unexpectedly high-pitched voice.

'*Ja*, Baas Cooper. It's his farm. Don't you work here?'

Hands on hips, legs apart. Confident. The men laughed. 'No.' One of them threw his empty skewer away into the bushes, and took a step towards us.

'Then what are you doing here?' said Sean. 'This is private property.'

I wondered if he was actually, properly insane, not just pig-headed. 'That's fine, we'll go,' I said. I tugged at Sean's arm, bony and cold.

'Wait a minute,' said one of the men. I was not waiting. I ran, pulling Sean by the arm. He did not resist, and started running with me. He had finally realised that we could be in big trouble.

I did not know whether the men were following us, but I imagined they were, and every snap of a twig made me think they were catching up. I ran through the darkness, in what I thought was the direction of the bike. All I could see were stars hopping and spinning above me, nothing else; thorns and low bushes snagged and snarled my feet.

'Where's the bluddy bike?' I hissed at Sean, but before he could answer me I was knee-deep in water.

'We're here,' he said. 'It's by the waterhole.'

I hated to think what was swimming around my feet in the dank water, or what was watching us from the bushes, waiting to have a quiet drink in the darkness. I splashed my way out towards the dim shape of the bike, and collapsed beside it. I could hear Sean breathing nearby, and smell his sweat.

'You stupid *domkop*!' I would have yelled, but I was afraid the men would hear us, so I yelled a whisper as best I could. 'You've lived on a farm your whole bluddy life, and you don't think to take a can of petrol or a radio with you when you go out on the bike! What's wrong with you?'

I could feel Sean's glare in the darkness. He stomped off, a few feet away from me, and sat down.

We sat in silence for what felt like a long time. Both of us were Bush-savvy enough to know that it was safer to stay put than to try to walk anywhere, but I was starting to think about moving when I saw twin gleams in the darkness. I thought for a panicked second that it was a pair of animal eyes, but then saw the beams of the headlamps and heard an engine rattling over rough ground. The *bakkie* juddered over the gravel and sand and came to a halt next to us.

Mr Cooper stepped down from the cabin.

Sean jumped up. 'Howzit, Dad.'

Mr Cooper clapped Sean on the side of his head. Sean held his ear with one hand and looked dazed in the harsh headlights. It must have been ringing.

'Don't you bluddy howzit me. What are you bluddy playing at, hey?' said Mr Cooper. 'You don't wander off without taking a radio. You know that. Wake up, *domkop*.'

He turned his attention to me. 'You all right?'

'*Ja*, I'm fine.'

'We'd better get you back to your Mum, hey.'

His voice was gentle, but changed when he spoke to Sean. 'Don't you get too bluddy big for your britches, boy. You're not as smart as you think you are, hey? You think being the farmer's son is going to help you out here?'

'No, man.'

'What did you say?'

'No, sir.'

'Right. You could have got both of you killed, you know that?'

Sean was silent.

Mr Cooper blew out his lips in a loud sigh. 'Right, hop in.'

I sat in the passenger seat. Sean sat in the back, and did not say a word. When we got back to the offices, Mum was frantic with relief, and Sean sank further into the seat cushions.

'*Ja*, sorry about that,' said Mr Cooper to Mum. 'I'll make sure he never goes out without a radio again.'

Mum told me there had been a farm-wide search for us, with all the workers on alert.

Finally, Jonah mentioned that he had told Sean about the elephant.

'Mr Cooper was bluddy furious,' she said.

'Poor Sean,' I said.

'Poor Sean my foot. Going into the Bush with no gun and no radio is just bluddy stupid. Thank Christ they found your hat on the road, or they may never have found you.'

When we got home, Mum fussed over me, making me cups of tea and running me a bath.

I thought about what Sean said. How I looked like a boy. When I had my bath, I stared down at myself. I was partly submerged, and the skin above

97

the water was pasty, with a pink line where the hot water touched it. Underwater my skin was green, with blue veins writhing through it. Blobby. Pale.

Mum banged on the door. 'Are you still in there?'

'Yes.'

'Don't be too much longer. Steve and I still need to have one.'

'I won't.'

'And leave the water in.'

'I know, Mum.'

I liked having first bath. If I had the last bath, I could not help thinking about all the things I was sitting in. Little bits of skin floating past like cornflakes. Hairs snaking along the water's surface. I pulled out the plug and watched the water gurgle and sputter down the hole.

Mum banged on the door again. 'Are you letting the water out? Why are you letting the water out?'

'Sorry.' I stood on the mat and watched the water pool around my feet.

'But I said . . .' Mum's voice moved away, until all I could hear was the faint sound of exasperation from the other side of the house.

CHAPTER TEN

I looked down at my breasts. They were just a slight bulge under my T-shirt, but Mum was making me wear a bra. She took me to Edgars department store especially to get measured and fitted; quite an occasion, as we hardly ever went into town.

'They're not big enough,' I protested, but she just laughed and ruffled my hair, which made me furious.

A fat black woman in the bra shop measured me with cold tape that tickled under my arms. She had terrible body odour and a sleeveless dress. I shifted position slightly.

'Stay still,' hissed Mum.

'Stay still,' hissed the woman and pulled the tape tighter, as punishment. I stood there, trying to hold my breath, the woman's armpit only a few centimetres from my face.

'You are A cup,' the woman announced.

'Is that the smallest?' I asked.

'Yes.'

'Told you, Mum.'

The woman wagged a finger in my face. Even her finger was fat. Each joint was like a sausage on a string. 'You still need proper bra. Everyone need support.'

I hugged my arms across my chest and left the rest to Mum and the saleswoman. They chose two white bras and one black one—flaps of plasticky fabric with mysterious hooks and straps.

It felt strange having something between my skin and my T-shirt. I felt like everyone could tell I was wearing a bra, although Mum swore faithfully that the outline did not show. I remembered when Hennie and I used to run around the garden under the sprinklers in just our underwear, and when Mum told me I could no longer do that. I must have been about six years old.

'Why not?' I had asked.

'It's just not right for girls to do that.'

'Why not?'

99

'Just because. I'll tell you when you're older, hey?'

'But boys do it.'

'Boys are different.'

'Why?'

'They just are.'

I also had to start using deodorant. It came in a little bottle and smelled like talcum powder. I had to slide it around my armpits until they were covered in slimy white which dried to flaky white.

I started getting spots on my face. This did not help matters at school, especially when one of the girls named a spot on my nose 'Old Faithful'. It got to the stage where Saru tutted in concern and made me turn my head this way and that to see how it was progressing.

'This one, it won't go away, hey?'

I pulled my head away. 'It's fine.'

The girls at school knew all about bras and make-up. I studied them. Everything from their walk to the way they reached their hands up to adjust their hair was designed to make the boys look at them. Most of them wore perfume and mascara, and some of them wore lip gloss that smelled like strawberries or bubblegum. Dallas even got her mother to shorten the school uniform to show off her legs. Mum bought my uniform a size bigger, so that I could grow into it.

The black girls were different again. They did not giggle and flick their hair like the white girls did, but they had an easy grace in their bodies. They looked like women already. They also had big boobs, some so big that the girls had to wear bras with wire and upholstery to keep everything pointing up and out. I saw them when they were in

100

the changing rooms after swimming or sports.

'What are you staring at?' asked Yevedzo, one of the biggest girls. I realised I had been watching the mysterious bulge and jiggle of her breasts as she put her shirt on.

'Nothing.'

When my period started, I did not realise it at first. I noticed a brown stain in my underwear, but I threw away that pair and thought I had an upset stomach. When it carried on for another two days, I started to get worried. It had a rusty, dark smell.

On the third day, I sat on the toilet, fully dressed, with the seat down, for almost an hour. I did not know what to do. Mum was not home yet. Finally, I asked Saru. I explained about the brown stuff and how I thought it might be a period.

'*Azwiite.*' It is forbidden.

'Oh.' I felt worse. 'Sorry.'

I wadded several folds of toilet paper into my underwear and waited for Mum to come home. I felt grubby, but I did not want to have a bath until this was sorted out.

'Mum,' I said when she got home. She was busy putting down her car keys, pouring a drink, taking off her sunglasses. I followed her around.

'What?' She did not snap, exactly, but she was preoccupied.

'Mum?'

'*Ja*, what is it?'

'Shhh.' I felt my abdomen contract. 'Mum, I've got my period.'

'You've got what? Stop mumbling.'

'I've got my period.'

Mum's face went soft. She reached out to touch my shoulder, but I jerked it away. I did not want mother–daughter bonding over this—not yet.

She seemed to understand, and became matter-of-fact. 'Stay here.'

She came back with boxes of pads, and told me what to do with them. The whole conversation was excruciating, especially when she offered to come into the toilet with me and help.

'No!'

'Okay.' She raised both hands. 'But give me a shout if you need help, hey?'

'Don't tell Steve,' I begged. I could not bear the thought of anyone looking at me and knowing what was going on in my body.

'Okay.'

I knew she would, but I appreciated the lie.

The next morning I prepared carefully for school. The pad felt strange and bulky inside my underwear, and I knew it was getting heavier with blood already, but I could not risk taking a spare one to school. Sometimes the boys took my bag and scattered my books on the grass. I could not risk something white and embarrassing coming out.

The school play was coming up. I was up a ladder, painting trees on the backdrop, when I heard a voice from below.

'What's that?'

I looked down from my perch on the ladder. Dallas was staring up my skirt at something.

'What?' I put my hands down to clutch my skirt.

She collapsed in giggles. 'Come and look.'

The others crowded around at the bottom of the ladder. I turned around awkwardly and tried to sit on the top step.

'What?' I asked again.

'Are you wearing a pad?' Dallas asked, still giggling.

I could feel my insides curling up small, like a *chongololo* when you poked it with a stick. 'Why?' I asked, and my voice came out too loud.

'There's blood all over your pants,' she said.

The laughter built like the sound of crickets, until the air was thrumming with it.

I came down the ladder as quickly as I could, banging my shin on one of the steps.

'What's going on here?'

One of the teachers walked over.

'She started her period,' said Dallas, pointing at me.

'Oh.' The teacher put on an understanding face. 'Come on, dear.'

She took me to the nurse's office, and gave me a pair of spare underpants they kept in the cupboard for occasions like this: once white, now grey.

Kurai sat with me in the girls' toilets while I cried. She picked at old nail polish on her fingers. 'I don't see why you get so upset about it,' she said. 'You know it's stupid.'

Easy for her to say. She was tall and magnificent.

'I can't go back to class,' I said.

'*Ja.*' She thought about it. 'Go sit behind the classrooms. I'll meet you after school.'

She came to meet me in our secret place. She sat with me in silence while I sniffled.

'It's not such a big deal,' she said.

'I can't go back to class again.'

'Yes you can.'

The borrowed underpants were too big, and bunched up under my skirt. 'I'm going to go home.'

103

'Call your Mum?'

'No, sneak out.'

'You'll never get past the guards.'

School security had tightened. There had always been a guard at the gates, but now there were two. New rules stopped us from venturing outside the gates during the day.

'Don't be stupid. They will have forgotten about it tomorrow. Besides, people like you more now.'

I shook my head.

'It's true. I've raised your street cred.'

I poked my tongue out at her.

'You're my entourage,' she said. 'Under my protection.'

I felt better.

There were food riots in town. People could no longer afford things like bread and milk, and they were protesting. We started having Riot Drills at school. When the alarm sounded, we had to put our hands over our heads and crouch down beneath our desks.

'How is this supposed to help?' whispered Kurai. She had braids put in the day before, and so was not quite resting her hands on her head. They hovered a millimetre or two above.

'I'm not sure.' I saw old chewing gum under my desk. 'This is disgusting.'

'Well, if rioters run through here, do they really expect us to sit under our desks and stay still?' Kurai was indignant. She was halfway through painting one of her nails with Tippex when the alarm bell rang, and it had dried into a strange shape.

'Why would they run through here anyway?'

'Get away from the police.'

I knew that the riots were about food prices. Bread, sugar and Coke were really expensive now. I had also heard that taxes were going up, which did not make much difference to me but made Steve stomp around the house glaring at things. Apparently the taxes were going to pay pensions to the War Vets.

'War Vets!' Steve snorted whenever he heard the term. 'Half of them weren't even alive during the bluddy war. Amazing how many war heroes pop out of the woodwork when it's all over.'

'Are you a War Vet?' I asked Steve. He laughed and laughed until I thought he was going to wet himself.

'You have to be black to be a War Vet. Or a War Hero,' he said.

I used not to pay much attention to the news. Mum and Steve had always complained about Mugabe, but I had almost felt affectionate towards him. He was like a hated headmaster, overbearing and incompetent, towards whom you felt a kind of loyalty. And we were always fine, no matter what happened. Sure, someone might get burgled, we might struggle through a drought or have to pay more for petrol, but our lives were essentially unchanged. Saru was still humming as she folded the clothes. The grass was still green; there was still tea in the silver teapot every day.

Now, however, when I saw a protester on television holding up a sign saying '19 years of corruption is enough!' I started to realise that this was not normal. This was not funny. Mugabe was not a comedy villain, and the people that were getting hurt were real people.

There were pictures on the news of police using

105

horse whips and *sjamboks* to subdue the crowd. I saw a shower of black come out of one man's head, as if it had shattered like a glass bottle into shards of skin. Then I saw the dark specks were blood.

It was hard to believe this was happening in our city. Archie purred in a dark, happy heap on my lap. I could hear the grandfather clock ticking, and I could smell the dinner that Saru was making for us. I wondered what she thought about all of this, but I knew I would never ask her.

*   *   *

The school sports day arrived. We piled off the bus and on to the field, which was looking festive with lines of bunting everywhere, fresh paint on the tracks and a table covered with a white cloth and dozens of trophies.

'Are you running?' I asked Kurai. She hated exercise.

'No way. I told them I have my period.'

Kurai wielded her period to great effect. It appeared every time there was a sporting event. One of the teachers told her that she was lying, that she could not possibly have four periods in a month, but Kurai got her mum to come in and shout at the teacher.

Since then they had left her alone.

We stood in neat rows. The headmistress was about to start proceedings when something stopped her, and she turned to look at the road. We heard drumming, and distant shouts.

We looked around at each other. Someone giggled. Someone else coughed. It was very quiet.

A crackle of static. A teacher had gone over to

the bus and was talking urgently into a radio. She walked back to us briskly, her skirt snapping against her legs. 'Sit down, everyone.'

The teachers moved around us in near-silence, making sure that everyone sat cross-legged on the grass. There were still some giggles, but my chest was throbbing with an unnaturally loud and painful heartbeat.

From the field we could see the main road. A crowd of black men with *sjamboks* and sticks marched down the road towards town. The traffic tried to weave around and past them, but there were too many.

We watched as the crowd passed an elderly couple sitting in their car. The old man gripped the steering wheel and stared straight ahead. The first few members of the crowd passed by with cheerful whistles and a few bangs on the roof. The next few stopped and started shouting things through the window. We could not hear what they were saying from the field, but we could see the old man's profile staring resolutely in front of him.

The wife looked more agitated.

Kurai eyed them. 'Must be scary.'

'My brother's cycling home,' whispered Dallas. 'I hope he doesn't run into them.'

'If he sees them he'll turn around and go back,' I tried to comfort her.

She shook her head. 'No. He'll call them bluddy Kaffirs and get beaten up. That's just the sort of thing he does.'

Now a crowd had gathered either side of the car. They started to rock it back and forth rhythmically. Some of the people streaming past were carrying flaming sticks. It seemed just a matter of time before someone decided to set fire to the car.

As I watched, I saw the old man bang his head on the window. A dark line appeared on his forehead.

'Don't look at them!' a teacher snapped, and I forced my eyes away again. We sat as quietly as we could, not even daring to brush the flies off our bare knees. My hand was in the grass, and I quietly tore off little blades and crushed them between my fingers.

Grip, crush, release.

After a long time, the shouts faded away. We sat surrounded by cheerful flags and trophies. The warmth of the sun had moved from my shoulder to the very top of my head.

I heard sirens. I did not look at the road.

'Back in the bus, everyone,' said the headmistress, and we trudged back. My leg had fallen asleep, and I had a cross-hatch of red lines on my shins where they had been pressed against the grass. Teachers put the trophies back in their boxes.

'Oh well,' said Kurai, 'at least we didn't have to run.'

'I suppose. I wonder what all that was about?'

She shrugged. 'Bread, probably.'

CHAPTER ELEVEN

The rainy season began. The clouds emptied as if Saru were wringing out a wet cleaning cloth, and the air was charged with electricity. Mum got her storm headaches, and lay on the bed with two slices of cucumber over her eyes. There was a blue crackle on Archie's fur when I stroked him.

I sat at my window and watched the rain. Storm clouds stalked the city on lightning legs, and I played the counting game between the lightning and the thunder. When I saw the flash of light, I started counting under my breath.

'One *chongololo*, two *chongololo*, three *chongololo* . . .'

The *chongololos* lined up. Three meant that the storm was three kilometres away. When you could not get to the end of the word before the thunder started, the storm was over you.

Our garden became red slush, the grass uprooting and floating on the water in tufts. We could not help tracking mud into the kitchen whenever we came inside, and Saru spent hours down on her knees, scrubbing at the tiles. A slumped pile of muddy flip-flops and *takkies* developed just inside the door, on a sheet of newspaper that soon became pulp.

Then came the flying ants, and Saru almost gave up on the kitchen floor altogether. When the rain touched the soil they came out of their underground burrows and corkscrewed into the air. Archie danced in the garden, twisting his long body in unlikely ways to claw them out of the sky.

Flying ants led pointless lives—one dance in the rain, and then they lost their wings and became weak, squishable things crawling on their bellies. They came into the house through every window and door, and flopped about for hours in long, melodramatic death throes. Their wings were crisp, with wiry veins connecting the sheets of brittle skin, and they floated through the house in great drifts, piling up against walls and catching in the bristles of Saru's broom. When she brushed them outside, the wind swept them back in.

With storms came the power cuts. We were used to these. They usually happened in the evenings, when a power line was struck by lightning or hit by a falling tree branch. The TV screen folded to a tiny white square, then blinked off. The lights flared, then darkened.

'Everyone stay still,' said Steve, as he did every time the power went off.

There was a thud as he bumped into the furniture, and a swear word. We heard him fumbling in the cupboard. A pale cone of light appeared as he switched on the torch. That was the signal for Mum and me to get matches and light the candles we kept around the room. Steve laid the fire, and Archie hovered near him, waiting for warmth.

Next came the camping stove on its little gas cylinder. Mum heated up some baked beans for supper. Steve tuned his radio to the BBC World Service, and we sat with our food on our laps, hunched over and huddled, our faces sunburned in the candlelight. The rain drummed the roof like impatient fingers on a table.

After supper there was nothing to do but play cards. It was too dim to read, and there was no television. We paused only to let Mum call ZESA and ask about the fault.

ZESA knew Mum well. 'It is the mad white woman again.' I could hear the tinny voice of the operator from the receiver. After five or six phone calls, we heard that someone had been sent to fix the problem.

'So it'll be another four hours then,' muttered Steve.

It was almost a pity when the lights came back on. The shrunken world sprang outwards again to touch every far wall. Interesting shadows became the same old furniture. Our eyes, dark and mysterious, returned to their normal washed-out selves.

In the morning, the garden was flattened and swampy, the plants drooping and grey. The world was a jigsaw of puddles linked by slim sections of solid ground, and the storm drains became bridges over slow-moving brown rivers. Dead rodents and insects floated on the surface of the water. The sun looked rinsed and paler than usual; the air smelled clean. I wanted to bottle the air somehow for those days when the world was stale and baked, but instead I plunged my hands into the wet soil and sniffed the secret, mineral smell of plant roots and the burrows of insects. Worms slid away from my hands and down tiny tunnels.

'What are you doing?' said Mum. 'Come and wash your hands.'

My fingers were red with mud. Mum helped me scrub under my nails in the kitchen sink, but we could not get all of it out. Red lines like veins snaked through every crack in my skin.

'Well, that was a bluddy stupid idea,' Mum said.

I did not care. The rains brought life. The yellow grass turned green and lush, and the plants swelled and sprouted to double their normal size. Birdsong sounded painfully loud in the mornings. The crickets screamed at night. The cane rats Archie lined up at the door were fat and robustly healthy. The soil was a rich blood-red, writing

111

with worms. Everything was alive, moving and growing, and the farm crops flourished.

White farmers and their land were on the news every night. Steve said that Mugabe wanted to take the land away from them. I was in favour of resettlement, after hanging out with Kurai and her friends.

'You think it's really going to go to the poor people?' said Steve. 'Bob wants to give it to his cronies, that's all.'

'Then why is he doing it?'

'Because there's an election coming up,' said Steve.

'Is he going to take Uncle Pieter's land? And Mr Cooper's?'

'Nah, it's not going to come to anything,' said Steve. 'It's just a lot of spear-rattling before the election. Mugabe needs the white farmers. They're the ones that keep the economy going.'

I could not imagine anyone making Mr Cooper leave his farm. He was so fluent in Shona and so respected by his workers that he seemed almost superhuman. I could not imagine Lettuce and Jeans and the other black foremen letting War Vets wander in and take over without a fight.

We were not worried, for the most part. The farm was always sunlit. The winds that blew across it smelled sharp and hot. There was energy in the air—machines grinding gears, people working in the fields, animals running in the paddocks, everything working towards prosperity and wealth. The whole farm shone with money spent and earned.

Although Mum had protested about the meat hooks being right outside her office, they were still there. Mr Cooper was in the office one day chatting to Mum, and I was sitting on the step outside, when a couple of workers came to the offices dragging a skinny *mombe* on a piece of rope.

'Sah!' They called from outside. They must have spotted his motorbike.

'I'll get him.' I went inside. Mr Cooper was sitting on the edge of Mum's desk, as he always did, chatting. Mum was leaning back in her chair and patting her hair with one hand.

'Mr Cooper!'

He came with me and saw the thin cow on the fraying rope.

'Sah, she is sick,' said one of the workers.

Even I could see she was sick. The cow was swaying. Every so often a shudder went through her bony frame.

'Any chance she's going to recover?'

'No, Baas.' The worker shook his head. 'Sorry, Baas.'

'It's not your fault, man.' Mr Cooper gave the cow a long, considering look. '*Ja*, okay.'

He strode over to his *bakkie* and pulled out his gun. It was an elephant gun. I fired one once, at a school camp, and it almost dislocated my shoulder when it kicked back.

'You might want to go back inside,' he said to me. 'It's not going to be pretty.'

'Nah, I'm okay,' I said, trying to be a blasé farm kid.

'All right, if you're sure.'

His eyes narrowed. He swung the blunt, snake-like head of the gun around until it almost touched the centre of the cow's forehead.

113

The cow closed her eyes, as if in relief. Her legs trembled, once, and then the gun went off with a crack that sounded more like a car backfiring than a gunshot, and she slumped to the ground.

I turned away, but not before I saw the first worker start to hack at the animal with a *bhadza*. He lifted it above his head, and the sticky, red edge of the axe blade caught the light. I felt a shiver. I reached my hand up to my forehead to brush away a piece of hair, and when my hand came away there was a dark smear on it.

'What's that?' Mr Cooper looked at my hand. He sucked his breath inwards in a whistle. 'Look at that. Must have sprayed some blood out after all. What are the odds, hey?'

He gave me his big, white handkerchief and I brushed it across my forehead. There were only a few spots of red on the cotton.

'Now you're one of us,' he said, and grinned. He had a smear of blood on his hand too. Noticing, he wiped it with his thumb and imprinted it on his own forehead. It looked incongruously like a lipstick stain, as if someone had kissed him.

'Blooded,' he said. 'That's what they do in the English fox-hunts, you know?'

I shook my head.

'They put some of the fox's blood on the forehead of the new hunters. Initiation. Stupid custom.' He smiled.

'*Ja*,' I said. I offered him the handkerchief.

'Nah, it's okay,' he said. 'You keep it.'

I crumpled the handkerchief up to hide the redness. Mr Cooper climbed into his *bakkie* and started it up.

'Cheers.' The red blood on his forehead shone

114

like a gummy smile. I felt a shiver of cold.

'Goodbye.'

The air smelled like meat. On my way back to the office I caught a glimpse of the workers cutting the cow into pieces to be hauled away, even though I tried not to look. They were humming as they worked. One of them flashed me a grin, and raised his hand, palm flat, in a wave.

I threw the bloody handkerchief in the bin as soon as I got inside.

*   *   *

Three ostriches went missing from the paddocks that week. I was with Mum on the day she found out about it, and called Mr Cooper to tell him.

'*Ja*, three,' she said. 'No, no one knows. I've asked Jeans. *Ja*. Okay.'

She hung up. 'He's going to talk to the workers.'

'Why?' I asked.

'Because one of them did it.'

'How do you know?'

Mum sighed. 'The whole thing is too well organised. It has to be someone from the farm. They probably took them for the meat.'

Mr Cooper gathered all the workers together and asked them about the ostriches. His Shona was fluent and colloquial, and his speech got a few laughs as well as the expected shame-faced shuffling.

'Come on, guys,' he said at the end. 'I'll be in my office all morning. Come forward and tell me who did it.'

He sat in his office all day, but no one came to talk to him. Streams of workers passed by on their way to or from somewhere else, but the streams parted and braided around the office. At the end of the day, when Mum and I loaded the car, we saw Mr Cooper come out of the office and light a cigarette.

'Good night, Baas.'

'*Manheru*, Baas.'

The workers greeted him and smiled as they passed. Their faces were empty of everything but friendliness. Mr Cooper lifted a hand to Mum and me as we drove off.

'I guess that's that,' I said.

'No,' said Mum. 'He has something else up his sleeve, don't worry.'

It sounded as if he were engaged in a war with the workers: a strange, amicable war of smiles and jokes that did not disguise the fact that it was always Them versus Us. Respect and affection on both sides, but a healthy dose of suspicion and cynicism as well. I thought Mum was right. Mr Cooper could not let this one lie, not if he wanted to keep up the rumour that he had eyes in the back of his head. He must have a plan.

He gathered the workers together again. They stood in front of him, looking everywhere but at his eyes.

Whites often thought Shona people were untrustworthy, because their ways of communication were so different. In Shona culture, it was rude to look someone directly in the eye, as it represented a challenge. If you tried to make eye contact with a Shona, their gaze would slide away.

'Shifty,' said people who did not understand, and 'untrustworthy'.

116

Shona handshakes were also misunderstood. The kind of people who say 'You can tell a lot about a man by his handshake' are the kind of people who grasp your hand firmly and pump it up and down while staring with great intensity into your eyes. Frank. Open. Firm. They will be disappointed by Shona handshakes, which are limp and slither out of your hand like a fish eager to get back to the water.

Mr Cooper waited, watching the workers' eyes look everywhere but at his face. He saw the sheepish smiles. He heard the nervous laughs. When no one came forward, he smiled and told them in perfect Shona that they would all be fined to cover the cost of the missing ostriches unless they gave up the culprits. Still nothing.

'Oh well,' said Mum when we got back to the office. 'At least you'll get the money back.'

'*Ja*,' said Mr Cooper. He was frowning. 'But I want to prove a point to these guys.'

'What are you going to do?' Mum asked.

Mr Cooper called in the witch doctor. He made a big show of welcoming him into his office, making sure that all the workers could see. The witch doctor was also a showman. He made a point of embracing Mr Cooper, and shook his rattle (a gourd filled with seeds) enthusiastically. The workers slid their gaze over to him, then away.

After an hour, the witch doctor emerged from the office. After another elaborate embrace and a lot of back-slapping with Mr Cooper, he left.

The next day, Mr Cooper called the workers together again. 'I have spoken to the *N'anga*,' he said. Instantly, everyone looked worried. The mood fell like woodsmoke sinking to the ground.

117

'If the bodies of the ostriches aren't returned,' said Mr Cooper, 'I am handing over the matter to the *N'anga*, and he will deal with it.'

The following morning, there were three dead ostriches laid out neatly in a row in front of Mr Cooper's office. They had not been touched.

'Magic,' said Mr Cooper to us with a grin. He left, whistling.

At lunchtime that day I sat outside, reading and eating a *naartjie*. The *naartjie*'s skin was thin and tightly bound to the flesh, and it was a messy business peeling it off. I was so involved in the operation that I did not see the woman walking past until she was right in front of me.

'Afternoon,' I greeted her, startled.

'*Masikati.*'

She was carrying a sack of mealie-meal on her head. She had close-cropped wiry hair and skin glowing like expensive dark furniture, or the parquet floors after Saru had polished them. Red earth powdered her feet and ankles, and the long yellow grass sweeping at her knees made her look as if she were walking through fire.

I watched her pass, fascinated. Her loose breasts swayed like ripe pawpaws on a tree, and she had the same stride as the slow-stepping ostrich that eyed her from behind the fence. I looked down to my own legs and saw knees scaly from scabs and grazes, and chubby white flesh. My skin looked an unhealthy colour in the noon light, veiny and blue. It did not have that polished-wood glow.

In reality, no one was really white (white like blank paper, or clean washing); people were pink, sunburnt red, sallow or brown. White was a state of mind. White was being shunted hurriedly to the

118

front of a queue, watched by a hundred resentful eyes. White was money, swimming pools, two cars. It was glow-in-the-dark, marking you at once on a black street. All those poems we learned at school about skin fair as snow, fair as petals or milk or cream, did not take the other side of it into account—the lack of pigment, the sickly, greenish tinge that white skin could have, the way it made us ghosts in a vivid country.

Sean roared up on the bike. Mum looked up from her work and gave me a knowing look, and I glared at her and stomped off.

I went out the back to sit with the ostrich babies, and watched one of them trying to run through a solid wall. They were even stupider than chickens, with long, adolescent legs.

Sean found me. 'Howzit! What are you up to?'

'Watching the ostriches.'

'All right.' He stood with his hands on his hips, unconsciously (or consciously?) copying his father's pose.

'Hey, come here a sec,' he said.

I stood up and made a big show of brushing the sand off my knees. 'What?'

'Come on the bike. I've got something to show you.'

'What sort of thing?'

'Just come, man.'

I walked with him, feeling the new bra move with my body. I crossed my arms over my chest, afraid he would see it.

'What do you think about this land redistribution stuff?' I said when we reached the bike. I wanted to show him that I was aware of the political situation, that even though he was older

119

than me and starting to think about leaving school, I no longer thought of him as a big hero.

'It's stupid, man. They'll never do it, *ek sei*? The farms are too important. We bring in all the money.'

Sean had started talking like this lately. 'I tuned him this'. 'What's the *gwan*?' It was the way the black kids in my class talked. I could not blame him—I had started wearing an Oliver Mtukudzi vest and wooden jewellery, and listening to the same music Kurai listened to.

'So you guys are staying here?'

'Of course.' Sean grinned suddenly. 'I've got to take over the farm, hey?'

'Not yet.'

'Nah, but one day. Think I'll make a good Big Baas?'

I looked at him. I could imagine him joking with the workers like his father did, knowing each of them by name. 'Maybe.'

'*Ja*, you know it.' He was still grinning. My skin itched, and I scratched my arm, hard, raising a pink welt.

'*Ja*, well, there's more to running a farm than speaking Shona.'

'Sure, I know.'

I shrugged. 'Doesn't sound like it.'

'Eeesh,' he drew his breath in through his teeth. 'You're like a bluddy porcupine today. What's up?'

'Nothing.' I did not know what was up, except that it had something to do with bras and periods and seeing that beautiful African woman walk past. 'I'm busy. I'm working with Mum.'

'Agh, fine.' He glared at me. 'Suit yourself.' He climbed back on the bike, gave me an exaggerated wave and kicked it into life. A few minutes later, Shumba came lolloping around the corner. He must have followed Sean from the house, and only just caught up. I poured him a bowl of water and watched as he gulped it down, smiling at me sidelong with his black lips and eyes.

'Dumb dog,' I said, and reached out to ruffle his ears. I heard the motorbike in the distance, and felt something watching me. A touch on the nape of my neck. I straightened up and looked around—nothing but gum trees. I thought I had imagined it, but the fur on Shumba's back was lifted, and his lips were pulled back in a half-snarl.

I felt like I had received a warning. The sound of Sean's motorbike had faded completely, but I felt an urge to run after him, call him back.

That night I lay awake for a long time. It felt like the land had taken a breath, and we were all waiting for it to exhale.

CHAPTER TWELVE

Whites, whites, whites, was all we heard on the news. We were being blamed for everything, but especially for taking land away from the blacks back when we were British and not Zimbabwean. I knew I was white, but I was a Zimbabwean too. Mum was born here. Steve was born here. How long did we have to be here before we were properly Zimbabwean?

The Shona said that killing a person tied you to the place where you committed the murder. The blood spilled on the soil had a power that would

121

draw you back, and *ngozi*—the vengeful spirits of the dead—would follow you. It must work with birth as well as death, I thought. There must be some primitive magic to tie you to the place where you were born, where you slid out of your mother bloody and gasping, mouth open like a dying person gulping for air.

Munyu was a smiling, blue-black man with teeth too big for his jaw. He was a worker, to begin with, but was soon promoted to foreman because of his smile and easy friendliness; a friendliness that did not step over the line of proper respect, and made everyone feel good.

'He knows his place,' said someone.

'He obviously loves his job,' said another.

'He's a bluddy good guy,' said Steve when he came home.

It occurred to me that white people often said black people obviously enjoyed their jobs, because they were so often smiling and laughing or humming as they worked. Tatenda sang all day in the garden, so much that Mum started closing the windows on whatever side of the house was closest to him. When he shifted to a different job in a different part of the garden, she got up and opened those windows, and closed others.

'Why don't you just ask him to stop?' I said.

'It's nice that he sings,' said Mum. 'I just don't want to listen to it all day.'

'Why is it nice?'

'Because it shows he's happy.'

The Shona sang all the time. I did not think it meant that they were always happy.

Mum suggested asking Munyu and his wife to our house for tea.

'*Ja*, maybe it's a good idea,' said Steve.

We were all treading warily then, trying to prove we were proper white Zimbabweans, not leftover Rhodies. Steve issued the invitation, and a date was set.

It was strange seeing Saru serve tea to Munyu and his wife. Munyu took the china cup with gracious thanks, and held it delicately. Saru was clearly disgruntled. She sighed heavily and deliberately clattered things on the tray as she placed it on the table.

'Thank you, Saru,' said Mum.

'*Mazvita tatenda*, *Amai*,' said Munyu. Saru gave him a heavy-lidded, expressionless stare and stalked back to the kitchen with a stiff back.

Mum made bright conversation with Munyu's wife, Nyasha. So what do you do, Nyasha? Really? How interesting. And how long have you been married? The men perched right on the edge of their chairs, with their legs apart in a manly way, nodding and smiling more than was required.

We had to avoid so many subjects. When we had white guests, Steve could relax in his chair and complain about the servants and that bluddy *munt* in charge of it all, and gossip about the farmers we knew. We could not talk about any of those things.

I noticed Mum was wearing a colourful print skirt, vaguely African, and Steve was in his Lake Kariba shirt. Even I was wearing my wooden giraffe necklace. Munyu and Nyasha were in carefully Western clothes—polo shirts, slacks. When Tatenda came around to water the beds by the verandah, we all sat and watched him— whistling, dousing the plants with far too much water. Normally Steve would have told him off, but not today. We sat and watched Tatenda, and felt a sense that the world was wrong, that things were not aligned properly today. Eventually Steve sent him off to the back of the house instead, which should have made things easier, but now we had nothing to look at but each other.

Soon Munyu cleared his throat and got to his feet. He was still holding his teacup and had to take a step forward to put it down, almost colliding with Steve, who had got up to shake his hand. The china looked delicate and too pretty in his big black hand, and he set it down far too carefully. He and Nyasha made their excuses. Thank you, thank you, lovely, must do it again, come to our place. Nyasha clapped her cupped hands before shaking Mum's.

When they were gone, the whole house took a breath of relief. We sat down for another cup of tea on the verandah.

'Six sugars, she had in her tea,' said Mum as if she were talking to herself.

'*Ja*, well . . .' said Steve, letting his sentence trail off. Everyone knew that blacks had lots of sugars in their tea.

'Nice couple,' said Mum.

'*Ja*, very.' Steve heaved himself out of his chair. 'Did you see Tatenda soaking those poor bluddy plants? I've told him a hundred times.'

'I'd better tell Saru about dinner,' said Mum.

Everything was all wrong. I felt a painful tenderness towards Munyu and Nyasha. I wanted to run after them and tell them not to worry, it was our problem. We were the ones who could not seem to get rid of our old ideas. Perhaps Mugabe was right, in some ways.

'What is the Baas thinking?' Saru said to me in Shona as she did the washing up. She had broken a glass already, as she tended to when she did the washing up in a heightened emotional state.

I lounged against the bench, drinking a Coke. If Mum were here she would have told me to do the drying up, but when I did Saru and I spent all our time apologising whenever we brushed against each other, and it was less stressful just to let her get on with it.

'What do you mean?' I asked.

'Bringing such guests.' Saru knew by now that I did not report any of our conversations to Mum and Steve. This meant that I heard a lot of the neighbourhood gossip, as well as some interesting insights into my own family.

'I don't know.'

Saru tutted to herself. I could see she was genuinely upset.

'Why . . .' I thought of how to phrase it. 'Why didn't you like the guests?'

'It is not right,' said Saru. 'I should not have to serve them.'

Saru and Tatenda had their own world within ours—their secret jokes, their Shona conversations, their good-natured pilfering of small items—like students passing notes behind a teacher's back. And, apparently, their own rules.

Maybe we were not the only ones still clinging to old ideas. We saw blacks on the news saying, 'These whites treat us like dogs. We won the war for Independence, and they lost. They should not be allowed to treat us like this. They should behave like people who lost a war, instead of like British Imperialists.'

We heard stories of the workers on white farms turning against their masters, just as we heard stories of the workers rising up to defend the big Baases. I could not imagine Tatenda and Saru having the same thoughts about us. Saru smiled constantly—the first thing I saw in the morning was her smile, and as she left in the evenings to go back to her family, her teeth were a white slash in the darkness. Tatenda sang, whistled and hummed all day, cracked jokes, flirted, played with the cat. Did they really wish us gone? Or worse?

Once I had this thought I started to notice things. I noticed how Saru would sometimes look at us with a cold, absent gaze, as if a mask had slipped for a moment. I noticed the way she smiled unapologetically after Mum reprimanded her (awkwardly and unwillingly—Mum had never learned the regal white way of dealing with servants) for some error. I listened to the songs Tatenda was humming, and I was sure I could hear some of the pro-Mugabe tunes in there. But I could have imagined that.

White farmers appeared every day on the news and in the papers.

Mum thought that the land should be redistributed. 'We did take it away from them,' she said, 'and we need to give it back if we're going to move forward as a nation.'

'Bluddy ridiculous,' said Steve. 'Half that land wasn't even arable until the whites sank wells and cultivated the soil.'

'That's not the point,' I said, siding with Mum. 'They were here first.' The word 'they' sat strangely in my mouth. I would rather have said 'we'. My whiteness felt like badly fitting clothes.

126

'*Ja*, well, the farmers now aren't the bluddy first settlers who took the land. They inherited it or bought it legally and they shouldn't have to give it up.'

'I'm not saying they shouldn't have compensation,' said Mum. 'And they wouldn't have to give up all the land.'

'*Ja*, and give it to people who'll grow five mealies for their families and export nothing. The economy will collapse, man.'

'Not if people are trained properly,' Mum said. 'I think this is a good thing.'

'I'm sure Mugabe will keep the whole thing legal and above board,' said Steve with heavy sarcasm.

'All I'm saying is that if they do it properly I think it is a good idea.'

'Bluddy *Kaffir-boetie*,' said Steve. He said it jokingly, but I saw him twirling his glass, watching the ice melt into the gin, and I wondered if he would be a bitter old Rhodie one day, when the harsh African heat and the dust and the relentless struggle had worn him down.

We hardly ever went into the central city. Our lives revolved around our house, the farm, the shopping centre and school. The rest of the country might as well not have existed for all we saw of it.

Biking down to the farm shop one day, I rode up on to the footpath and almost hit a little black girl who was walking with her dad. The girl's hair was braided close to her head and fixed with little pink ribbons at the end of each stiff ridge. Someone must have spent hours getting her ready. She squealed and jumped aside, and I swerved.

'Sorry!' I said, but her father had already started

shaking his fist.

'You bluddy white kids, you think you own the place!' he shouted. 'You could have killed my daughter!'

'I'm sorry.' I stopped a few feet behind them.

'You think you can do whatever you want, but this is our country! Go back to Britain!'

I felt like I should stay there and debate this with him. Convince him that I was a real Zimbabwean, despite my skin, and that I was not going to run away to a country that was not truly mine. Instead, I jumped back on the bike and pedalled as fast as I could.

The next time I realised that I was a 'White' with a capital letter was when I accompanied Kurai to the driver's licence office. She was desperate for the freedom of a car. Technically you had to be fifteen to get a learner's licence, but everyone knew you could bribe the officials to give you one earlier.

'Sha, imagine being able to go wherever you want, whenever you want,' she said.

Our world had shrunk so much that it was difficult to think about going somewhere new.

We went to the licensing office and joined the queue. It snaked out of the main buildings, out of the iron gates, and out on to the road. There were over a hundred people in front of us.

'And, of course, I need to pee,' said Kurai. 'Typical. See a loo?'

'No.'

'Typical.'

We stood in line with the others. I noticed that I was the only white person there. A group of men stood a few metres away, not in the queue. They pointed at me and talked rapidly amongst themselves in Shona.

'What's going on?' I asked Kurai.

She shrugged. 'No idea.'

One man split away from the group and came over to us.

'Hello,' he said, with an ingratiating smile. He was missing his two front teeth.

'Hi,' I said. Kurai just raised her eyebrows.

'You want driver's licence?' he asked me.

'Um . . .'

'I get it for you, cheap-cheap.'

'Uh, no thanks.'

'Five hundred dollars,' he said. His face was close to mine, and I could see the shine of sweat on his upper lip.

'We're not interested,' said Kurai.

The man shrugged and went back to his group, waving his hand at us in what I hoped was a friendly way.

An official poked his head out from the office and spotted us. A couple of minutes later, a man in uniform came down the line.

'Are you queuing for a driver's licence?' he asked us.

'Yes,' said Kurai.

'Come.' He led us into the office, past a row of accusing faces.

'Is it just because I'm white?' I asked Kurai in a whisper.

'*Ja*.'

'But they hate me.'

'Maybe, but you have money. Or, at least, they think you do.'

'That's not fair.'

129

'No, but it's better than standing in that queue for another two hours. I still need to pee.'

When we got inside, the officials were smiling and friendly. Kurai got her licence without any trouble.

'Have a nice day,' said one of the men when we left. We walked past the accusing faces again.

My skin had such power, good and bad.

*   *   *

Several weeks later, I asked about Munyu and his wife.

'Oh,' said Steve, 'I thought I'd told you. Munyu died last week, suddenly. Turned out he had AIDS.'

'What about Nyasha?'

Steve shrugged. But we both knew.

CHAPTER THIRTEEN

The workers on the farm started to complain about *tokoloshes*. According to legend, they hid under beds and attacked their victims in the night. The workers raised their beds high on bricks, so that they could spot any lurking *tokoloshes*. Others claimed to see leopards walking upright like men. A child went missing from one of the compounds.

'He wandered into the Bush,' said Mr Cooper. 'Probably got snapped up by a mangy lion too slow to catch buck. Nothing mysterious there.'

But the workers thought differently. Some of them stopped coming to work.

'Bluddy ridiculous,' said Steve.

The farm was built on old blood and bones, and something had freed them. I remembered the words of the witch doctor in Chinhoyi. 'You have misfortune following you.'

I woke up in the middle of the night, my head alert and fizzing with thoughts. Someone stood in my doorway.

'Mum?'

I could not tell who it was—it was too dark—but it looked like a man's figure.

'Steve?'

The person just stood there, turning his head slightly to look at me. I made no sound. The world slowed down and congealed, and I had to force my lungs to expand and contract, suck air in and blow it out. My heart felt sluggish and strained. I tried to call out for Mum again, but it took effort to force the tiniest sluice of air through my throat.

The figure disappeared, and my voice came out in a rush, far louder than I had intended.

'Mum!'

Mum came down the corridor. Her voice was late-night hoarse, with a thread of panic.

'What?'

I told her about the man.

'You were dreaming. Go back to sleep.'

'I was wide awake.'

Mum leaned against the door frame. 'You know you're always talking yourself into seeing things. Remember the *tokoloshe*?'

'The *tokoloshe* was there too.'

'I'm not getting into this now, hey. Go to sleep.'

Later in the night, I woke up to the sound of someone talking. It sounded like a radio or

131

television had been left on. I lay in bed for a while, trying to disentangle the voices into separate words.

Mum appeared in my doorway with a torch. 'There's a power cut,' she whispered. 'Can you hear that?'

'*Ja*. What is it?'

'I don't know. I thought it was coming from the lounge.'

'I thought it was coming from your room.'

'It must be from the *khaya*,' said Mum. 'I'll have to tell Tatenda not to play his radio at all hours of the night.'

'What time is it?'

'After two.'

I followed Mum down the corridor. The radio voices faded out. I clicked the switches automatically as we entered the lounge, then remembered there was no power.

'Does it sound like it's coming from outside to you?'

'Let's not go outside.' Outside was snapping twigs, velvety darkness, spirits calling like owls across the night.

'*Ja*, no, hey, we'll stay indoors.'

The lights came back on with blazing force. A bulb popped somewhere.

'Shit!' said Mum, then clapped a hand over her mouth, giggling. 'Don't you start saying it just because I did, okay?'

'Okay.'

I started giggling too. We stared at each other. Our eyes looked naked and hollow, bigger than usual, like the pale eyes of bushbabies.

'What the yell is going on?' said Steve from the

bedroom.

'Nothing.' Mum clicked off her torch. 'Do you want some tea?'

'Well, I'm awake now.'

The noises came the next night, and the next. Even Steve heard them. Archie's tail was permanently half-fluffed.

'Jeez, man,' said Steve at breakfast, 'this is getting ridiculous.'

He took Tatenda aside. I could only hear bits and pieces of the conversation until their voices became raised.

'Well, someone around here is playing a bluddy radio!' said Steve. 'You must have heard something.'

Tatenda replied, but he spoke softly.

'Then who is it?'

Steve listened to Tatenda's reply, then threw up his hands and stormed over to us. 'He says it's not him.'

'We heard.'

*   *   *

Mum and Steve went out to dinner. They paid Saru to stay later and look after me. I lay on their bed watching television, listening to dishes clinking in the kitchen.

Archie made himself comfortable at the foot of the bed and started washing. I could hear the rasp of his tongue. Suddenly he stopped, and was very still. The room felt colder, and the television screen developed uneven grey lines across the picture. The bedside light flickered.

I looked over to the open door leading to the

bathroom. I could hear a tap dripping. Archie sat upright, his eyes very wide and yellow. The hair rose on his spine, starting from his head and moving down to his tail. Finally his tail puffed up, and his ears flattened. I felt something watching me from the doorway. I wanted to speak, but my tongue seemed to have doubled in size.

The open doorway grew, looked darker and more gaping the longer I stared at it. The hairs on the back of my arm rose with a crackle and snap. Static. The television screen went fuzzy too, and only vague shapes of people appeared before being whisked away into a grey snowstorm. An arm. A hand. A face. A collection of letters, indecipherable.

The air was thick and tasted like metal.

After a minute of this, Archie slowly started to relax. Watching him, so did I.

The television image cleared, and the room seemed warm again.

I took no chances, though. Hauling the duvet after me, I trotted down the corridor to where Saru was sitting in the living room, and without a word sat next to her on the couch.

The strange incidents mounted up. Footsteps followed us from room to room, and even out into the garden. Pictures fell off walls, little objects went missing and turned up in strange places. Steve found his car keys in the fridge. Glass vases fell off shelves and shattered. There were spots in the house that felt cold for no reason. The cat became skittish, jumping sideways down the corridor or suddenly bristling up.

Mum asked the other farm managers about it.

'*Ja*, we've had some strange stuff happen,' one

of them said. 'Thought it was the servants.'

Every white on the farm was on edge. None of them admitted to believing in spirits, but all of them did. It felt like the farm did not want us there.

That weekend, I went to Mr Cooper's house to take the dogs for their walk. As soon as I entered his garden, I tripped over nothing at all and fell over.

Jonah watched me with empty eyes as I floundered. I felt like he knew more about what was going on than he would say. To get out of his line of sight, I walked down towards the back fence.

'Go carefully,' he called out. 'There are snakes down there.'

I walked faster. The garden was poisonous green, humming with bees. I called the dogs, but they did not come. I would have to look for them.

I saw a brown shape out of the corner of my eye. One of the dogs, playing games? When I looked around, however, it had moved just out of sight again. This happened so often that I decided to try to track whatever-it-was down. When I saw the flicker of movement at the edge of my vision, I started walking towards it, keeping my head turned away. Doing this, I ended up at the far edge of the garden, near the compost heap. There were so many flies that their buzzing was not so much a noise as a throbbing in the air.

I stepped carefully over kitchen scraps—banana skins, avocado pips, potato peelings—and walked towards the strange movement. It was that time of day when the sky was leeched of colour and the first mosquitoes were starting to whine, just before the sun dropped abruptly off the edge of the earth.

I heard a crunch, and looked down. I had crushed a *chongololo*, and it was not quite dead. Its body was flailing on the ground, spewing yellow liquid, and its little blind eyes stared up at me. It had a fine fur of tiny yellow legs along each side, and they furled themselves into clenched claws of pain.

Chongololos emerged from all over the compost heap. Maybe it was going to rain—but I had never seen so many at once. The flies hovered in the air, watching me.

I caught the movement again, just on the edge of my vision. I felt something tickling the back of my neck and put up a hand to brush away whatever flying thing had landed on me, but realised that it was not an insect. The air thickened with static, and my hair gently lifted itself off my scalp. Something snapped my feet out from under me. The ground rushed up towards my face, and my nose spurted blood. I did not realise I had actually hit the ground until the pain arrived, a couple of moments later.

I lay there, watching the blood drip red on to the ground, turn brown and sink into the thirsty earth. My bleeding had somehow released the tension in the air, as if whatever knocked me down would only be satisfied with an offering.

I looked up and saw a crowd of people staring at me. They were not transparent or pearly white, like the ghosts I had seen on television; they were stained with dirt, sweat and blood. Some were black and some were white, but all of them were silent and staring at me. They reeked of decay and body odour.

I screamed. Jonah came—not running, but walking.

'Medem?'

I looked at him, and then back to where the crowd had stood. They were gone. 'Did you see them?'

Jonah shook his head. 'I have to get back to work,' he said.

I watched him go. I knew he had seen them too.

Mum and Steve called in a priest from church to say a prayer in our house. He came with his Bible, wearing full regalia. I sat with my knees drawn up to my chest and watched. He had a bottle of water that he sprinkled on the rug and he said prayers in English and Latin.

'Thank you,' said Mum as he left.

'You're very welcome,' he said. 'I don't think you'll have any more problems.'

That night was worse than any of the others. As well as the voices, there were footsteps up and down the corridor, and a painting fell off the lounge wall. None of us got any sleep.

'For Christ's sake,' said Steve at four in the morning. His skin looked crumpled, like slept-in sheets.

'Maybe we could try something else,' I said.

'Like what?'

I asked Saru the next day.

'Black man's medicine does not work on white spirits,' she said. Her face was implacable.

'Please, Saru.' I had great faith in the powers of the *N'anga*. 'Just ask. They might not be white spirits, anyway, we don't know who they are.'

'I will ask,' she said, 'but I do not think he will come.'

137

He came. Our electric gate intercom buzzed and Mum answered it.

'Who did you say you were?' she said into the speaker. I heard muffled Shona from the other end. Mum turned around to stare at me and I jumped up and pressed the button to let him in.

'It's the witch doctor, Mum,' I said.

'What witch doctor?'

'I asked Saru to ask the witch doctor to come to the house. To get rid of the spirits.'

'You did what?'

'It's worth a try, isn't it?'

Mum looked at me. She picked up one of the walking sticks that we kept by the door. 'All right. But we'll keep an eye on him, hey? And if he steals anything, it's your fault.'

The witch doctor was a small man, wearing jeans and a shirt. I could only tell that he was a *N'anga* from the string of wooden necklaces he wore, and the little bag of rattles, powders, feathers and stones that he carried.

As soon as he got inside he stopped and sniffed the air. 'Ah yes,' he said, 'there are definitely *vadzimu* here.'

He shook a gourd rattle in the air and chanted something in Shona. Mum gave me a meaningful look, then asked Saru to make some tea for us all. She glanced down to where the witch doctor's bare feet were leaving greasy marks on the floor and closed her eyes briefly. There was a faint smell about him: body odour, yes, and fresh sweat, but also something spicy and unfamiliar.

'What are *vadzimu*?' I asked.

'They are the ancestors.'

'But it is usually good to have ancestors around,

138

isn't it? These ones are causing trouble.'

'Ah, yes, usually it is good to have one's ancestors around, but not when they are not at peace. When someone dies, their spirit wanders until they are asked to come home and look after their family. Come with me.'

We walked from room to room. In each, the witch doctor shook his rattle and chanted. Mum followed us, looking anxious.

The witch doctor stopped at the door to my room. 'It is strong here.'

I told him about the man I had seen in the doorway.

He nodded. 'That does not sound like the ghost of your ancestors. But when a spirit is unhappy, it attracts other spirits to the place.'

Mum sniffed. The witch doctor spent a few minutes cleansing the doorway and then went down the hallway into the bedroom. Mum stood in front of the cupboard where she kept her jewellery, arms crossed. The witch doctor spent some time standing over the bed, murmuring. Mum rolled her eyes.

'It is done.' The witch doctor straightened up. 'I have asked the spirits to come home. They are still here but now they are not wandering. They are happy because they know you are here and they can watch over you.'

'The priest tried to get rid of them,' I said.

'Ah.' He shook a finger. 'That was a mistake. That would just make them angry. You do not want *vadzimu* to go away. You want them to stay and make your family stronger. No wonder they were *shupering* you.'

Mum did not offer him tea, in the end. She did

offer him money, which he did not accept.

'No, no. You tell your friends about me, yes?'

Evidently he imagined that there might be a run on exorcisms in the white community. We managed to give him some avocados and vegetables from our garden in thanks, and ushered him off the property. It was getting close to the time when Steve came home, and if he saw the *N'anga* there would be hell to pay.

I was given the job of closing—and locking—the gate behind the witch doctor.

Before he stepped out, he turned to me and smiled. 'All they want is to be remembered. That is all *vadzimu* want. When you do not remember, you condemn them to wander.' He tapped his nose as if he had shared a great secret with me, and stepped out into the road.

CHAPTER FOURTEEN

The workers had started wearing T-shirts showing their support for Mugabe or the MDC. I noticed the opposition leader for the first time. Steve had told me about the Movement for Democratic Change, but I had not paid much attention to them before; now, I saw photographs of Morgan Tsvangirai in the paper. He had a big, wide face like a frog's, and he lifted his open hand as a symbol of his party. Mugabe's symbol was a closed fist.

'Don't wave at anyone unless you mean it,' warned Steve. 'Showing an open hand can be dangerous these days.'

No more Sweet or Sour games, then. But I had not played them for years.

I still went to the Coopers' every week to take the dogs for their walk. Jonah's expression was darker and darker each time I saw him. He stopped greeting me, and just grunted instead. After a few weeks he did not even bother to grunt—he kept his head down and ignored me.

'What's up with him?' Steve asked Mr Cooper. 'He has a face like a baboon's bum.'

'I didn't give him the day off to go to the ZANU PF rally in town,' said Mr Cooper.

'Bluddy right,' said Steve.

One morning when I arrived to pick up the dogs, Mr Cooper was there. The dogs, delighted to have him home, worshipped at his heels as he strolled. I hovered, feeling like I was intruding, but he spotted me.

'Howzit, Elise?' he said.

'Fine, thanks, Mr Cooper.'

'Surveying my kingdom,' he said, sweeping out a hand to indicate the garden—half-joking, half-not. 'Your parents are well?'

It still bothered me to hear Steve described as one of my parents. *Ja*, they're fine, thank you.'

Mr Cooper took a breath as if to say something else, but then stopped as if he had noticed something. I followed his gaze. A monstrous bougainvillea plant, draped over the fence, sagging under the weight of a thousand bright blossoms. 'I thought I said to cut that bougainvillea back?' he said to Jonah, who was clipping the dead heads off some roses.

'Yes, Baas.'

'And you haven't done it.'

141

'No, Baas.'

'Why not?'

'I don't know, Baas.'

'Did you forget?'

'No, Baas.'

'All right, then. I would like you to cut it back today.'

'Yes, Baas.'

'Thank you.' Mr Cooper looked at me, 'Cheers, Elise,' and went back into the house.

I avoided Jonah as much as I could. When I was in the Coopers' garden I felt his eyes on me, like a cold finger sliding down my spine. When he and Mr Cooper talked, Mr Cooper looked shorter, suddenly, and younger, while Jonah's face looked like a dark soapstone carving: definite and bitterly chiselled.

I kept an eye on the bougainvillea. It was heavy and lush with life, like everything in the garden, and it spilled over the wall and hung over the flowerbeds. By the next week, it was still not cut back. I noticed Mr Cooper was watching it too.

Jonah did not cut it back the next week, or the next. The bush grew larger and even more luxuriant.

'That is bluddy stupid,' said Mum when I told her.

The bougainvillea continued to grow, taking over the fence and drowning the other plants in its shade. Its flowers darkened, turning from bright pink to a poisonous red. It dropped blossoms on the ground, and I trampled them when I came to pick up the dogs.

Soon there was a smashed, bloody carpet of red mingling with the mud and grass.

Mr Cooper's manner towards Jonah changed. He started to bark out orders. He started treating him like a servant. When I saw Mr Cooper shaking his finger in Jonah's face, I realised that their relationship was not as cosy as I had imagined.

One week, I was crouching to attach the dogs' leads to their collars when I heard shouting. Jonah and Mr Cooper. I knew I should have straightened up, but instead I stayed, listening.

'Do not speak to me that way!' shouted Jonah. The deferential servant voice was gone.

'You are a bluddy employee in my house, living on my land!' Mr Cooper shouted back.

'I have lived here since before you were born!'

'*Ja*, and you're bluddy lucky to have kept your job.'

'Your father would never have spoken to me that way! I have known you since you were a boy. How dare you . . .'

'Shut up!'

'*Machende arimuhapwa*!'

'Don't make me bluddy fire you, boy!' I heard Mr Cooper say to a man almost twenty years his senior.

I knew what Jonah had said. I remembered it from Chinhoyi. It meant 'your testicles are under your armpits', which sounded strange in English but was one of the most terrible insults in Shona.

On the following weekend, I saw Mr Cooper talking to Jonah in the garden again. They were calmer this time, but they stood with their arms crossed, further apart than you would normally stand if you were having a conversation.

'The bush is practically dead anyway,' said Mr Cooper.

143

The bougainvillea bush was no longer green. It wilted, browned and slumped over the wall as if it were tired. The blossoms at its base had become a pinkish sludge.

'It has been here ever since I have.'

Mr Cooper waved his hand at the sad, straggly bush.

'Look at it!'

'I can fix it, Baas.'

'I don't want you to fix it. I want you to take it out. I have a cycad that I want to put there.'

'The old Baas planted that bush.'

'*Ja*, I know he did. He planted everything in this bluddy garden.'

'The Baas planted that before you were born.'

'I know he did. But I want it taken out.'

'The old Baas would not have done it this way.'

'The old Baas is dead!' The word thudded in between them like a bird shot from the sky. 'Now, you go take that bush out quick-quick,' said Mr Cooper. He had, consciously or not, slipped into Kitchen Kaffir.

Jonah said nothing. He hoisted his *bhadza* over his shoulder and walked to the bush. He struck its trunk once, twice, three times. It came away from the fence and started to fall. Jonah stood back, and Mr Cooper made an involuntary movement as if to catch it. Its leaves shivered and rustled as it hit the ground.

'Well. Good,' said Mr Cooper.

The marigolds that edged the flower bed were crushed into juicy orange mush by the falling bush.

*   *   *

144

Mr Cooper's house and garden started to be quietly sabotaged. Tools went missing from the shed. This was not unusual—there was a complex barter system between the gardeners of all the farm managers and they regarded tools as communal property.

Everything from the lawnmower to the hedge clippers disappeared from our shed at intervals, to be replaced by something that very clearly did not belong to us. When we needed something that was missing from the shed, Steve phoned up one of the neighbours, and they rolled their eyes ruefully at each other down the line, chuckling at the Africanness of it all.

Everyone had heard the story of the gardener whose Baas asked him to bury two cans of petrol. We were all storing extra petrol those days, just in case (of what? A flight to the border?), and so we could all sympathise.

'So this *oek*, he gives the two cans to his gardener and he tells him to bury them in the garden. The gardener says "Yes, Baas" and goes away. A few weeks later the Baas needs the petrol, so he asks his gardener to show him the spot where it is buried and dig it up. The gardener starts digging, but there is nothing there.

'"Are you sure you put it here?" says the Baas.

'"Yes, Baas, I buried it, just like you said."

'The guy scratches his head. He just can't understand it. Then he asks, "When you say you buried it, what exactly do you mean?"

'"I dug a hole, opened the cans and poured the petrol in, Baas."'

Howls of laughter.

This time, however, Mr Cooper's tools vanished

and were not replaced. The hedge trimmers, the big spade, even the saw. Jonah came to Mr Cooper every day with hands outstretched, palms up.

'Baas, I cannot chop the hedge because the clippers are gone.'

'Then use the secateurs.'

'Sah, they are gone too.' There was a light in Jonah's eyes as he said this.

Mr Cooper knew the tools had some help in disappearing, but he played along. He bought new clippers. The new clippers went missing.

Mr Cooper's chickens stopped laying eggs—or, at least, there were no eggs there when I went to collect them. A dead rat floated in the pool. Slugs infested the rockery. Torrential rain blocked his gutters and pooled water in the ceiling.

'Jonah doesn't control the weather,' said Mum when Mr Cooper listed the problems.

I was not so sure. Our gutters had become blocked as well, and Tatenda was away visiting his family in the *gwash*.

'Can I borrow Jonah?' Steve asked Mr Cooper.

'You're bluddy welcome to him,' said Mr Cooper. 'Good riddance.'

And so Jonah came to work for us that week. I avoided him as much as I could. He hunched over the gutters, high up on his ladder. Whenever I went outside I saw his dark shape on the roof and felt his eyes on me.

I started finding dead things everywhere. A baby bird, fallen from a tree. A sticky ball designed to catch flies, covered in crawling things, dropped as if by accident just outside my window.

'The wind must have blown it there,' said Mum.

A neat line of shrews, their tiny triangular

146

mouths open in shrewish laughter, lined up on the back doorstep.

'Archie must have been hunting,' said Mum.

Archie showed no interest in the shrews at all, after giving them a disdainful sniff.

'But there aren't any marks on them,' I said.

'Cats can be so cruel,' said Mum, which did not really answer my question.

'Don't worry. We've had a run of bad luck, that's all.'

A few nights later, Archie stumbled in through my bedroom window, his mouth filled with green froth. His eyes were wide and mad.

'Looks like he tried to eat a frog,' said Steve. He prised Archie's jaws open.

'We'd better take him to the vet.'

'Good thing he came back,' said Mum, trying to comfort me. 'When cats are sick, they sometimes just disappear.'

I knew Archie would not. He stared at me with milky, panicked eyes as I wrapped him in a towel ready to take to the vet. His legs were stiff and his whole body trembled.

We woke our vet by banging on the door.

'What the yell is it?' he said out of the window. He was the hairiest man I had ever seen, and that night he was only wearing boxer shorts. His chest hair was fascinating, but Mum hissed at me to stop staring.

The vet forced something into Archie to make him vomit. His little jaws worked as he emptied his stomach, and his ears were flat back on his head.

'What do you think caused it?' Mum asked.

'Poison,' said the vet. 'Could be he licked some rat poison one of your neighbours laid down. Or

147

perhaps some insecticide.'

Mum and the vet bemoaned irresponsible people who left these poisons lying around where anyone's pet could lick them up. I stroked Archie, seeing the familiar blue flicker of static along his black back.

The next morning we were pale and dark-eyed. Saru made us a big pot of porridge, as always, and we poured molasses and milk on to it. That morning the molasses seemed to ooze even more slowly, and the porridge seemed even stodgier and more difficult to eat.

'Morning, Medem,' said Jonah when he came to the back doorstep to get his cup of tea. His eyes flickered to me, and then down to Archie in my lap.

'Archie was sick last night,' said Mum. 'He ate some sort of insecticide or poison.'

'I am sorry,' said Jonah.

'Have you laid any poison down anywhere, Jonah?'

'Yes, Medem. For the rats.'

'Well, I would rather you didn't do that. Go and get rid of it, please.'

'Yes, Medem.' He disappeared.

'Well, mystery solved,' said Mum, and went back to eating her breakfast.

I felt uneasy all day. I watched Jonah working in the garden. He was whistling to himself.

I watched as he took a barrowload of compost to the heap at the end of the garden, then wheeled the empty barrow back. It had a squeaky wheel that shrieked with every turn.

When it was Jonah's lunchtime, he disappeared for a while. Now that I could not see him, I felt even more uncomfortable. In the morning, Archie was recovering from his poisoning, stretched out on a hot water bottle wrapped in a towel. In the afternoon, he had disappeared.

'Mum, Archie's missing.'

'He probably just wandered off. Cats do.'

'He always comes when I call him.'

'Don't worry. Go inside and ask Saru to make us some tea, hey?'

I went inside and sat, pretending to read, listening for the sound of Archie coming in through the window. The light went purple with evening, and cold stars punched holes in the sky.

'He's still not here, Mum.'

'He'll be back when he gets hungry.'

I could not sleep. I was listening for the sound of paws on the windowsill, waiting for a weight on my feet. They did not come. In the morning I was out on the dewy grass before anyone else was awake, calling.

He did not come home that day, or the next. By now Mum and Steve were worried too, and we expanded our search. Steve set Jonah to searching as well, and he thrashed the hedges with a stick, whistling under his breath.

We found him. A neighbour's gardener came running. He had found a cat in a bush at the side of the road. It looked like our little *katsi*.

Archie was limp, his black fur plastered with mud. His tail was still fluffy, though, and it twitched in greeting.

'Do you know what happened?' Mum asked the gardener who found him.

'It must have been the boys, Medem,' he said. The blacks generally thought whites were mad for

149

treating their pets like people, but there was real sorrow in this man's voice.

We had all seen the gang of local boys, ranging in age from eight to twelve, who wandered around our area from time to time: ringing gate bells and running away; vandalising walls and gates; teasing dogs. It seemed a logical conclusion. And yet. Archie's back was clearly broken. Someone had picked him up and snapped him as you would snap open a cream-of-tartar pod to get at the flesh inside.

I did not know whether to pick him up or leave him lying still. His nose was dry and coated with mud—he would never put up with being so grubby if he was well. His pink tongue came out weakly, whisk whisk, tried to clean, but flopped back into his mouth.

'Go and get Steve,' said Mum. She bent down and picked up Archie. His little cat mouth opened in a pained triangle, but he made no noise. 'I'll take him to the vet.'

At home, I waited for Mum to come back from the vet's. I could see Jonah working in the rockery. He was smiling and humming. All the darkness and fear of this day seemed to cluster around him.

He looked up. I ducked my head down and pretended to be reading. When I lifted my eyes again, he was still looking at me. He smiled, slowly, and lifted a hand in greeting.

When Mum returned, it was with a cardboard box. I looked inside and saw limp fur and a paw, pink and dry. We took the box outside and Mum asked Jonah to dig a hole in one of the flowerbeds. He was still humming something under his breath as he dug.

150

I watched him as he leaned on the spade. Mum lowered the box into the ground, then stepped forward and shovelled a spadeful of earth into the grave. It hit Archie's fur with a soft patter-patter, like rain. A grain of soil rolled down his face and settled in one pink nostril. I waited for him to twitch, and then remembered.

Mum put her arm around my shoulders, and I did not shrug it off.

Jonah smiled, and filled in the hole.

*   *   *

Jonah painted the outside of the house that weekend—another job Steve had put off for a long time.

'Will you keep an eye on him?' said Mum. It was Saturday, and she and Steve were off to get the groceries. Everything kept going up in price, which made the weekly shop a long process. Mum spent most of it rummaging at the back of the shelves, hoping to find something with the old price tag on it.

'What am I supposed to do?'

'Just keep an eye,' said Mum.

'What do you think he's going to do?'

'I don't know.' Her voice was sharp. 'Look, just stay in the house while he's there, okay? Just in case.'

Theft by servants was a common complaint among the whites, and people almost assumed that it was going to happen.

An idea settled under my skin like a putzi fly, coiling and curling.

Mum and Steve were going to a party that night.

Mum needed her gold necklace.

'Steve' Mum's voice from the bedroom was distant.

'*Ja?*'

Mum came through with a jewellery pouch. She unrolled it, and we all stared at its complete lack of jewellery.

'I saw Jonah standing in the bedroom,' I said.

'When?'

'This afternoon.'

'I told you not to let him in the house.'

'*Ja*, well, I went to the bathroom, and when I came out he was in the bedroom.'

'Did he say why he was in there?'

I shook my head. Mum and Steve exchanged glances.

'Well, that's that then,' said Steve. He looked relieved.

We went around to Mr Cooper's house to tell him, and he fired Jonah on the spot. I hugged Mercy when we said goodbye. She was in tears, but her husband was standing straight and ominous beside her.

'Goodbye Jonah,' said Mr Cooper. He had a no-hard-feelings voice and he held out his hand. Jonah stared at him until he dropped it.

'I did not steal from you,' said Jonah to Steve as he left. He had his arm around Mercy's waist, and they looked small and shabby as they walked out of the iron gates. All their possessions fitted in one suitcase. It had Mr Cooper's name printed on the side.

Steve snorted. 'Typical. Even after the fact.'

Jonah looked back as he shut the gate behind him, and stared at me. And then, with a clang, he shut it and was gone.

'Good riddance,' said Mr Cooper.

I went into the *khaya* after they had gone. It smelled of pine cleaner and floor polish.

Mercy had scrubbed the red floors to such a high shine that I could see my reflection looking up at me from beyond my feet.

The last time I had been there was over a year ago, when I came to play with the girls. The house looked even smaller empty. There was an enamel pot sitting in the dead centre of the kitchen floor, upright. I wondered if they had forgotten it, or just left it behind. It looked like an offering.

There was something pale in the dirt outside the *khaya*, by the gutter. I bent down to pick it up. It was the snapped-off arm of a Barbie, with its disproportionately small hand cupping a handful of dirt on the end of a gleaming tube of pink plastic. The girls were in high school now and probably did not want it.

I carefully scooped out a handful of earth, dropped the arm into the hole and covered it up.

We celebrated the year 2000 in our backyard, with fireworks. Steve propped them up on the lawn, lit the fuse and then ran backwards saying 'Shit, shit,' as they started to fizz and crackle sooner than expected.

Mum was indoors. She had washed her hands of the whole thing. 'If you set the hedge on fire, don't come running to me,' she said.

The adults drank on the verandah.

'Here's to a better year,' said Steve.

'Cheers.'

I heard the glasses clinking. An owl flew above me, white and dusty as a moth, and landed on the roof of the house with a clatter of claws. Owls were a bad omen.

'Happy New Year,' said someone from the verandah, and drunken voices started singing what they remembered of 'Auld Lang Syne'.

CHAPTER FIFTEEN

We got a call from Uncle Pieter and Auntie Mary, from their farm.

'*Ja*, hi,' said Auntie Mary in a bright voice when I answered the phone. 'Can I talk to your Mum?'

I passed the phone over. I could still hear Auntie Mary's voice, higher than usual. Mum said lots of yeses and nos and nodded her head as Auntie Mary talked.

'Don't worry, Mary,' she said. 'I'm sure it won't come to anything.'

When she hung up, I asked her, 'What's wrong?'

'Nothing,' she said. 'Auntie Mary just had a visit from some people saying they were going to take over the farm.'

'That's not nothing.'

'Well, it's going to come to nothing. Don't worry.' Mum touched my hair.

The farm invasions had begun. Unofficially. At least, officially unofficially. Everyone knew that Mugabe supported them, but he was still insisting that the War Vets acted on their own. Police were slow to respond to distress calls from white farmers, and the squatters were cocky and unafraid.

Auntie Mary kept in touch on the terrible

Chinhoyi phone lines. She sounded like she was shouting from the bottom of a well.

'*Ja*, everything's fine,' she said every day.

From five in the morning until eleven at night, a gang of War Vets beat their drums, sang revolutionary songs and waved clubs and *bhadzas* outside the gates of the farm.

'They're a bluddy nuisance,' said Auntie Mary.

'Aren't you scared?' I asked.

'No, I'm not scared.' And I knew she was not. 'I've already been through one bluddy Bush War, I can cope with this. But I'm worried about Hennie and the poor bluddy workers.'

I passed the phone to Mum. I could still hear Auntie Mary's voice through the receiver.

'What are the workers doing?' asked Mum.

'Getting on with their jobs,' said Auntie Mary. 'We don't want them to get involved. Pieter thought about getting some of them together to throw the squatters off, but I think that would just cause more trouble. And he doesn't want them to get beaten up because of us.'

'Are they sympathetic to the War Vets?'

'What War Vets? All I see is a bunch of bluddy ZANU PF youths.'

They had a good laugh at that, and then Auntie Mary said, 'No way, man. They know what side their bread's buttered on. No farm means no wages. And they're bluddy stupid if they think Bob's going to give the land to the squatters. He just gives it to his cronies.'

'Do you need us to come down?' Mum asked.

'No, we're fine, hey. I'll give you a call if anything changes. Here's hoping they stop banging those bluddy drums soon.'

155

'Here's hoping.' Mum hung up. 'See? She's fine. We've been through all this before, except worse. So stop worrying.'

*   *   *

On the weekend, we heard that Uncle Pieter's farm had been invaded, properly. While he and Auntie Mary were out doing their shopping in town, the War Vets went into the farmstead and made themselves at home.

'Chinhoyi is the breadbasket of Zimbabwe,' said Mum. 'Mugabe is a fool.'

Uncle Pieter and his workers threw the War Vets out, but they came back. Their chanting and drum-beating doubled.

'We're getting no sleep,' said Auntie Mary. 'They came up to the house today and demanded that we kill them a *mombe*. We said no, at first, but then Pieter said he'd rather kill one of the cows himself than see them try to do it with a *bhadza*, so he killed one and had it sent out. They're cooking it now. At least they've stopped singing.'

'Did they take anything from the house?' asked Mum.

'*Ja*, a few things. Beat up Phineas a bit too, poor bugger.'

The Trinepon Man. 'Is he all right?'

'*Ja*, he'll be fine.'

Whenever I saw Mugabe on the news, I wanted to reach in through the screen and shake him by the neck as if he were the scrawny rooster painted on the ZANU PF building. He had a way of speaking and pausing that made each word sound like a prophecy.

156

'There have been very few cases of violence,' he said about the farm invasions, 'but if the farmers start to be angry and start to be violent, then, of course, they will get that medicine delivered to them. And it can be very, very, very severe, but we don't want it to get there.'

He pronounced each 'very' slowly and with weight. We had been given a warning. Behave, or suffer the consequences.

In the middle of all this, we had another dry spell. The ground cracked like the dry skin on our heels, and our dry skin cracked like the crust of the ground. The grass was yellow, when there was grass at all. Mum put a brick in the toilet cistern so that it would use less water. We went back to leaving wees in the toilet and only flushing for something larger, or when the urine started to rot in the bowl and smell like old vegetables. We were not allowed to water our garden any more, or wash the car. We had shallow baths and we shared them, one after the other. I usually got the hottest, freshest water, because I had to go to bed earlier. Mum usually went next, and Steve was left to sit in the cooling, grubby remains.

In the evenings, I used the remains of our rain-water barrel to water the vegetables.

Tatenda was uprooting the sad, limp carrots. 'It is because the land is being taken,' he said. 'Because of what Mugabe is doing.'

If I were indoors, I might not have believed him. But we were outside, looking at a pale fingernail of moon, and it seemed perfectly reasonable.

Mum and Steve were drinking gins and tonics on the verandah.

'Tatenda says the rains won't come because of

what Mugabe is doing,' I said.

Mum raised her eyebrows and Steve spluttered into his drink. 'Well, I suppose that's one theory,' he said.

Mum pulled out a chair for me, and I sat with the adults.

'Can I have a sip?'

Mum sighed and passed me her drink. '*Ja*, but just one, hey.'

I took a sip. It tasted like medicine. By the time it reached my throat, all the liquid had gone and it was nothing but fumes.

'Medicinal,' said Steve. 'Been used by the colonials for generations. The tonic water protects against malaria.'

'And what does the gin do?'

'Painkiller.' They all laughed.

'I'm sick of this bluddy drought,' said Mum. She had her eyes closed and her head tipped back. The sky was starting to turn lavender. I heard the first whines of mosquitoes and saw the dusty shape of moths start to move towards the house.

'You could do a rain dance,' said Steve, and snorted.

'Shut up and make yourself useful,' said Mum.

Steve sighed and heaved himself out of his chair. He closed the door into the house and lit a mosquito lamp.

I slid my legs off the chair on to the cool tiles.

'Where are you going?'

'Outside.'

'Take a jacket,' said Mum.

The evening air felt like a light blanket clinging to the hairs on my arms and legs.

'All right, Mum.'

158

I did not take a jacket, but I did slide my feet into flip-flops. In the dark it was hard to see the fallen acacia thorns lurking in the grass.

I walked down to the end of the garden, to the avocado tree. I could feel the squish of ripe fruit under my flip-flops.

I spent my days making bargains with the gods. If I could climb to the highest branch of the avocado tree, the farm would not be invaded. If I picked up a stone every time I went outside and put it on a little tower of stones beside the door, my family would be safe. I trusted the old gods. They were not compassionate or merciful, but they understood things like sacrifices and offerings.

Maybe a rain dance would have some effect. Even if the dance was danced by a white girl in Harare. I started by moving some sticks into a circle. I was not sure why, except that circles seemed to be important for magic. A fire would have made the whole thing more effective, but Mum and Steve would get suspicious if I went back for matches.

The only rain dances I had seen were Native American ones in the movies. I started to hop on one foot around the circle, making vague chanting noises, but then I felt silly and stopped. Instead I stood and listened. I could hear crickets more as a shivering in the air than a sound, and the rustle of creatures in the hedge and in the trees.

I sat in the middle of my circle and let my breathing slow down until I could not hear it any more. I knew that *N'angas* would go into a trance and let a spirit possess them if they wanted rain. I wondered if I could do it. The idea would have seemed ridiculous in the hot, hard sunlight, but

159

was perfectly reasonable in the rustling night.

I closed my eyes. I saw myself from above, sitting on the ground with my legs crossed. At first I thought it was just my imagination, but then I felt like I was floating further away from my body. I panicked and opened my eyes. My body was wide awake again, heart thumping, legs itching from the rough grass.

I decided to try it again. I closed my eyes and felt myself float away. I wondered if I really had gone somewhere outside my body and, if so, what was left down there inside the skin and muscles and blood. I wondered how *N'angas* welcomed spirits in. A hot red light hung in front of my eyes, as if I were tilting my closed eyelids up at the sun, and I drifted into a warm sleep.

When I woke up, I was thrashing on the ground and my mouth was full of saliva. I spat it out in a white glob on the grass, and coughed. Tatenda was crouching a few feet away, watching me with wide, white eyes.

'Are you all right, Medem?' he asked me.

'*Ja.*' I took deep breaths. It felt like I was trying to catch the air in a net. I could not draw nearly enough into my lungs. 'What happened?'

'I heard you shouting,' said Tatenda. I saw sweat on his forehead and I realised that he was afraid.

'What was I saying?'

He shook his head.

'Was I saying something?'

He stood up. 'You should go back inside,' he said. 'You are not well.'

When I got back to the house, Mum and Steve were drinking tea in the living room.

Steve looked at his Blue Duiker head. 'Hey,

160

when's the last time Saru dusted?'

'Yesterday.'

'Well, there's bluddy dust all over Bluey.'

Mum followed his gaze. 'I'll tell her to clean it.'

I poured myself a cup of tea and did not say anything. I lifted my hand up to my head.

'Are you okay?' said Mum.

'Headache.' I never got headaches. Mum had migraines sometimes, and when she felt one coming on she drew the curtains and lay on the bed with a beanbag over her eyes to block out the daylight. She knew when she was getting a migraine because she could see tadpoles swimming in front of her eyes, she said. I could see little black dots in front of my eyes now and I wondered if that was what she meant. I told her.

'Migraine,' she said. 'Must be a storm coming.'

She put me to bed, and I lay in the darkness feeling my head swell and fill up with blood until there was no room for thoughts. I felt the heavy clouds outside pressing down on me.

Whatever spirit I talked to must have listened to me. The rain came and felt like a release, like when you really need to pee and have crossed your legs for hours and finally reach a toilet. The heavy, throbbing blood seemed to rush out of my head, leaving it clean and sharp. I listened to the fingers of rain drumming on the roof and realised that there was still some tension left behind after the storm had broken. The world was not washed as clean as usual. We were not just waiting for the rain, but for some other release.

161

CHAPTER SIXTEEN

The first time I heard someone outside at night, it was just a slight crunch on the gravel. I thought it was an animal until I heard another crunch: measured, deliberate, as if someone were placing their feet very carefully and listening for a response between each step. There was a human mind behind those feet.

Silence fell again. I decided to go to the curtain, count to three and pull it back suddenly. Then, when I saw nothing, I could relax and go back to sleep. It was better to do it quickly, like ripping off a plaster.

I did not turn on the light, because it would make everything beyond the window an impenetrable wall of black. I slid my feet out of bed and on to the floor, and stood shivering with one hand on the curtains, feeling the chill from the glass. I counted silently, and pulled back the curtain with a clatter and ring of runners.

A face flashed into view, so close that if there was no glass I could have touched it. I felt the air rushing up from my lungs and then heard my own voice screaming, slightly muffled by the swoosh of blood pulsing through my ears.

The face was gone as quickly as it had appeared. Mum and Steve ran in. 'What the yell?'

Steve had his old school cricket bat. Mum had brought a pillow. I told them about the face at the window.

'Are you sure?'

'*Ja.*' It was a flesh-and-blood person, not a

tokoloshe or a ghost.

'Oh well.' Steve lowered his bat. 'There's no point calling the police now. He'll be long gone, whoever he is.'

The next night, I heard footsteps again. I ran through to Mum and Steve's room in my pyjamas. This time Steve went into the garden armed with a rifle and a torch. He found nothing.

This happened every night for a week.

'Probably bluddy Jonah,' said Steve, 'coming to see what else he can steal.'

Once he had said that, I lay rigid in my bed waiting for the footsteps. Of course, I thought. It must be Jonah. He must know what I did. He is coming back to find me. I could not sleep, and in the mornings I was grey and limp.

'What's wrong with you?' said Mum, laying a cool hand on my forehead.

'Nothing.'

'These prowlers getting to you?'

'*Ja*, a bit.'

'Don't worry,' said Mum and ruffled my hair.

I tried to remember if it was Jonah's face I had seen on the other side of the glass. I imagined him coming into my room with his angular face and angry stare. I woke Mum up with my screams the next time we heard the footsteps.

'For God's sake,' she said, 'this is getting bluddy ridiculous.'

'What do you expect me to do?' said Steve. 'Call the police? They're worse than useless. I can handle them.'

Mum and I did not trust Steve's cricket bat and ancient rifle as much as he did.

On the next night, I woke up to the sound of

shouting and bumping and banging from the study. I poked my head out of the door and saw Steve charging down the corridor, wearing only a pair of boxer shorts. Mum pursued him with his ratty dressing gown.

I followed them. When we arrived in the study, it was a rather pathetic crime scene. The window was open, the computer was gone, and there was a perfect, red-dust shoe-print on the windowsill. The raw-onion smell of body odour hovered in the air.

'Agh, hell,' said Steve. He ran into the garden, but returned after a few minutes.

'Couldn't find anyone. I think he's buggered off.'

Mum put on the kettle and brewed a pot of tea. We sat in the kitchen sipping it while we waited for Steve to call the police.

Steve came in again, jingling his car keys.

'What the bluddy yell are you doing?' said Mum.

'The police don't have a car available,' said Steve. 'I'm going to pick them up.'

'You're going to pick them up?' Mum repeated. She gave a snort of laughter.

'Back soon,' said Steve.

Mum and I sat and drank our tea. When we had finished, Mum poured us another cup. It was from the bottom of the pot and tasted like tar. When we had finished that cup and were staring at the dregs, we heard Steve's car in the driveway.

'About bluddy time,' said Mum.

Steve came in, followed by two policemen. One was obviously more senior; smiling, obsequious. His eyes slid around our faces, never quite landing on our eyes.

Steve took them into the study. They stood

looking at the footprint, making concerned noises.

'Eh-eh.'

'Oh-oh.'

One made a few desultory notes. Steve was red-faced and desperate.

'Pointless,' said Mum under her breath. 'The police are worse than the criminals.'

I did not know if it was my imagination, but it seemed to me that one of the policemen eyed our television in a suspicious way.

They accepted tea from us. Mum even brought out the best biscuits. The policemen sat and drank their tea, smiling at us, and then left. Apparently one of their colleagues could pick them up now.

'Good night Baas, good night Medem.'

'Useless,' said Mum after they'd gone. 'Oh well.'

'*Ja*, well hopefully it gave the burglar a fright, if he's still somewhere around,' said Steve.

Mum shrugged. 'So why did it take you so long to get back?'

'The police station was empty.'

'The one you called?'

'*Ja*. All the lights were off.'

'So where the yell . . .'

'Well, I thought they must have gone home or something so I drove to another police station and couldn't find anyone there, either. Then on the way back I spotted a couple of them drinking a Scud outside the shopping centre.'

'You picked them up from the shopping centre?' Mum said.

'*Ja*. Not like they were doing anything. Poor buggers,' said Steve. 'You can't blame them half the bluddy time.'

The next morning, we examined the scene more

closely.

'Shouldn't we leave it for the police?' I ask.

Mum snorted. 'No.'

'But there might be fingerprints.'

'They won't bother with fingerprints. Come on.' Mum studied the window. 'It may well have been Jonah,' she said.

'Bluddy Kaffir!' shouted Steve.

'Steve!' Mum shushed him.

'How do you know?' I asked.

Mum fiddled with the window catch. 'This was painted over. We never opened the window. But someone has chiselled the paint away and worked it loose. You could only do it from inside.'

'Shit!' Steve kicked the doorframe. 'I'm going to find him,' he said. 'I'm going to track the bugger down.'

'*Ja*, you'll get your pack of dogs and track him across the Bush,' said Mum. 'This isn't bluddy Rhodesia, you know.'

'I've got my rifle.'

'*Ja*, and your father's bayonets. So?'

Steve subsided. 'Would be more trouble than it's bluddy worth, anyway,' he said.

The police did not contact with us again. We did not expect them to. Mum superstitiously refused to clean the footprint away, in case we ever found Jonah again. After a few weeks, I stopped noticing it.

Even though Steve consulted the neighbourhood jungle drums, he could not find Jonah. No one seemed to know where he had gone.

'Good riddance to bad rubbish,' said Steve.

We got a big, red panic button installed. Steve

166

instructed Mum and me in its use.

'What's to teach?' said Mum. 'You just press it.'

'*Ja*,' said Steve, 'but there is a code to type in to cancel it.' He showed us. If we set off the panic alarm, the armed response unit would phone us. If we answered the phone and gave the five-digit code, they would cancel the response. If we gave the wrong code, or the phone rang and we did not answer it, they would send a team of men to the house.

'Better than the bluddy police,' said Steve with satisfaction.

We had a rape gate installed as well—a bolted gate that separated the bedroom wing from the rest of the house.

The next time we thought we heard a prowler, Mum pressed the panic button and the alarm went off. Steve ran outside with one of the old guns and a torch to check the garden.

'No one there. Or he ran off,' he said.

We watched the phone for a while, waiting for it to ring.

'Should I call them?' said Mum, worried.

'Nah, they'll call,' said Steve.

We waited a little longer.

'Something must be wrong with the transmission,' said Steve. 'I'll call them in the morning and get someone to fix it.'

We went to bed.

Not long after I fell asleep, I was woken up by shouts and barking dogs.

Something bright shone through my window, and I heard Steve saying 'Shit, shit, shit.'

About a dozen black men in uniform stood outside the house shining huge torches at the house. One of them had a megaphone. One was holding the leash of a snarling Alsatian. Behind them, our front gate hung off its hinges.

Steve appeared in his dressing gown and slippers. He waved at the men, gesturing and explaining. They looked grim.

Mum stood behind me at the window.

'They look angry,' I said.

'*Ja*.' She watched Steve. 'Apparently they might fine us for a call-out.'

'Are they allowed to do that?'

'It doesn't really matter if they're allowed to. They can.' Mum leaned past me and reached in past the burglar bars to open up the window.

'Hello, guys,' she shouted, cutting off Steve. 'We're really sorry you came out here for a false alarm. Would you like some beers?'

A few smiles appeared.

'Come round to the back,' said Mum. She shut the window and pulled her dressing gown closer around her.

'It's two in the morning,' I said.

'*Ja*, well, better than having to pay a thousand-dollar bribe,' said Mum. 'Come on. You want a beer?'

I sat on the back doorstep of the kitchen sipping a Castle Lager while the men sprawled on the dew-soaked grass, laughing and chatting. Mum and Steve stood in the kitchen doorway. There was a party atmosphere.

'Sorry again for calling you out,' said Mum.

'Eh-eh, don't worry,' said one of the men, waving his hand. 'It was a mistake.'

*　　*　　*

168

Mr Cooper came to our house for dinner the following night. Steve told him the story of the burglary and the false alarm.

'Could well have been Jonah, I suppose,' Mr Cooper said. 'Would surprise me, though.'

'*Ja*, well.' Steve stabbed a piece of meatloaf with his fork. 'Bluddy Kaffirs. I'm sick of the lot of them.'

'They're not so bad, Steve,' said Mr Cooper. 'Just struggling to get by, like the rest of us.'

'After everything we do for them,' Steve said. 'They never bluddy appreciate it. They're just waiting for the chance to stick a knife in our backs. I should have left when Mugabe came to power.'

'You thought things would get better,' said Mum. 'We all did.'

'We failed,' said Mr Cooper.

We all stopped eating.

'We did our best,' Mr Cooper said. 'We tried to be fair. I know I did. We wanted the best for everyone. But we failed.'

'Don't say that,' Mum began. Her eyes flicked to me, then Steve. Say something.

'Potholes in the roads, police accepting bribes, Mugabe's thugs doing whatever the yell they want,' said Mr Cooper. 'The whole place is going to hell. And d'you know what the worst thing is? We are going to be remembered as colonialists who didn't care about anything except staying in power. They won't remember any of the good. They have forgotten it already.'

I was halfway through chewing a mouthful, but I did not dare move my jaws.

'And these young *skellems* like Sean, they're

spoiling for a fight again. That, or they think that all these problems are our fault, that the whites did all this. Don't know what we were thinking,' said Mr Cooper. He shook his head, and he was still shaking it when Mum got up to pour him a glass of water.

When Mr Cooper left, I walked him to his *bakkie*. Something rustled in the bushes next to us. The moon was a slice of orange rind in the sky, and the air smelled like night-time.

He paused before he got in, and cleared his throat. I waited. 'Don't worry about what I said, hey?' he said. 'I didn't mean it. Not really.'

He was waiting for an answer. 'I know, Mr Cooper.'

'Good. Good.' He opened the car door. 'I wouldn't change this for anything, you know.'

We stood there in the dark. The stars were white pinpricks; the air was humming with night-time noise.

'Not for anything.' He smiled and climbed back into the car. 'Cheers.'

'Come on,' said Mum from the kitchen door. 'Come back inside.'

I inhaled the night before going in. There was nowhere on earth like this, and I would not change it either.

CHAPTER SEVENTEEN

Steve told a story about boiling a frog in a pan of water.

'The trick is to heat the water up gradually,' he

said. 'Then the frog doesn't notice the water's getting hotter, and he doesn't jump out. When the water gets to boiling point, the frog still won't jump out because the change has been so slow that he doesn't realise.'

'That's ridiculous,' said Mum. 'Of course he would realise.'

'You haven't actually done it, have you?' I asked, feeling sorry for the frog.

'No, man, of course not. But it's true. You can kill a frog by degrees without him knowing.'

This had always been the land of Make-a-Plan. People were proud of it. 'Zimbabweans are resourceful,' they said. 'We can cope with anything.'

No power? Simple. Hook up a generator. No bread in the supermarket? No problem. Buy some on the black market. You could always make a plan, work something out. And we all stuck together, calling our friends when we found a garage with petrol, sharing what we had.

Going to school became optional. Whether because of lack of petrol or riots in town, I stayed home almost all week, and when I did go to school it was half-empty.

Skipping school was fun at first, but after a few weeks I wanted to go back. Scratch my initials on the desk. Sit through boring assemblies. Study for exams.

On Uncle Pieter's farm, the War Vets and the farming families seemed to have reached an uneasy truce. The War Vets were not venturing any further into the farm. Instead, they were camping outside. The revolutionary songs and drumming were not as unrelenting. Occasionally Uncle Pieter would send them a cow to eat, and occasionally they would take one without asking. They also chopped down trees on the farm for firewood and pilfered vegetables and mealies when they could, but no one seemed to be very concerned.

'Could be worse,' said Uncle Pieter on the phone. 'And if they start to *shuper* us again, we'll boot them off.'

Over the past two years this had become normal, this strange, limited life. Only sometimes did I feel like we were under siege, behind our high walls topped with glass.

On the days when I could not go to school, I spent a lot of time on the phone with Kurai.

'I am so bored,' said Kurai every night. 'I can't stand it.'

'Me neither,' I said, but I was lying.

Boredom was a luxury. You could not trust ordinary. Ordinary was not safe. You could wake up on an ordinary day, drink a cup of tea, eat a piece of toast, and be killed by a mob outside your door. You could drive to work on an ordinary day and end up in the middle of a riot.

I held the times I had been bored in front of my mind like beloved photographs. All those hours spent in doctors' or dentists' waiting rooms. Sitting in the hot sun at school prize-givings. I looked back at myself then, kicking the legs of a chair or pulling up tufts of grass, and I tried to remember that feeling. Nothing to fear, nothing to think about.

The petrol queues were getting worse. I left the school gate one day to see backed-up traffic, bumper to bumper, disappearing in both directions. Petrol queue. A record, this time. The Shell station was a good couple of kilometres away.

172

'Bluddy yell,' said Steve when he came to pick me up. He had to park several blocks from the school, and it was a long way to the car.

The atmosphere in the petrol queue was festive. Someone had set up a *braai* and people were leaving their cars to get *boerewors* and burgers. Several people had brought cooler bags with Castle Lager inside. There were a lot of empty cars, sitting deserted while their owners ate, drank or made the long trek to the nearest bathroom.

'What if the line moves forward?' I asked. 'What will happen?'

'It won't,' said Steve. 'The petrol station doesn't have any petrol yet. These people have probably been here all night, waiting for the delivery.'

A man in a suit got out of his car and gave the keys to a woman—probably his wife.

'Her shift,' said Steve.

There was a joke we told at school about petrol queues. A man who had been sitting in a petrol queue for several hours grew gradually angrier and angrier. When he could stand it no longer, he jumped out of the car and told his friend, 'Look after the car for me. I'm off to kill that bastard Mugabe.'

His friend sat in the car and waited for the man's return. After another few hours, the would-be assassin returned looking crestfallen.

'What happened?' asked his friend.

'The queue was longer there,' said the man.

We fell about laughing at this one.

'You know, I used to be able to see him in his office when I was having clarinet lessons,' said Kurai one day.

'Who?'

173

'Mugabe.'

'Seriously?'

'*Ja*. The College of Music looked right over his wall and into his office.'

'You could actually see him?'

'*Ja.*'

'What was he doing?'

'Nothing. Boring as hell. Just sitting writing or reading papers. But I missed an opportunity.' Kurai hefted an invisible gun on to her shoulders. 'Great place for a sniper. Bang! Problem solved.'

If only. I prayed for an assassination.

The news had become a fearful, hated ritual. When we heard the familiar drumbeat, we dropped what we were doing and went into the lounge. We did not sit to watch the news; we stood with our arms crossed and our feet planted firmly on the ground, facing it. What was he saying about us today? What did this mean? Sometimes it was not translated into English and I could only pick up a word here and there.

I watched him yelling at the camera. The television's sound was muted, but I still felt each word landing on me like a physical blow. There were little sequins of sweat on his upper lip. It had a very clearly defined line down the middle, filled with a tiny moustache. I felt my own lip. I had the same line.

Mugabe had very beautiful eyes. People always said that you could read someone's character in their eyes: if they were shifty, or too close together, or had a mad light. Not so with Mugabe, who had a neat fringe of almost feminine lashes along his top and bottom lids, and brown eyes that seemed to glisten with feeling.

Sometimes I tried, really tried, to understand him. I stared at the screen and tried to read his expression, to see what was going on in his head.

People said it was after his wife Sally died that Mugabe went mad.

I looked at Mugabe's face, leaning in so close that the television image disintegrated into coloured dots of light, and wondered why we were all in thrall to him, this little old man with the long eyelashes.

Mum found a place that exchanged goods for cash, no questions asked. It was outside the city, in a new development that was abandoned when inflation rose and the money ran out. We piled furniture and electronics into the car and drove out there. When we had the cash in our hands we went straight to the shops and spent it, giddy and giggling.

'Hey, chocolate!' said Mum, spotting some of the imported stuff on a shelf. 'Get six bars.'

We bought twelve tubes of toothpaste at a time, acres of toilet paper, enough canned food to build a pyramid. Prices were strings of 0s looped together on long chains, and they went nowhere but up.

The summer was hotter than usual. I wished I could run around in nothing but my underwear, like I did when I was five, but the best I could do was drink continuous glasses of iced water.

Mum came home from the farm office with bright eyes and something exciting to tell us.

'Mr Cooper has offered to put a pool in for us,' she said.

Steve had no expression. 'Put in a pool?'

'*Ja*. He's going to pay for it.'

'Why?'

'Well, because he likes us. It's a present.'

'A present.'

'*Ja*. He's going to get some of the workers to come over and measure for it this afternoon.'

I could feel the water on my skin already.

'We don't need a pool,' said Steve. He flapped his newspaper out to straighten it.

Mum stood still. 'Come on, Steve. It's free.'

'We don't need it. Tell him no thanks.'

'Agh, come on, Steve.'

'Come on!' I said, sitting right on the edge of my chair. It would be so wonderful to be able to dive into our own pool.

'I said no.' Steve got up. 'I'm going to talk to Tatenda about those beds by the rockery.'

'All right.'

We watched him go.

'Mum!' I began, ready to launch into a tantrum that would somehow persuade her to persuade Steve.

'Shush.' Mum was pale. She gave me a quick smile and went out after Steve. I watched her walk to him and slide a hand around his back.

I did not whinge about the pool. Instead, I did what I used to do in Chinhoyi—turned on the sprinkler on the lawn and ran through the water in my swimming costume until I was almost too cold and could lie on the grass, letting the sun warm me through.

There was a letter in the paper that said, 'If white farmers think they are so good at farming, why can't they go back to Britain and farm there?'

'They're bluddy Zimbabwean, just like the blacks,' said Steve. 'Can you imagine Mr Cooper

176

farming in England?'

I could not imagine Mr Cooper anywhere but on the farm. Like Steve, he was part of the landscape.

Mugabe announced that he was putting forward a referendum to give him almost unlimited powers. As a side note, it allowed the government to take white farms without any compensation.

'What a bluddy surprise,' said Steve.

People could say 'Yes' or 'No' to the change. Mum and Steve voted and sat back, laughing and giddy with pessimism, joking that it was probably rigged anyway and there was no point.

I started to see people wearing 'Vote No' T-shirts—even some of the farm workers. There were big 'Vote No' adverts in the paper, too.

Mum and Steve threw a party to hear the results of the referendum. All the farm managers came to the house for a *braai*, to grow warm and drunk in the February sun. It felt like the end of the world. Everyone had been throwing those kinds of parties lately—where people got so drunk that they could not move, voices were brittle and laughter had a hysterical edge. We had a perfect life here, in this perfect weather, with our servants and sunshine and silver teapots, and we were determined to make the most of it while we could. If we were going down, we were going down with a gin and tonic in one hand and a cigarette in the other.

The time came. The results were going to be announced on the radio. The party trooped into the living room and sat around the transistor, waiting for one word.

It came. 'Fifty-five per cent of Zimbabweans have voted "No" to the proposed amendment to the Constitution.'

177

There was a silence, and then, 'Bluddy yell,' said Steve.

Everyone broke out in excited talk. Surely Bob would have rigged the vote? He always did. Was he really that confident? Had he really thought that he could intimidate enough people to guarantee a 'Yes'? People jumped up and clapped their hands. They were euphoric. They could not believe something they did had actually made a difference. They started to think that perhaps they could change things after all. On the news that night, people cried and laughed.

'We have the old rooster cornered,' said a Shona woman. 'He can't hang on much longer now.'

Everyone thought it was just a matter of time, that this meant the end of Mugabe's rule. The people had spoken against him.

I remembered this, and tried to freeze it in my mind like a photograph. The time when we did make a difference, despite everything. When we wrote something on a piece of paper and it changed history.

The Shona people were fatalistic. If you were run over by a bus, it was your time. They did not rail against God and fate, which could be why they were so good at religion—any religion, be it Christianity or the older, less forgiving ones. It was so easy to adopt this attitude, living in Zimbabwe, and to think that we were on an inevitable slide downwards, and that no one could do anything to change it. That night, I felt hopeful. I remembered Mr Cooper telling me that our duty was to leave things a little bit better than we found them. It was the idea that we could make changes, redirect fate, that made the colonists build roads and schools

178

and hospitals. We were in charge of our own destiny; that was the philosophy of the West. We could make things better. I could almost believe it.

Mugabe made a speech after the results were released. He was very calm, staring over the heads of the crowd, saying that the people had spoken.

'Shit, man,' said Mum, staring at his face.

I knew what she was seeing. I saw it too. There was a powerful anger in Mugabe's face that seemed to come right out of the TV screen and jab me in the chest. You, it said. You will pay for this. You will be next.

Mugabe had started wearing his old army fatigues again. The trousers were too short on his spindly, old-man legs, showing a few inches of blue sock. His ankles poked out, knobbly and thin. For a moment I felt sorry for him, this old man who was petulant at not getting his own way.

Articles started popping up in the government newspaper, blaming the whites for the referendum results. The farmers forced their workers to vote 'No', the paper said.

'How the hell is this supposed to be our fault?' said Steve. 'There's only a bluddy handful of us.'

We went to another farm manager's house for yet another celebratory party. When we got home that night, the house was ankle-deep in water. The parquet floors were drowned and stained, and the paint on the walls had started to bubble.

'What the bluddy yell . . .' said Steve as we splashed our way into the kitchen.

He pressed the light switch, but nothing happened. Power cut. We did not bother putting the candles and torches away now, because there was one almost every night. The camping stove

179

had a permanent place in the corner of the kitchen.

Steve switched on the torch, and we followed its optimistic light down the corridor. All the floors were underwater.

'What happened?' asked Mum.

'The water tank.' Steve gestured with the torch, making the light flicker and dance on the walls. 'Looks like it sprung a leak. Must have emptied itself into the ceiling, and then come through and run down the walls.'

Mum splashed back down the passage to put the kettle on the camping stove.

We needed tea before we could tackle the water.

'I don't understand it,' said Steve, looking up at the ceiling. 'Nothing has ever gone wrong here before. There hasn't been so much as a termite.'

We watched the water snake down the wall, coiling and hissing into puddles when it reached the floor.

'Not a bluddy thing,' said Steve.

CHAPTER EIGHTEEN

One morning we awoke to the smell of cigarettes. The tobacco fields were burning. Steve jumped in the *bakkie* and drove down there, shouting into his radio. I hopped on my bike and followed.

Workers scurried like dark ants, hosing down the flames and chopping down plants to create breaks in the fire's path. White teeth flashed in their faces. This was a Drama, and they enjoyed drama.

180

Sean was there too, leaning against his bike, watching the blaze.

'What happened?'

'What do you think?'

'Don't be smart.'

'Mugabe's lot,' he said. 'At least, that's what Dad thinks.'

'Not an accident?'

'Nah.' He flicked some ash off his cigarette and it was whirled into the cloud of ash that settled on our shoulders and in our hair.

'Steve says it's like another bluddy Bush War.'

'*Ja*, maybe.'

'I hope not.' I watched the flames soak and die under the weight of the water.

'I wouldn't mind,' he said.

'What do you mean you wouldn't mind?'

'Well, it wouldn't be so bad, would it?'

'Of course it would, it's a war.'

'*Ja*, well.' He crossed his arms. 'Give us a chance to show Mugabe's bluddy thugs what-for, hey?'

'Don't be stupid. We don't need to fight any more. This whole land thing can be peaceful, we're not in Rhodesia any more.'

'You might not be,' he said. 'The cities might be Zimbabwe, but out here, things haven't changed.'

I punched him on the arm. 'Stop talking like that.'

'What, you're worried someone will hear?'

'Just stop, all right.'

We stood and watched the workers tramping among the burned and sodden tobacco leaves.

Harare was known as the Sunshine City.

'Sunshine City my arse,' said Steve. 'Whole place is going to hell.'

181

The city was fraying around the edges, and everyone was on strike. Like the rubbish men. For a week the whole city smelled like rotten vegetables. And the rumblings about land invasions had not gone away as Steve had predicted—if anything, they had grown stronger.

We saw the people called 'War Vets' every night on the news. They were meant to be veterans of the war for independence, but most of them were far too young. No one talked about the War. We did not study it at school, either.

'Steve,' I asked one day. 'Did you fight in the Bush War?'

He surprised me by flicking open his old leather wallet. Inside, there was a picture of Mum, a picture of Steve's parents in black-and-white wedding clothes, and one of Steve with a couple of other boys.

In the picture he was young, with a shock of curly hair and bony knees pulled up under his chin. His hand rested on the barrel of a long rifle and he was in uniform. His uniform did not look all that different from what he usually wore—a khaki shirt with a collar, shorts and long socks.

'How old were you here?'

'Seventeen.'

'What were you doing?'

Steve gave me a Look.

'Was it during the War?' I felt very daring. I did not know much about the War, except for a vague idea that it was blacks fighting against whites to rule the country. I knew that a little while before I was born Zimbabwe was called Rhodesia, after Cecil John Rhodes, and Harare was called Salisbury. I knew the War was called the Second

182

Chimurenga or the Bush War, depending on who you asked. The War felt like a death in the family—someone whose name was never mentioned, who was cut out of photographs.

'I was on an army base in the Bush,' said Steve.

'Were you guarding it?'

'*Ja.*' Steve glanced down at the photograph again. 'It was my birthday.'

'Oh.'

'The boys sang "Happy Birthday" to me,' said Steve, 'and I got a beer and a Rubik's cube.'

'Do you still have the Rubik's cube?' I asked.

'Nah, some other bugger nicked it. I didn't care, I couldn't figure it out.' Steve scratched at a little mark on the photograph. 'We had to sit like that, looking out into the Bush. The bluddy terrs moved like snakes on their bellies and you wouldn't see them until they were right up close. You didn't know whether there was no one around or whether they were all-bluddy-around you. They were guerrilla fighters, you see.'

'Gorillas?'

'*Ja.*'

'Like the monkeys?'

'No, man, guerrillas, terrorists, Bush-fighters. We called them floppies,' he said.

'Who?'

'The terrs.'

'Why?'

'Because they'd flop over when you shot them.' He laughed a little. 'Shit, man. I'd love to know what they called us. Seems like anyone would flop over if they were shot, hey?'

'Oh.'

'They'd sneak up on you. My sergeant told me

to look for the whites of their eyes and teeth, and shoot at that.'

I was breathless. 'Did you shoot someone?'

Steve's eyes flickered up and down. 'What sort of a question is that?'

'I just thought . . .' I did not know what to say.

Something had woken that had been sleeping for a long time. Steve would say it had been sleeping since the last war. But whatever it was, I could hear it circling the house at night and breathing in my ear while I slept.

*   *   *

Kids started to vanish from school, pulled out to go overseas. They left without any warning, usually. The rest of us were trying to study for our exams, but it was difficult to concentrate. I found that my mind skittered like a flying ant, landing on something and then jumping somewhere else, leaving barely a footprint. I had to read the first line of a book several times before the meaning sank in. Everyone else seemed to have the same problem, even the teachers, and our lessons were disconnected and strange—when they happened at all.

Kurai and I lay on a blanket in the garden, talking. A storm was roiling up, eating the blue sky and moving towards the city. Clouds were piled like pillows to the east, and the air smelled of copper.

'I'm trying to concentrate on my bluddy exams,' said Kurai. 'But some days the teachers don't even turn up.' She uprooted grass in great green tufts as she talked. 'All this political stuff is a pain. I just

184

want to get into a good university.'

'So you can become an executive,' I supplied.

'*Ja*. And have a corner office with a view.'

'And a secretary who has a secretary.'

'Exactly, sha.'

'*Ja*, Mugabe's awful,' I said to Kurai. I waited for her to join in. This was a familiar and much-loved game.

She paused, then made a non-committal noise.

'Don't you think?' I said.

'*Ja*, well.' Kurai did not meet my eyes. 'He wasn't so bad in the beginning, you know?'

'He's always been bad,' I said. My voice came out louder than I had intended.

'So what?' said Kurai. 'You think you guys should still be running the show?'

'What do you mean "you guys"?' I asked. It took me a moment to realise what she meant. 'You mean whites?'

'That bastard Smith,' she said. 'Mugabe may be a dickhead, but at least he's our dickhead.'

I laughed, but it came out sounding not like a laugh at all. 'You don't think he's doing a good job?'

'No, but I'd rather have him doing a bad job than some White doing any kind of job.'

'Some White?' The word acquired a capital letter. I was suddenly very aware of Kurai's otherness: the way her skin was coloured and oiled differently to mine; the way her hair grew out of her head; the shapes and curves of her face. Her eyes looked exotic and very, very dark. Looking into them, I saw no reflection of me at all.

We stared at each other for a moment, and I backed down. 'Sure,' I said, and 'All right.'

We started talking about school and exams and friends again, but something had changed. The air between us was a different colour.

*   *   *

Mr Cooper sent us a guard. I saw some of the farm workers building a guard hut by our gate.

'What's going on?' I asked Mum.

'It's for the guard,' she said.

'What guard?'

'Our guard.'

'When did we get a guard?'

'Mr Cooper gave him to us.'

I felt something press at the back of my eyes, like the beginning of a headache before a storm. Mr Cooper heard things that we did not. He talked to the farm workers. He knew about things before they happened.

'Why?'

'He just wants us to be safe.' Mum smiled at me with just her mouth, not her eyes.

Our guard arrived the next day.

'Cephas!' I had not seen him in a long time. I shook his hand and felt the familiar stump of his half-finger. 'How are you?'

'Good-good, Medem,' he said, grinning.

'Mum, you remember Cephas? He used to be the compound guard.'

'Yes, yes, of course,' said Mum, who had no idea. She showed Cephas where the guard hut was.

'Have any new books?' I asked him once he was settled in.

'Ah, no,' he said. 'I am busy, too busy for reading.'

186

That night I lay awake listening to him walk around the property: the crunch of gravel, the crack of twigs in the grass, a cough. And then again, crunch, crack, cough, around and around. Every time I dropped off to sleep, I heard a noise and jerked awake, my heart leaping, until I remembered that we had a guard and it was not another burglar or prowler. When I woke up in the early hours of the morning, I looked out of the window and saw the quick orange flare of a cigarette from the guard hut. I found the small flame comforting.

After a week, Cephas went missing. He did not turn up to work in the morning.

Mum called Mr Cooper to arrange a replacement.

'Of all the times to have a hangover,' she said. 'We need a bluddy guard more than ever.'

Soon a worker appeared at the gate and took up Cephas's post. He was a fat man with a face like a toad's, but an amiable grin.

'Do you know Cephas?' I asked him.

'*Hongu.*' Yes.

'Do you know where he is?'

The man shrugged. 'He has been at the shebeen every night. He is probably sick.'

It seemed Mum was right. Until he did not appear the next day either. Or the day after that.

'He's scarpered,' said Steve.

'He wouldn't leave without saying goodbye,' I insisted.

'Jesus, Elise.' Steve was exasperated.

I went looking for Cephas on the weekend. I cycled along the edge of the dirt road that led to the workers' villages, swerving into the bushes when a truck or tractor passed me.

The soft white dust of the road was like talcum powder in its consistency, but showed a terrible persistence when it came to sticking to things. Things like the underside of your car, your hair, your hands, your eyeballs. If I did not get out of the way, I would be coated in the stuff and look even whiter than a White.

When I came to the workers' compound, there was the usual crowd of *piccanins* kicking a football around and fooling with an old, abandoned car on the side of the road. When they saw me, they came running up. 'Money for sweets!' 'Do you have sweets?'

Their eyes glittered with simple greed and a more complex acquisitiveness.

Whites had money, everyone knew that, and it was your right to pester them until they gave it up. What gave them the right to hang on to it?

I dispensed the few coins I had in my pocket. The little kids loved the two-dollar coins especially, because they had pictures of pangolins on them, but they were next to useless those days.

'Do you know where Cephas is?' I asked them.

'Cephas the cook?'

'Cephas the guard.'

The *piccanins* were the best people to ask if you wanted to know anything. But it came at a price. I found a mint in my pocket, befurred with lint. It disappeared into someone else's pocket.

'He has gone.'

'Do you know where?'

They consulted. 'He went into the Bush.'

'The Bush?'

'*Ja!*' They giggled and ran away before I could

188

ask them anything more.

I biked into the compound. Most of the men and women were at work, but I found an elderly woman cleaning clothes in a tin basin and asked her where Cephas had gone. She pursed her lips together and shook her head with great significance. I knew that this meant she knew, and disapproved.

'Where is he?'

She spoke in Shona and her accent was thick. I only understood a word here and there. I heard 'young men' and 'angry' and 'camp', and I heard 'the Bush'.

'Do you know where?'

She traced a map for me in the dust. Just outside the farm boundaries, in the scrub land where no food would grow, not even mealies. And mealies would grow everywhere, from the dirt in a pothole to a pile of sand in the back of a *bakkie*.

I thanked the old woman. It was turning into a long expedition, but I was too curious now to leave it alone.

Before I had left the compound, one of the *piccanins* grabbed my arm and tugged on it. 'They took them away,' he said in a whisper.

'What?'

'ZANU. They came with trucks and took them away from the compound. The man said it was for correction. He said the boys needed to be re-educated.'

'Who's "he"?'

The boy shook his head.

'All the boys?'

'Some of us ran and hid, but they took the rest. My father went.'

'What are they going to do to them?'

'They are going to teach them,' said the boy. He pursed his lips suddenly and turned away.

'Wait! Where did they go?'

He did not come back.

I hopped back on my bike and pedalled down the dirt road, towards the Bush. I knew I had ventured beyond the farm boundaries when potholes appeared in the road and the wire fences sagged and bent. I turned on to a small dirt road, startling a goat that had been grazing on the verge. Soon I passed more goats, in lean-to pens. I knew there had to be people nearby, but I saw no one. It was a surprise when I turned a corner and came across a makeshift camp in the grasses. Lean-to houses made from boards and a surprising number of people. Rough and uneven fencing, topped with razor wire. A man with a rifle, guarding the entrance. There were dozens of people inside: men, women and even some children. The children were all boys, as far as I could see. I wheeled my bike into the bushes and stood, one foot on the pedal, watching.

A group of men sat, smoking, around a cooking fire just outside this gate. They looked familiar, I thought. There was a cow hung up on meathooks—one of Mr Cooper's cows, I recognised the brand on its flank—and a hunk of meat over the fire. It smelled good, greasy and hot.

Cephas emerged from one of the shacks, holding a Chibuku Scud. He walked over to the edge of the fence, near to the clump of bushes where I was hiding. I stood with one foot on my bike pedals, ready to take off. His eyes were striped red with veins, absorbed in their own world.

190

He was not seeing the Bush and the camp, but something else.

'Cephas!' I hissed. 'It's me.'

I stepped out of the bushes a little way, still holding the bike by its handlebars. He turned his head to stare at me, and I did not know if he had recognised me or not. His mouth opened, and his jaw moved slowly. 'Bluddy white kid,' he said.

I felt like someone had clasped my head in cold hands. 'What?'

'Bluddy white kids think they can do whatever they want,' he said. He was speaking very slowly, and his eyes were not focused.

'Cephas! What are you doing here? Who brought you here?'

He put his face close to the wire. I thought he was going to whisper something, so I moved forward as well. He pursed his lips and spat a yellow glob of saliva that landed at my feet. His blank eyes glared. 'Bugger off.'

And I did. My legs shook, and my bike swerved left and right before I could straighten it out. Stupid—and cocky. Why did I think my smart-alec Shona comments and my supposed farm-girl toughness would impress anyone? Why had I come here? It took me a long time to cycle back to the farm, and I looked over my shoulder the whole way.

The new guard's footsteps sounded different at night. He was a good man, who enjoyed chatting in his breaks, but it was not the same.

CHAPTER NINETEEN

We were Whites, and nothing else. We did not have lives outside of our whiteness. We huddled together with the rest of the community like pale maggots in a dusty corpse. All we could do was watch the news, and wait.

Every week, my grandparents posted us what they called aid packages. They did not put anything valuable inside, because parcels were always opened at Customs.

When we got them, they were battered and haphazardly taped together.

They sent us videos taped from the BBC. They sent me teenage magazines with pictures of smiling white girls on the covers and articles about boyfriends and clothes and pop stars. I was fourteen, nearly fifteen, but I had nothing in common with those girls. I read the magazines anyway.

We all went to church every week, even Steve. We gathered together, sang songs and comforted each other.

'God is working in Zimbabwe,' said one of the banners above the altar.

We prayed for peaceful change. Our priest was openly political, and in his sermons he talked about Mugabe and his plans to take the white-owned farms.

'He's going to get himself into trouble,' said Steve.

'It's his duty to speak out,' said Mum.

'*Ja*, well, sometimes it's better to fly under the

radar and not get yourself arrested,' said Steve. 'When he's chucked into Chikurubi Prison he won't be any use to anybody, will he?'

When we sang 'Jabulani Africa', people stood with their hands up and tears leaking from their eyes. It almost felt like we were talking to God.

There was a march for peace planned for the first day of April. April Fool's Day, a Saturday. They told us about it at church. Lots of people were planning to go, even the children and the very old people. They would carry banners. 'No to violence'. 'No to intimidation'. 'No to military rule'. We all helped to make them.

'Can we go on the march, Mum?' I asked.

'Don't be bluddy stupid,' she said.

'Kurai's going.'

'Kurai's mad, you know that.'

'Why can't we go? We have to do something.'

'No, we don't.'

'It's a peaceful protest.'

Mum turned to me. 'Do you still think there's such a thing as a peaceful protest? Don't be bluddy stupid.'

I locked myself in my room and sulked, but Mum paid no attention. And neither did Steve, who I thought might be more sympathetic. 'There will be trouble,' he said. 'You just watch.'

It took a great deal of careful planning. Kurai's parents were not happy with her going either, but her older brother was going into town under the pretence of getting a part for his car. Kurai had persuaded him to let her tag along, and I was going with.

'Is it all right if I go to Kurai's house on Saturday?'

193

'I thought she was going to that bluddy march.'

'No, her parents won't let her.'

'All right then.'

'Tafadzwa's going to pick me up.'

Mum was suspicious of Tafadzwa. He drove with his windows down and rap music on his car radio, and he wore thick sunglasses that hid his eyes.

'He's a good driver,' I said.

'I don't know how he can be a good driver with all that racket in his ears.'

'Can I go?'

'*Ja.*'

I considered asking Sean to come too, but I had an uncomfortable feeling he would tell me I was being stupid, as Mum had.

*   *   *

On the day of the march, the house was very quiet. Steve sat in the dining room, pasting newspaper clippings into a scrapbook. Mum was gardening. Tatenda and Saru went about their work.

The gate intercom rang. 'I'm off,' I shouted and ran down the driveway.

'Take care!' Mum shouted back.

In Harare, the air was fresh in an early-morning way that overrode the smell of petrol fumes and garbage. Hundreds of people stood around, letting their placards hang by their sides. Black and white. More black than white, probably. I stayed close to Kurai and Tafadzwa.

'Welcome, welcome,' people said to us. Complete strangers clasped my hand. Smiles, laughter. Even the drifting jacaranda flowers seemed like confetti. Kurai and I did not have banners, but we positioned ourselves behind someone who did. There was a white family a few feet away from us who were sharing a Thermos flask of tea—parents and two little children. I could see at least two people in wheelchairs.

'So many people,' said Kurai. She smoothed lip balm on to her mouth. 'Hey, it's starting.'

The crowd had started to shuffle and murmur expectantly.

'Is that the police?' said someone. I saw a brown uniform skulking several metres away from the crowd, then realised there was more than one.

'Kurai.' I nudged her and pointed.

'What?' She followed my gaze. 'They'll leave us alone.'

'Let us pray,' said someone into a megaphone. We all bowed our heads. I kept my eyes open, so I could see who squeezed their eyes tight shut, who mumbled words along with the leader, and who just stared at their feet. The policemen did not come any closer. I thought the prayers had spooked them.

'There are blockades around the city,' I heard someone saying. I turned round.

'What was that?'

The speaker was an elderly white man. 'Blockades around the city,' he said.

'Why?'

'To stop people joining the march.'

'But it's a peace march.'

He turned away from me. I tugged at Kurai's arm.

'It's fine,' she said. 'Typical Mugabe, he just doesn't want the media to see us. Don't worry.'

'Ready, everyone?' said the voice from the megaphone, and we started walking down the main street. The tarmac was satisfyingly hard beneath our feet. The banners flapped and snapped in the breeze. It was a beautiful day. The tiny purple balloons of jacaranda flowers popped beneath my feet. Even the Zimbabwean flags on the street lamps seemed to be complicit in what we were doing; they took on a cheerful air, like bunting.

Passers-by waved and smiled, some of them joining us. Tourists in the pavement cafés stood up to take photos. Even people in cars, who could not drive down the road because of us, honked their horns in support. It felt like a big party, but it also felt like we were doing something important. My heart swelled in my chest, and I walked with my head up.

'It's going well,' said Kurai.

Someone started singing a hymn, and people joined in. I did not know the tune, but I sung along anyway, as loudly as I could.

We turned a corner and saw a group of young black men jumping down from *bakkies*. A ripple of fear went through the crowd, and people's steps faltered. 'Keep walking!' someone shouted.

We moved our feet forward, but the young men were advancing too. They carried makeshift weapons—clubs, *sjamboks*. They looked purposeful, and organised. This was not just a group of youths causing trouble. This was something that had been planned. The crowd shifted, uncertain. One of the black women from church started singing again and others joined in. This gave us courage, and we stepped forward.

I did not see who was hit first.

People started to scream, and run. The War Vets—I was almost certain they were War Vets—did not discriminate. The orderly lines of marchers disintegrated and scattered. I saw an elderly couple stagger past, the man's white hair smeared red and gleaming against his scalp.

'Where's Tafadzwa?' said Kurai.

'I don't know.' We had lost him. 'Where shall we go?'

Kurai grabbed my arm and pulled me towards the side of the road, where the shops were. We saw a couple of tourists sitting outside a pavement café, untouched cups of coffee sitting in front of them. The woman's mouth was slack with shock, but the man was taking photographs.

'Don't be bluddy stupid!' Kurai yelled at them, but it was too late. A *sjambok* cracked across the man's skull and he slumped forward on to the table. His wife did not scream but let out a strange, ladylike yelp before leaning over the table to cradle her husband's head. His camera had fallen from his hands. As we watched, a young black man snatched it and ran off.

I lost Kurai. She was beside me, and then she was not. I could not see where I was going—whether I was headed towards the worst of the conflict, or away. I was carried along by the press of bodies.

'Tear gas!' someone shouted. I could not see the police, but when I looked up I could see the still blue of the sky and the lilac jacarandas, and then a mist of droplets settled on us. It felt like a very fine curtain of rain, the kind we called *guti*. There was a second when it was almost pleasant, and then it burned. I felt like all my insides had turned to liquid and were leaking out wherever they could—through my eyes, my nose, my mouth. It was difficult to breathe. Whatever air I managed to suck in seemed to go straight back out again without giving me any oxygen.

The tear gas had made me close off into my own body, doubled over, clenched inwards. I realised everyone else was doing the same. Everything in the world melted and swam. Shouts. Bodies pushing. An elbow in my side. I saw many faces that were so clear and vivid they almost seemed like hallucinations. I could see right down to the pores on their skin and the yellowed veins in the whites of their eyes. I had lost Tafadzwa, I had lost Kurai, I had lost everyone and I should have listened to Mum when she told me that there was no such thing as a peaceful protest in Zimbabwe.

A white boy bumped into me and I tripped and fell, landing with my hands and knees flat on the tarmac. My hand was covered in little shards of glass. I realised the street had disappeared under debris. There was something small and cold under my hand—a tooth.

I was right outside the Edgars store, where we bought our underwear. A black man I did not know pushed me into the doorway. I fought against him.

'Get inside!' he yelled. His eyes were streaming and red.

'My friend . . .'

'Get back inside! They are targeting you Whites.'

Then he was gone, sucked back into the crowd. But I obeyed him, and ran into the cool, carpeted shade of the department store. Even as I ran, I hated being lumped with 'you Whites'.

The Edgars store was in chaos. Someone had set up a makeshift first aid centre, and people were bandaging their cuts with bits of clothing. An elderly white woman was holding her cardigan to her head, and red was seeping into the beige wool.

'Elise!' Kurai was there. For a moment I did not recognise her—everything was so strange that her familiar face seemed suddenly alien.

'Kurai! Where's Tafadzwa?'

'Don't know.' She did not seem concerned. 'He can take care of himself. You all right?'

'*Ja*, you?'

'*Ja*. But you have a big cut on your head.'

I raised my hand to my hair. It was sticky and had arranged itself into little wet spikes. 'How big?'

'Doesn't look too bad.'

We looked out of the windows, just in time to see a War Vet crack a *sjambok* across the head of a black boy.

'Shee-yit.'

There was no way I could hide my presence at the march from Mum and Steve now.

*   *   *

Mum came to pick me up, hours later, when the crowds had dispersed and all that was left was litter, blood and vomit on the streets. She did not talk to me in the car on the way home. Her freckles stood out against the white of her face.

When we got home, Mum cut my clothes off me and threw them away. They were still infused with tear gas, and every touch burned. Then she washed

199

me, as if I were a baby again. I stood up in the bath and she sponged me down with soap and water. She kept her lips tight together and her face set, until she came to the top of my head, where blood had formed a bird's-nest of hair and dirt. Then she sat down on the edge of the bath and cried.

I stood in the pink water, watching.

No one shouted at me. I was not sure if Mum had spoken to Steve about it or not, but he showed no reaction when I came through to the dinner table with a bandage on my head. We ate in silence. And then we heard the sound of a helicopter.

'Traffic helicopter?' said Mum.

'Too early,' said Steve. 'Police.'

We sat, and chewed, and listened to the whop whop whop of the blades cutting the air. It faded. And then we heard a siren, very far away.

'It's fine,' said Steve.

When the setting sun cracked like an egg yolk on the horizon, Mum poured us all a cup of tea. The steam smelled like burning wood.

We sat there, holding our cooling cups of tea, and did not drink.

When we went into town the next day, the street was still littered with broken posters, blood and pieces of brick. It smelled of tear gas, a smell that closed up my throat and made my stomach lurch into my chest.

We saw footage on all the news channels. 'Why, why? We came in peace,' said one black woman into the camera.

I saw the woman with the 'No Violence' banner struck by a policeman. Her face looked surprised as her legs buckled and she fell to her knees. A

200

middle-aged white man had a bloody split in his head. We watched as the marchers hoisted him on to their shoulders. The white man looked embarrassed.

'A judicial order for the march to proceed without interference was presented to a senior policeman,' said the smooth newsreader voice, 'who took it and threw it on to the pavement.'

The blind singer who performed at the corner of First Street and George Silundika Avenue had his guitar destroyed and his money and CDs stolen in the fight.

'I am appealing for help to raise money for a new guitar,' he said into the camera with dejected, puckered eyes that were even blanker than usual. There was a postal address at the bottom of the screen for anyone who wanted to help him raise the money. I giggled, clapped a hand over my mouth, and stopped. It wasn't funny.

We lived a strange life. We got up, went to school and work and lived our lives during the day, then came home to watch the news and see what was happening in the country. Obsessively, we checked all the channels we could. ZBC. CNN. The BBC. Sky News. It was like living two lives. As if nothing had really happened until we saw it on the television that evening. Our own lives had all but disappeared—absorbed into the wider drama.

That night, the sky was streaked pink, like my blood in the bathwater.

'Red sky at night, shepherd's delight,' said Mum.

We sat and watched the sky change colour. Saru left for the day, jingling her keys in her pocket and calling, 'Goodnight Baas, goodnight Medem,' as she crunched down the gravel. Tatenda let her out

201

of the gate, tipping an imaginary cap, then ran whistling down to the *khaya* where he would probably get ready for a night in the shebeen. Mum dished up roast chicken, *sadza* and vegetables. Steve poured beers with creamy heads. Black began to leak into the sky, leaving a trail of stars.

The moon was big tonight, and orange, like a *naartjie* hanging on a celestial tree. I could see the pockmarks in its skin.

'It's an optical illusion,' said Steve. 'Look.' He stretched out his hand and measured the moon with his fingers.

I tried it. The moon was swollen and juicy, but when I pinched it between my finger and thumb it shrank to its normal size.

'It's not real,' said Steve. 'It just looks that way. It's always the same size.'

I watched it rise above the broken glass on top of our wall.

Kurai called me that evening. 'Hi, howzit?'

'Good.'

There was silence on the other end. This was unusual with Kurai.

'Look,' she said after a moment, 'Can I come over tomorrow?'

'Of course.'

'Because I'm moving to the States.'

'You're what?'

'I'll tell you tomorrow.'

*   *   *

Kurai and I sat on a rug in the back garden. There were Cokes and a bowl of crisps in front of us, but we hadn't touched them.

'It's not like we're not going to see each other again,' said Kurai. 'I'll probably bump into you at some glamorous party in New York.'

She was moving to America to live with her older sister.

'What will you be doing there?'

'I'll be some kind of executive. With a corner office. And my secretary will have a secretary.'

'And what will I be doing there?'

'How the hell should I know?'

'Right.'

'Are your parents staying?'

Kurai shrugged. '*Ja*, well, it's not so bad for them.'

'Because they're . . .'

'No, because they're rich.'

'Sure.'

'I'll probably be back in the holidays.'

'Will you come back here to live? After uni, I mean?'

'Who knows?' She took her first sip of Coke.

'That's very sad for the country,' said Steve when I told him.

'What?'

'Well, that people like Kurai are leaving.'

'What do you mean, people like Kurai?' I was in a combative mood.

'It's not going to be people like us who change this place,' said Steve. 'You know that. Kurai is the future.'

He was right. Kurai was the future. And I was not.

Our minister at church gave a special sermon that Sunday. 'We will not give up,' he said, and

'God is watching over us.'

'Good will triumph,' said one of the banners on the wall. We bowed our heads and prayed in special, robotic praying voices for God to bring us peace and justice and democracy.

When I was at church, I sometimes forgot the horror and the hopelessness. I looked around as we sang and saw all the faces tilted upwards, looking at a God I could almost believe was there somewhere. For a moment I believed that it would all work out. That our prayers would be heard.

But when we prayed, the words were sucked into a vacuum. There was just darkness out there. Darkness and the old vengeful gods of Zimbabwe, the ones who wanted blood-offerings and sacrifices. On a blazing blue-sky day, I could not imagine a God somewhere up there. Instead it felt like a bright, merciless eye, pinning us to the world like bugs to a board, watching us squirm with a compassionless gaze. There were older things here than Christianity. They were here first. They were stronger.

CHAPTER TWENTY

Once again, I was home from school. I sat in the farm office with Mum, addressing envelopes for the monthly invoices. Mum turned the radio up for the news. It was bad, as always. All we hoped for was less bad news than the day before.

Mum's parents had called us from England the night before. They sounded frail and old on the phone. I knew they were asking us to leave, because Mum poured herself a big gin and tonic before speaking to them and said '*Ja*. No. *Ja*. Yes, Mum. I know, Mum,' for a long time.

When I spoke to them, they made their voices bright and cheerful. 'How's school?'

'Not too bad. Things have calmed down a bit in town so I haven't missed too many days.'

'Good-oh.'

They did not mention their worries to me.

'Morning,' said Sean, raising his hand as he passed the offices. He had to stay home from school as well, as the War Vets threatened to attack wealthy boarding schools in the country. Instead, he had started working with his dad on the farm. The workers still called him Mini Cooper. He had his dad's easy smile and grasp of Shona slang. And swear words. I watched him walking through the tobacco silos and the ostrich paddocks, his hair lit up like the dusty yellow of the grasses.

I heard something on the radio. 'Mum, turn it up.'

Mum turned the dial. 'Airlines have stopped flying out of Harare International Airport.'

'Mum?'

Mum pressed her lips together. 'It's not a big deal,' she said. 'It's only temporary.'

I felt my chest tighten. We were trapped.

'Don't look like that,' said Mum. 'It's not a big deal.'

'But we can't fly out,' I said.

'We weren't going to fly out anyway,' said Mum.

That was not the point.

'I'm just going outside for a sec,' I said. The sky was a hot blue, and the farm buildings were so white that every time I blinked I could see them imprinted on my eyelids. I walked away from the office to the dirt road.

Every face on the farm was a threat. Every laugh was a menace, a joke with no punchline. I walked, trying to shake off the feeling, but everyone I saw looked like a potential killer. I did not know whether their smiles and greetings were real, or whether underneath they were thinking of me as a White, a White that needed to be eliminated.

I sat in the shade and tried to control my breathing. We were trapped. Nothing was flying out.

I had not realised how much I relied on our ability to escape. Even though I had been telling everyone in my loudest voice that we would never leave, some secret part of me relied on my British passport and the fact that we had enough money to jump on a plane if things got really bad.

I dipped my head between my knees. I heard my heart slowing down, then speeding up when I took a breath.

'Are you all right?'

I could not look up.

'Medem?'

The voice was young. I looked up. It was Lettuce, one of the workers.

'I'm fine, thank you,' I said.

'Okay.' His teeth flashed white in a smile as he walked away. I watched him go.

I thought I was one of them, almost. I was not a White. Not really. Was I? I thought of Beauty, all those years ago. How could I possibly grow up with two mothers, one black and one white, and still be just a White?

My brain was not working properly. Maybe it

was the heat. I started to walk back towards the offices, where things would be more normal. Despite the farm invasions, everyone was concentrating on end-of-month accounts.

Mr Cooper pulled up on his motorcycle.

'Howzit?'

'Good.' I pulled my lips back over my teeth in what I thought a smile looked like.

'How's school?'

'Good.'

'You all right?' He ran his hand through his hair, which was sticking straight up. He hardly ever wore a bike helmet. He said it was because he wanted to hear what the workers shouted at him as he went past, in case they were being cheeky.

'I'm fine.'

'You're not worried about all this government nonsense, are you?' he said, smiling. 'Agh, sure, they talk big, but we've been here for years and we'll be here for years still. These bluddy *munts* can't force us off our land.'

I nodded.

Mr Cooper was about to say something else, but stopped to shout in Shona to a passing worker. Something about his girlfriend. His Shona was very colloquial, and I could not understand it all. The worker shouted something back, and laughed.

'The boys would never stand for it,' he said, turning his attention back to me. 'D'you think they'd let some rabble come in here and *shuper* us?'

'No.'

'No, they wouldn't. Now, is your Mum inside?'

'*Ja.*'

'Good stuff.' He started up his bike, walking his

feet along the ground a little way before it sprang into life. 'Cheers.'

'Okay.'

I watched him pull up to the offices and walk in. When he left, I went back.

'You all right now?' said Mum.

'*Ja*,' I said, and sat back down to work on the envelopes.

When I had finished writing an e-mail to my grandparents that evening, Steve sat down to read over it with me. He checked my e-mails every night, to make sure there was nothing incriminating that could be caught in the government filter and traced back to us. I forgot, sometimes, how careful we had to be. We were not allowed to say anything bad about the President in case someone heard and reported us. We knew that the government opened any letters we sent to England, and that our e-mails were checked for keywords. All the Whites developed a code. In our e-mails and our conversation, we called Mugabe Tim. I asked Steve what it meant.

'That Ignorant *Munt*,' he told me. I was surprised that he answered so quickly. I thought it would have gone under the heading of Things He Would Tell Me When I Was Older.

It occurred to me that perhaps I was Older now, that magical age when everything would be revealed. I certainly felt older, as I watched my mother's skin go loose on her bones, and saw the first grey hairs appear at her temples. When I touched her hair it no longer felt glossy and oiled, but crumbling. New lines had appeared—one between her eyebrows, a sharp, deep cut, and two at the corners of her mouth.

In bed that night, I wondered what it would be like to live in England. I was so hot that sweat was trickling down the backs of my knees and pooling in the crooks of my elbows, as if my whole body were crying. I imagined lying in bed in a cold country where there was no need for a mosquito net and no mysterious sounds from outside. I wondered if I could prepare myself for it if I started imagining myself there. If that would make it easier.

Mugabe told us that we had to hand in our foreign passports or lose our Zimbabwean passports and be declared aliens. If we did not renounce our British citizenship, we could not vote.

'Mum, we have to be able to vote,' I said.

'Don't be stupid,' said Mum. 'Do you think our votes will make any difference? The whole thing is rigged.'

'But we have to make a stand!' I said.

'No, we don't. We're giving up the Zimbabwe passports and that's that,' said Mum.

'Bluddy stupid,' said Steve.

It was not even a decision, really. Of course we would keep our British passports. We would be mad not to. But handing the Zimbabwean passports over was hard. Steve left it until the very last minute.

'I'm keeping my Zimbabwean one,' he said on the morning of the last day.

Mum and I stared at him. 'Are you mad?' said Mum.

'I'm a Zimbabwean,' said Steve. 'I'm not a bluddy Brit.'

'You can't give up your British passport.' Mum

209

crunched down on her breakfast toast as if that settled the argument.

'I'd rather give up my British passport than my Zimbabwean one.'

I felt hollow. Our British passports were the most important things we owned. Mum kept the three maroon pamphlets in a locked cupboard, and she had always told me that they were the first things to grab if we had to leave quickly. Our passports represented civilisation, freedom, the possibility of a future somewhere else. I had a superstitious attachment to mine, as if it were one of Beauty's totems. The thought of Steve just handing his over made me feel sick.

'That's stupid,' said Mum. 'Come on, Steve. It doesn't mean you're not a Zimbabwean any more. It's just a piece of paper. Mugabe wants you to give up your British passport so you're trapped here.'

Steve shook his head and stared at his tea. Mum put out a hand and touched his. I saw the shiny patch on his knuckle where he had had a piece of skin cancer cut out.

'It doesn't mean anything,' said Mum.

But we knew it did.

Steve gave up his Zimbabwean passport. The people at the office grumbled because he had left it so late, and made him wait for an hour before they brought him the paperwork. For the rest of the day he was silent and brooding.

'It is too much,' said Tatenda, shaking his head. I was sitting with him and Saru while they had their tea. 'Mugabe must go now.'

Saru and I exchanged glances. It was not safe to say things like that.

'I worry about that one,' said Saru later. She was

making the dinner while I sat on the back doorstep. 'My husband has heard him in the shebeens. He is always yelling about Mugabe and the MDC.'

I was silent. I did not want to voice any opinions. Even to Saru.

Mr Cooper was the only person we knew who handed in his British passport. He handed in his South African passport as well, and then threw a party.

'Celebrating the burning of bridges,' he said, 'and the beginning of the end.'

The house was covered in Zimbabwean flags, and everyone got splendidly drunk.

'You're mad,' someone told Mr Cooper every ten minutes.

'I know,' he said.

We were illegal aliens. The name made me smile. It made us sound like we had two heads, rather than just being white Zimbabweans with British passports.

Mum started to have low conversations with Mr Cooper in her office that I strained to hear from the other side of the door. I knew, somehow, that Steve did not know about those conversations, and I did not tell him. I heard the odd word— passports, airport, money. I knew that Mum had a bank account that Steve did not know about, that she used for emergencies, but she told me not to say anything.

'It's our secret,' she said.

Mum's wages went straight into the family account along with Steve's. This money was coming from somewhere else. But I did not ask. We needed everything we could get.

Mum and I drove back from the farm shop with meat for dinner. She was making Steve's favourite, to cheer him up. He had been in a foul mood since giving up his passport.

'What do we do now?' I asked.

'We go home.'

'No, I mean, now that we're not citizens any more.'

Mum kept her eyes on the road. 'Mr Cooper thinks we should leave,' she said finally.

My stomach felt empty. Leaving was something we would do in the future. It was always just around the corner, after some vague event that made it necessary, far enough away that it might not come at all.

'Oh.'

'And Steve doesn't.'

Steve was made of biltong, woodsmoke, khaki and cowhide. He could not survive anywhere else.

'But we're not going yet,' I said.

'I don't know,' said Mum. 'If we get enough foreign currency, there's no reason to stay.'

'But we can't leave. Not unless we have to.'

'Things aren't going to get better,' said Mum. 'It's not a matter of "if", it's a matter of "when".'

When we got home I sat on the back doorstep in the sun. I could smell clean laundry and the dark, bitter smell of fresh tea. I could see Saru and Tatenda sitting on the grass drinking from enamel mugs and eating thick bricks of peanut butter and bread. I could not imagine living anywhere else.

Mum brought up the subject of leaving at dinner, while I was there. I knew she had done this so that they would not have too big a row. Steve did not like fighting with Mum in front of me or the servants.

'We always said we'd leave when we got burgled, Steve,' she said.

'They only took the bluddy laptop.'

'I know. But it might be time to seriously consider it. We can stay with Mum and Dad . . .'

'I hate England.'

'I know you hate England.'

'Too bluddy cold. Too many people.'

'I know, Steve, but we can't carry on like this. It's just a matter of time before everything falls apart.'

'It could get better. The election's coming up . . .'

'*Ja*, as if that will make any difference. You know how it works. Mugabe's the big chief, he's not going to give up power.'

'I don't want to talk about it now.'

I stared at my plate, pushing a piece of carrot around with my fork.

'I've spoken to Mr Cooper about it, and he thinks . . .'

Steve was tight-lipped. 'So you've been discussing this with Mark Cooper.'

'Not discussing this, Steve. He's just concerned.'

'Concerned for you.'

'For all of us. Bluddy yell, Steve, he just wants to look after us. You should be bluddy grateful.'

'*Ja*, like I should be grateful for the bluddy pool he wants to put in, and the guard.'

'You're just pissed off because you don't want to leave.'

'No, I'm pissed off because my wife discusses our private business with another man.'

'He's not another man, he's my boss. And yours. For Christ's sake, Steve.'

'*Ja*, well, you can go and tell him that we don't need his money.'

'Don't be bluddy stupid! We need as much money as we can get. How else are we going to get into a country overseas? I haven't got a degree. I have almost no points. We need money to get in, and you know it. Get off your bluddy high horse.'

'My bluddy high horse! When my wife . . .' Steve realised I was still sitting at the table. 'Go to your room.'

I did not go to my room. I ran down to the bottom of the garden, to the avocado tree. I could hear Tatenda whistling from somewhere in the garden.

Living in Zimbabwe was like having a demanding younger brother or sister. It was loud, disruptive and badly behaved. It demanded everyone's attention, sucked up everyone's energy, ruined family holidays and dinner conversations, kept everyone up at night worrying about its future. All our problems centred around Zimbabwe's problems.

I wondered what would happen if we lived somewhere where we didn't have to worry constantly about money. Where we no longer had servants wandering about the house who forced us to speak in lowered voices when we had an argument. Where we could not exchange rueful glances with people in the supermarket when the bread had run out.

It would be disorientating to be suddenly free of it—to make choices that were not dictated by its rowdy, unignorable presence. In Zimbabwe, Mugabe was to blame for everything. Away from Zimbabwe, some of our problems might actually be our own fault.

The next day, Mum and Steve were still not speaking. Steve went into the garden to order Tatenda around, which always made him feel better. I went with Mum to the office, as usual.

'Are the Coopers going to leave?' I asked. Mum's radio crackled at her side.

She never put it down, just in case the news everyone dreaded came through.

'I don't know.'

It was well known that they had received threats. Theirs was one of the biggest farms in Zimbabwe. What War Vet wouldn't want a piece of it?

'Mark Cooper won't leave,' said Mum. 'He's more Shona than the Shona. They love him.'

We sat in silence for a moment, thinking about all the farm workers that joked and laughed with Mr Cooper when he roared around the farm on his motorbike.

'I don't think it matters,' I said.

CHAPTER TWENTY-ONE

The first white farmer died. He was abducted from his farm and shot. The five farmers who followed to try and rescue him were attacked and beaten. They were not young men. They had beer bellies from years of standing over a *braai* with a Castle Lager in their hands. They had greying hair and floppy white hats. They had short shorts and *veldtskoens*, and a tan that stopped at their sleeves and the folded tops of their socks.

They looked like people we knew.

On Easter weekend we heard about the white farmer who was killed in Nyamadhlovu, down near Bulawayo—comfortably far away. For me. Not for Steve, who was born there.

The story was dramatic, a dawn raid, the last stand of the white farmer against the War Vets. It sounded like a western. A man locking himself in his house with ammunition and dogs. His wife and children fleeing. A crackle on the radio telling him that 'they' were coming—the news we all dreaded. Seventy attackers. A two-hour siege.

Roadblocks placed to stop an ambulance getting through. Molotov cocktails thrown through the windows.

And then: two shots in the face as the farmer stumbled out. Beatings with an iron bar.

We saw a picture on the BBC news.

'Don't look,' said Mum, but I did, and I saw a pulp of white and pink that used to be a man. He had been mashed into the ground. He did not even look human. He looked like meat.

'What's that on his leg?'

'Apparently he made himself a splint,' said Steve. 'When his leg was shot.'

I imagined him carefully strapping his home-made splint to his leg. So much care for his body, the same body that was blown apart and chopped up as soon as he crawled outside.

The attack was organised by Comrade Jesus. The killing happened on Zimbabwe's Independence Day. The place was called Compensation Farm. It was all straight out of a film script—ironies so great that no one even bothered to mention them.

One of the farm workers was interviewed. He

216

was sobbing. He said his employer did not deserve to 'die like a dog'. The news showed pictures of the body, covered with a sheet. The War Veterans were shipped there in busloads from Harare, and given weapons. Local, genuine War Veterans were horrified by the attacks, and made sure to say they were not involved. The dead farmer quickly became a mythical figure, a folk hero.

'He's not bluddy Ned Kelly,' muttered Steve, but we all saw ourselves in him. And we were scared. It had started, and we all knew where it would go.

The war was back. No one said it, but everyone knew it. People dug out their old guns. Mum went to bed with a migraine. My heart was scudding on quick waves of blood, and I heard it like a drumbeat in my ears, always. I started to say 'Pardon?' every time someone spoke to me, because I could hardly hear them over the drums. The same drums that announced the start of the ZBC news.

This was the second farmer to be killed. And, as if something were hungry for more blood, the killings kept on coming.

Steve watched the news over dinner. Even after he swallowed a mouthful, his teeth kept grinding. We sat in silence, watching Mugabe gesticulate with chopping motions of his hands. There was spittle at the corner of his mouth.

'I'll burn the house to the ground myself rather than let those filthy Kaffirs get their hands on it,' said Steve suddenly. He got up and took his plate to the kitchen.

There were more and more white farmers on the news these days. They all looked the same: so easy to caricature. The dreadful cartoons in the newspaper showed them as comical figures, the Big Baases who owned the land.

I started having nightmares about War Vets invading the farm and destroying our house. We had heard stories of what they did inside the farmers' homesteads. I imagined them smashing our ornaments, burning the family pictures.

Auntie Mary and Uncle Pieter called every night. Mum held the receiver as if she were gripping Auntie Mary's hand.

'They made us invite them in for a drink the other night,' said Uncle Pieter. 'I had to go and buy six crates of beer. And they made Mary cook them dinner.'

'What do you make for thirty War Veterans?' said Mary when Pieter gave her the phone. 'It's not in any etiquette books, is it?' She laughed. And she laughed again when Mum asked how she was. '*Ja*, I'm okay. We've got the dogs if they get too cheeky.'

Mum did not remind her of what the War Vets did to dogs. We had seen the pictures of pets hung on chicken wire fences, dogs shot and crumpled in farmhouse driveways.

Sean seemed to feel personally affronted by the attacks. He folded in on himself, grew shorter. One evening he packed a rucksack and disappeared into the Bush, just took off.

'That boy behaves like a bluddy idiot sometimes,' said Mr Cooper. There was a raw edge of worry to his voice. 'I told him he needs to just put up and shut up. We'll be fine. I can't have my workers seeing him panic like this, it won't make anything better.'

'Bluddy stupid thing to do,' said Steve. But I

218

could understand it. There were things that would hurt you in the Bush—insects and snakes and animals and *tokoloshes* and ghosts—but they would not try and justify the blood with laws and long speeches.

Sean returned the next day. Grimmer and older in the face, he stopped by to apologise for worrying us.

'That's fine,' said Mum. 'Are you all right?'

'*Ja*, thank you, I'm fine.'

I tried to talk to him. 'How are you feeling?'

'I'm fine,' he said. 'Was just being a sissy. I've got my act together now.'

'You weren't being a sissy,' I said. 'We're all scared.'

'*Ja*, well,' he said. 'I'm not any more.'

We went for a walk, leaving the motorbike behind for once. Sean lit a cigarette, and offered me one too.

'No, thanks.'

'Gone off them, eh?' He tapped some ash on to the ground. 'So what are you guys going to do?'

'What do you mean?'

'Are you staying here?'

I shrugged.

Sean straightened up and took the cigarette from his mouth. 'Did you hear something?'

'Like what?'

'Shut up.'

I heard voices around the bend of the road, and the crunch of footsteps.

'There's nothing to worry about.' Steve's voice.

'Don't be bluddy stupid, man.' Mr Cooper.

'Shee-yit.' Sean stubbed out his cigarette. 'He'll kill me if he sees me smoking.'

219

'He doesn't know?'

'What do you think? Come on.'

He grabbed my hand with his sweaty one, and pulled me over the fence and down among the tobacco plants.

'Have they seen us?'

'Shush.' Sean was listening. His hair had taken on a greenish tinge from the reflected light of the leaves.

I shifted position and bumped a plant, setting it shaking.

'Stay still.'

We breathed shallowly, trying to take up as little space in the world as possible.

'Do you think they'll hear us?' I whispered.

'Well they bluddy will now, won't they? Shut up.'

'You shut up, you're doing it too.'

Our shoulders were close together, but self-consciously not touching. I could smell the intimate, nicotine-stained scent of his skin.

'Just be quiet.'

On the road, the voices grew louder again.

'They're coming,' I said.

'Did I not just tell you to shut up?'

'You need to take Elise out of the country,' we heard Mr Cooper saying. 'It's not safe here.'

'*Ja*, well,' said Steve. 'We'll see. We're not making any decisions yet.'

'Listen, man.' The footsteps stopped. 'I'm serious. I can feel it coming. It's not going to be pretty.'

'You don't think they'd invade Cooper Farms?'

'It's hard to tell. I don't think things are going to get better, put it that way. You need to get Elise out of here.'

'That's my decision to make.'

'No, it's not. You have a kid, it's your responsibility to go.'

'What the yell are you talking about? You have a kid!'

'Sean is different.'

'How?'

'He has to run this farm one day. He has to know what it's like. I don't want him to go running when there's trouble. You need to stand and fight.'

'And why should Elise be any different?'

'For one thing, she's a girl. For another, there's no need for you to stay.'

'Don't you bluddy tell me what to do with my stepdaughter!' said Steve.

There was a short silence. Steve coughed. 'Look, Mark, we'll cross that bridge when we come to it.'

I could not hear Mr Cooper's reply. The voices moved out of earshot again. Sean and I sat in the cool, waxy shade of the tobacco leaves.

'I guess you might be going after all,' he said.

*　　　*　　　*

The fabric between the old world and the new one started to tear. Shapes moved in the night, a whisper of a darker black. Older gods than ours had woken up, and they lived by older rules. Mercy was not one of them. Nor was forgiveness, nor happy worship songs, nor 'The Lord is My Shepherd'. As we crowded around the BBC World Service listening to the stories of violence and murder, I could feel the night pressing on the windows of the house like black hands cupped over ears.

221

We were under attack from the world around us, too. Army worm infested our garden. Steve and Tatenda launched a counter-attack with foul-smelling chemicals that burned our grass to a peroxide blond. The army worms, which were really caterpillars, marched on tiny legs with their blind, blunt faces pointing towards our house. I did not walk on the grass those days.

I caught bilharzia from swimming in the waterhole. We used to study the lifecycle of the parasite at school, but I could not remember anything about it except that it was carried by snails and entered your body through the skin—which was disgusting. The doctor gave me a fat pill almost too big to swallow, and told me to stay in bed after I had taken it.

'Why?'

'Because it will upset your balance.'

When I got home and swallowed the pill, I lay back carefully on the pillow and waited for it to take effect. Then I realised I needed to go to the bathroom. I swung my feet on to the floor, and the ceiling seemed to wheel around under me while the floor shot up to where the ceiling used to be. Gravity was not working. Strangely, this was a relief; all the other laws had failed, so why should physics be any different? Finally, the world looked the way it felt—upside down and spinning.

There were more crows than usual, too. They sat on the branches of the pecan and macadamia trees, laughing at us and throwing empty shells. Steve decided to try shooting a crow and hanging it from a branch, as Mr Cooper did.

He did not trust Tatenda with the pellet gun.

'Sure you can manage it?' said Mum.

'Of course I can bluddy manage it,' said Steve. 'I was in the army, wasn't I?'

I went outside with him. Tatenda was there too, grinning. This was the most exciting thing to happen to him all day.

The crows snickered down at us. They cocked their heads on one side and eyeballed Steve.

'Right,' said Steve, and raised the gun to his shoulder. There was a commotion among the crows. They knew about guns. They scrambled to take off, tripping over each other, but before they could escape Steve fired once, twice into the crowd, and a bird fell.

'Got the bastard,' said Steve, but when the bird hit the ground it got to its feet and started staggering towards us.

'Shit.' Steve lowered the gun.

'It's not dead,' I said.

Steve gave me a look. 'I can see that. We'll have to shoot it again.'

The bird was turning in a circle around its injured wing and flapping with the other, trying to get off the ground.

'I can't hit it while it's moving,' said Steve. 'Hold it still.'

I hesitated.

'We have to put the bluddy thing out of its misery.'

I did not want to touch it. Its black eye revolved in its head as it looked for a way out. Its beak clicked.

'Hold the bluddy thing still!'

I grabbed the crow's wings and held them closed. It snapped its beak at me and rolled its eyes.

'Right,' said Steve, and rested the gun right against its head. He pulled the trigger. The crow's brains fell out of the back of its head, looking like chewed gum.

'Good stuff.' Steve picked it up by one foot. 'Tatenda, grab the ladder. We'll string the thing up.'

Tatenda did not bother with the ladder, just shimmied up the tree with the agility of a vervet monkey. He tied the crow's feet to one of the higher branches. 'Is that good, Baas?'

'*Ja*, good.'

The crow revolved slowly. The sun reflected off its dead eye.

'Kill one and the rest will go away,' said Steve.

The crow cast a pall over the garden. All I could see from the back doorstep was its dead, slowly spinning body. It rotated one way, then, when the string had wound itself too tightly, it started to spin the other way. It was hypnotic.

When I looked out into the night, I did not see the bright fingernail of moon or the pale shapes of moths. Instead, I looked for shadows where something might be hiding, the glint of eyes that did not belong to any animal. We were besieged. We had always locked every door and had burglar bars on every window, but now there was no sense of safety, even when we were barricaded indoors.

I lay awake for an hour every night listening for sounds outside. Sometimes I listened so intently that I forgot to breathe, and my chest surged up with a laboured puff of air, startling me out of my trance. I knew Mum and Steve were awake too, in their bedroom. I could not hear anything, but the silence from their room was a listening silence, a watchful silence.

We were woken up at nearly midnight by the phone. It rang and rang in the darkness while we swam up from our dreams and back into the quiet house. I heard Mum answer. A light was switched on; I could see the band of yellow under my door. When people started moving about and I heard the hiss of the kettle, I climbed out of bed and walked down to the kitchen.

'What are you doing up?' said Steve.

'I heard the phone.'

'Oh.'

Mum was pale and red-eyed. 'That was Auntie Mary,' she said. 'They're about half an hour away.'

'From here?'

'*Ja.*'

'But it's the middle of the night.'

'They had to leave the farm,' said Steve.

'Why?'

Mum and Steve looked at each other through the steam from the teapot. 'Just had to,' said Steve.

'Do you want some tea?' said Mum.

She poured me a cup. I sat down. Steve pulled his little radio over to him and started fiddling with the dials to tune it. Whistle, crackle, hiss, a voice, then a snatch of sunshiny trumpet music that could be from South America. Steve loved to tune the radio, and he was fussy about getting the perfect sound. The static scraped over my nerves and the voices, when they came, sounded startling.

The light from the kitchen window shone into the garden, and I could see the dead crow revolving slowly in its dull gleam.

CHAPTER TWENTY-TWO

They piled into the house. My aunt and uncle looked thin and tired, older and smaller than I remembered. My cousin was fuzzy around the edges and half-asleep. They carried two bags each, and all the bags were bulging.

Mum had thrown blankets and pillows on the sofas in the lounge. Soon it was awash with people and luggage. There were awkward hellos and hugs.

Hennie was disconcertingly large and masculine. Equally disconcertingly, he reminded me of Sean. His voice had broken. The thin, vulnerable curve of his neck that I remembered so well, bent before me as we rode the farm pony, had become thick and strong, studded with freckles.

'Hi Elise.' His voice walked a tentative line between low and high. He shook my hand, an oddly formal gesture.

'Hi, Hennie.' It was so strange to see him again. Especially then, when circumstances were too serious to allow us to laugh and swap stories. 'How is everything going?' I said.

'All right,' he said.

'I'll make some more tea,' said Mum, and vanished. She popped her head around the door to add, 'Better call Mum and Dad.'

'*Ja*.' My aunt took the phone out of the lounge, smiling apologetically at us all.

My uncle leaned his elbows on his knees.

'So,' said Steve. 'What time is your flight tomorrow?' He glanced at the clock. 'Today.'

'Five,' said my uncle.

'Early.'

'You still okay to give us a lift?'

'*Ja*. Is there going to be any trouble with . . . ?'

'No, I don't think so. We're saying we're going on holiday. They wouldn't have had time to . . .'

'*Ja*.'

'What happened?' I asked.

My uncle looked at my cousin, then me. 'We thought it would be a good time to go visit Granny and Grandpa for a while,' he said.

I supposed that in his head Hennie and I were still barefoot, grubby *piccanins* wandering around the farm.

'The farm was invaded,' said Hennie in a flat voice. 'They said they were going to kill us unless we left.'

'Hennie!' My uncle tried to silence him.

'What? Why shouldn't I say?'

'Don't talk to me like that, *domkop*.' Uncle Pieter clapped him across the ear.

He turned to me. 'They wouldn't have killed us, hey, but I thought it was better safe than sorry.'

Better safe than sorry—a good enough reason to leave your home, your livelihood and all the possessions you had worked for? Yes, I thought.

Steve and Uncle Pieter started talking in murmurs about the trip. I was left with my cousin, but I did not know what to say.

'We had to leave the dogs behind,' Hennie whispered. 'And all the horses.'

'I know.'

'We gave them to a friend. We didn't just leave them.' His face was fierce.

'I know.'

We had all heard the stories of dogs and cats left

227

to forage on farms, or dumped out of car doors on the airport road.

Soon, Hennie fell asleep. He was exhausted. Mum came through with a tray of tea and toast spread with butter and anchovy paste, the meal she always made for me when I was sick. When she had poured the tea and sat down, and we were all clutching hot cups, the real business began.

My aunt came back with the phone and sat down. 'They're going to pick us up from the airport,' she said to Uncle Pieter.

'*Lekker.*'

There was a silence, and then 'Those bloody Kaffirs,' she said.

'*Ja.*' My uncle nodded slowly. They did not say anything more. We all knew that this was how things worked in Zimbabwe. You had to be strong, you had to shrug these things off and Make a Plan.

Steve and my uncle sat together, unconsciously mirroring each other's bowed heads and clenched knuckles, chins resting on fists.

I thought of the farm—the stretches of white road lined with dead flowers, the blue gum trees, the horses with their dust-powdered coats, the endless ear-splitting racket of the chickens. I did not know what the War Vets would do to it, but I imagined them rummaging through the closets and drawers, using every pan in the kitchen, running themselves baths and using all of Auntie Mary's expensive bath salts. I knew this was ridiculous.

'What about the workers?' said Steve.

'*Ja*, well, they tried,' said Uncle Pieter. 'That poor bugger Phineas got himself beaten up for his trouble.'

'What will they do?'

228

'Hell, I don't know, hey,' said Uncle Pieter. 'Some of them might stay on, but, shit, if they break it up and use it all for growing six mealies each, there'll be no work.'

'*Hapana basa*,' said Steve. The men laughed a little.

My uncle was rooted in the soil like a baobab tree. There was dirt under his fingernails that no amount of scrubbing would clean, and every crease in his palms was a thin brown line. His skin had been burnt by forty African summers to the consistency of horse-hide. He spoke Shona more readily than he spoke English, which is why his words came out in short, sharp bursts, as if he had to think before each one.

'*Ja*, well,' said my uncle again. I could see him already looking ahead to the next step. There was always a next step.

'Auntie Mary,' I said, 'what really happened to the dogs?'

She looked at me. Her face was grey. 'They shot them,' she said. 'Shot them and hung them on the fence as a warning. We took them down before Hennie got home from school and told him we had given them to a neighbour.'

Those beautiful dogs. The little black spaniel, the big golden retriever. Friendly animals with names and personalities and warm breath. Dogs and cats, horses, pets of all kinds were being killed.

'Don't tell your cousin, okay?' she said, and I nodded.

They left in the grey concrete light of morning, just as the sun was hardening in the sky.

Steve drove them to the airport. There was not enough room in the car for Mum and me to come too, so we waved them off at the gate. Their luggage weighed down the car so much that it barely scraped over the speed bumps.

Mum let me have a cup of coffee that morning. It was bitter and gritty, and the milk swam in pale, scaly puddles on its surface.

'Are they going to come back?' I asked.

Mum smiled. 'Maybe.' She reached out and smoothed the hair off my forehead with a dry hand, as if I were five years old again. For a second I imagined I could smell the stale, furry air of an airport, hear the roar of planes. I would hate to leave, but part of me wished I was going with them.

We got a call from my grandparents two days later—quavering, elderly voices that sounded far away. Hennie came on the line too, to tell me about playing football with the local boys on muddy fields, and to tell me about snow.

'It didn't settle,' he said, 'but we saw it falling.'

'Cool,' I said.

We started keeping a suitcase packed and ready to go in the corner of Mum and Steve's bedroom. It was called a Grab Bag, and every white had one—just in case we had to fly out in the middle of the night, like Auntie Mary and Uncle Pieter, or drive to Beitbridge or the Mozambique border. We were meant to fill it up with all the essentials and leave it alone, but we could not seem to stop packing it. Passports and important paperwork were in a box under lock and key in Mum's cupboard, also ready to grab in the middle of the night.

This suitcase was for things we could not bear to leave behind. It started sensibly—photo albums, some precious jewellery—and then became

230

steadily less so. Mum's ancient teddy bear, who was missing an eye and most of his nose, went in. My stuffed toy cat went in and out on a daily basis. In the mornings I put him in the suitcase, since I could not bear the thought of accidentally leaving him behind, and at night I took him back out because I felt sorry for him, alone in the dark. In the morning, back he went.

Mum was relentlessly cheerful, even more than usual. She jollied Steve and me along. She created meals out of whatever we were able to buy that week. She bought us chocolate from the petrol station whenever there was any for sale.

I managed to go to school almost every day that week. A friend's mother dropped me back home one evening.

'Mum? Mum!' I slammed the door and heard it echo through the house. I knew Steve was out that night, but Mum should have been there.

'Mum!'

The lights were all off. I switched them on as I went—the switches snicked, and the fizz and crackle of the fluorescent bulbs settled down into a steady hum.

I heard something from the lounge. 'Mum?' I could suddenly see in sharp focus, and the hairs on my arms rose up. I pulled a walking stick out of the tub by the front door and walked through to the lounge. There was a shape in one of the chairs. I flicked the light on. 'Mum?'

Mum was sitting in her bathrobe, surrounded by crumpled tissues, a glass, and a half-empty bottle of Scotch. She was pale and waxy, her nose a bright red spot in the middle of her face.

She turned her head to look at me. She was not

231

wearing her glasses, and her eyes had a naked, unseeing look. 'Oh, hello, darling.' Her voice sounded thick.

'What's the matter, Mum?'

Mum waved her hand. 'Oh, I'm fine.'

I touched her shoulder. 'Have you had anything to eat?'

'No. But I'm not hungry.'

I went into the kitchen. I did not know how to cook—I never had to learn—but it could not be too difficult to heat up a can of beans and frankfurters. I opened the tin and poured the orange gloop into a pan.

'Do you want some tea, Mum?' I called. There was an indistinct noise from the lounge which I chose to interpret as yes. I switched on the kettle. The beans started to bubble and I poured them into a bowl. They had crystallised at the bottom, but once I had stirred them around they looked pretty appetising—and Mum probably would not notice the difference.

I took through a tray and a cup of tea. She had tried to tidy herself up while I was in the kitchen— her hair was smoothed down and she was wearing her glasses again.

There was a white speck of tissue on the side of her nose.

'Thanks, treasure.' She sipped the tea. I perched on the arm of her chair.

After a while, 'What's the matter, Mum?'

'Oh . . .' She pinched the bridge of her nose. 'It's nothing, really, I'm just a little tired.'

I had never seen Mum cry properly before. For the first time, I looked at Mum and saw her as a person. I looked at her pale, freckled face and red-painted lips and saw her as someone else, removed from me. She was like any mother in Zimbabwe, in so many ways. She knew all the black-market places to buy forex and food. She could deal with snakes and spiders, even though they made her squeal. She did her best with the servants, she kept her sense of humour even in the worst situations, and she managed to get to her hair appointments even when there was rioting in the streets.

'Come on, Mum.' I wanted her to tell me.

Mum smiled and downed the rest of her tea. 'I called your grandparents today, that's all.'

'What did they say?'

'Oh, you know, the usual.' Mum took a spoonful of my concoction, but the spoon hovered in the air and did not move towards her mouth. 'They're getting old, so they worry. And it's so long since they lived here, they've forgotten what it's like. I've told them not to worry about us.'

'Okay.'

Sometimes I wanted to leave. There were lots of people who had gone already—to South Africa, England or even places as far away as Australia or New Zealand. 'They've gapped it,' or 'Rats deserting a sinking ship,' Steve said whenever we heard about someone else leaving. I did not want to be a rat, but if the ship was sinking I did not see any other option.

'Thanks for the tea,' said Mum. She looked like herself again, and I could almost forget the dark, silent shape in the chair.

'That's okay. Do you want me to run a bath? You can have it first.'

'No thanks. I think I'll just go to bed.'

'Okay.'

I had a bath that night. I left the lights off, and sat in the hot water staring out of the window at the scudding clouds and the wild thrashing of the trees in the wind. I could hear the television from the bedroom—first the drums of ZBC, then the dramatic, film-score music of CNN and SKY, then the BBC. I saw myself from above, sitting in the cooling water, as if I was remembering myself from somewhere far in the future, safe on another shore.

I knew that Mum wanted to leave. 'We can't just sit here and wait to be killed,' she said to me. 'We have to make sure we have somewhere to go. We need to get the ball rolling. If I could just get over there, I could make a start.' She did not say these things to Steve.

I heard her on the phone to my grandparents, when Steve was out. She half-covered the phone with one hand, as if her voice could escape and betray her. 'I can't,' she said, and 'Not just yet.' I pretended I had not heard.

'I've booked a ticket to England,' she said at dinner one evening.

Steve looked up from his shepherd's pie and chewed while he looked at her. He swallowed. 'What?'

'I've bought a ticket,' she said. 'Just to see Mum and Dad, and Pieter and Mary.'

Steve picked up another forkful. 'And when were you planning to tell me?'

'I'm telling you now.'

'*Ja*, well.'

'I leave next Monday.'

'What about work?'

'I've already got time off.'

234

Steve stared at Mum, then pushed his chair back. 'So Mark Cooper doesn't mind?'

'No.'

Steve took his plate into the kitchen. I looked at Mum. It felt strange. Mum had made plans that did not include me or Steve.

'Is there anything you want me to bring back?' asked Mum.

I knew that she would stay with my grandparents, and I thought that she would probably be investigating places for us to live. That was what we did. There was always a back-up plan, always an escape clause.

At the airport she looked young and excited. 'I'll phone you when I get there.' She even smiled at the men with rifles who guarded the gate. One twitched his lips a little, but the other kept staring straight ahead.

As we hugged I smelled her perfume.

'Bye, treasure.'

'Bye, Mum.'

She walked through the gate. She was wearing jeans and a long-sleeved sweater, even though it was thirty degrees, so that she would be warm when she stepped into winter on the other side.

Steve and I went up to the observation deck to watch. The plastic chairs were scaly and on the table in front of me was a white plastic cup ringed with old lipstick. Everything smelled of cigarettes.

'Look.' Steve pointed. 'There she goes.'

The Air Zimbabwe plane pointed its nose up and took off. Out of the country.

'Come on.'

We went back downstairs. The airport looked even dirtier and shabbier. And outside, the sun

235

made everything flat and hard.

On the way home, we passed groups of black people walking or resting by the side of the road. War Vets? Or workers leaving the farms? They looked too tired and defeated to be War Veterans, but it was difficult to tell.

Steve grunted as if he were about to say something, but when I looked at him he was staring straight ahead. Steve and I had never been alone before, and Mum would be gone for two weeks.

That night I dreamed of tobacco. I was walking through a field of giant plants, their smooth, blade-like leaves arching over me and blocking out the sky. I felt a terrible heat and saw flames tearing through the leaves. I smelled burning. I smelled cigarette smoke.

I woke up to a warm rush of liquid which quickly turned clammy, and a rich, yeasty smell. I reached my hand down between my legs and felt the dampness. I could not believe it. I had wet the bed.

I turned on my bedside light and stripped back the blankets. They were damp and embarrassing. I could not let Steve see this. I changed my pyjamas, took off the bedclothes in one damp, ungainly bundle and threw them into the washing machine.

Would Steve wake up if I turned it on? I had to risk it.

Back in the bedroom, I remade the bed. The red light of my clock blinked at me—half past four in the morning. Just two more hours of sleep before school.

Steve and I had long-distance, crackly conversations with Mum. She called us, not the other way around, because phone calls were so expensive. We heard about how pretty it was in England, how clean, how easy.

'The supermarket shelves are full,' said Mum. 'And there's petrol at every station. And no queues.'

'*Ja*, well,' said Steve.

'Mum and Dad don't even lock the doors when they go out,' Mum said.

'That's a stupid idea,' said Steve.

'The point is, Steve, that it's a safe place.'

'Too many bluddy people,' said Steve, which was strange, because there were millions and millions of people here, swarming like worker ants in the cities. I thought Steve meant there were too many bluddy white people. I wondered what it would be like to be just another white person, rather than a White with a capital W.

We picked up Mum from the airport. She hugged us and said she was happy to see us, but I could tell that she was sad to be back. She smelled different, of English washing powder and new perfume.

She brought out a picture of the house she was planning to buy for us in England. It was a grey box against a grey sky. 'It's lovely inside,' she said.

We watched BBC World and saw the War Vets taking over another farm. The chief War Vet pounded his fist against his palm, shouting so loudly at the old white farmer that little globs of spittle flew on to the camera. But the old man said nothing. He was nothing special—he could have been anyone, someone we knew. His face was blank as he listened to the shouting, his head tilted to one side.

Some of the farm workers defended their Baas

and Medem against the War Vets and got beaten for their pains. Mum and Steve would not let me look at the pictures on the international news channels, but I saw some of them anyway—heads with blood and flesh blossoming like roses from their temples, faces that were all bruise. The foreign journalists came in for a kicking as well.

I thought of the dark glow of the floor that Saru polished every day, rain thundering on the roof, the sharp smell of morning and the blue bowl of the sky overhead. Was living here worth the danger?

'We're not going,' Steve kept saying. 'Not yet.'

CHAPTER TWENTY-THREE

We followed the plan. The plan had been stuck up on the walls of the offices for months, complete with numbers to call, places to hide and supplies to bring. There were even little diagrams of how the farm managers were meant to deploy themselves. It was like a miniature campaign map.

Although no one really thought we would have to use it.

I came with Mum to work most days now, as school was often cancelled or it was too dangerous to drive into town. I was filing invoices in the office when we heard a crackle on the radio.

'Come on,' said Mum, picking up her handbag and a file bulging with papers.

'What's happening?'

'War Vets on the farm.'

My hands and feet felt suddenly cold. The tip of

Mum's nose turned white. We packed up our papers and Mum drove the car up the dirt road to Ian's house. Ian was one of the farm managers and his house had been chosen as the Safe House because it was so far away from everything, up on the *kopje*. It was surrounded by granite rocks that looked like the great bald heads of gods, with long grass making comical tufts over their stone ears.

'Hello, hello, howzit,' said Ian when we arrived, ushering us in. He had his rifle slung over his shoulder and a Castle Lager baseball cap on his head. His wife was inside, laying out trays of sandwiches. The atmosphere was brittle, fear shimmering in the air like a heat haze. Mum went straight to Steve, who stood looking out of the window.

'Oh good, you're here,' he said when he saw us.

'Have you heard anything?' asked Mum.

'Just that they're heading up to the farmhouse,' said Steve. He had a grin on his face that did not seem to belong there. It hovered like a pale moth in front of his sun-reddened skin.

The wives and children of the farm managers were inside the house, as well as the other female office workers. The children played in the corner while the adults stood around the food table with drinks in their hands and talked in low voices. Whenever there was the crackle of a radio, everyone fell silent, even the babies.

'Where's Mark?' someone asked.

'At the homestead, I think,' said Ian. 'He knows they're coming.'

We had all heard the stories of what the War Vets did when they came to 'talk'. Mr Cooper's perfect Shona and easy smile would not help him then. I looked out of the window. The trees up on the *kopje* were blackened and scarred. Lightning was attracted to granite, and this was the highest point on the farm.

After about an hour, we heard the sound of an engine coming up the hill. Ian went to the door with his gun.

'It's just Lettuce,' he said. The room relaxed. Ian went to meet Lettuce, who was riding his motorbike barefoot.

'The Vets are going up to the Coopers' place,' said Ian when he came back in. 'But Mark has hidden. He's not going to meet with them today.'

'Good,' said several people.

'Where is he hiding?' asked Mum.

'In the generator shed,' said Ian.

We all imagined Mr Cooper crouched down in that hot metal shed, his ears filled with the thrumming of the generator. How ridiculous if they found him. He would have to crawl out of there into the crowd of War Vets, blinking in the sunlight, shading his eyes with his hand. And no one knew what they would do to him if they found him. Sometimes they talked. Sometimes they beat the farmers up. You could never be sure.

'I did find this *skellem* wandering around the farm, though,' said Ian, pushing Sean into the room. There was a rush of relieved conversation as everyone tried to touch Sean and ask if he was all right.

He shrugged them off. 'Leave me alone, sha.'

'Sean!' I waved to him, and he came over. 'You all right?'

'*Ja* man, of course.'

'You weren't at home?'

'No, I was out on the bike till Lettuce told me everyone was here.' He sat down on the floor and folded in on himself, drawing his knees up to his chest.

'Have you seen your dad?'

'Nah.' He picked at a scab on his leg. 'But he'll be fine, hey.'

Conversation died down, and we sat in silence. Dozens of whites in the thatched house on the *kopje*, pale and waiting. After a while the novelty wore off. I wanted to go home. I was almost willing to risk the War Vets just to end the tedium, and I could see Mum thinking the same thing.

When Lettuce toiled up the hill again, he told us that the War Vets were angry that no one came to talk to them. The workers refused to tell them where the farm managers were hiding.

I started to worry. 'Mum, what if we can't get home tonight?'

'We will.'

'But what if we can't?'

'It'll be fine.'

'But what if it isn't?'

'For Christ's sake.' Mum was exasperated. 'It'll be fine, all right?'

I sat still. The radios crackled every few minutes. A farm manager, checking in. Nothing from Mr Cooper.

'I can't believe he's still hiding in the generator shed,' said Mum.

The sun set over the granite hills and the sky turned pink. A hyena whooped in the distance. Ian's dog barked back, standing on trembling legs, ready to run away if his bravado produced any results. Mosquitoes started to bite our ankles. Ian's wife closed the fly-screens on the windows and doors, but it did not help much. It was too hot to close the doors and windows properly, and the air smelled of night-time, faint wafts of it blowing away the hot, dusty smell of day.

When the first stars spilled like grains of sugar, Lettuce appeared again. 'They have gone, sah,' he said to Ian.

'You sure?'

'Yes, sah.'

Mr Cooper's voice crackled over the radio. He was out of hiding. He laughed a static laugh. Everyone in the lounge straightened up and stretched. My foot was asleep. I did not realise it, but I had been sitting in the same position for hours. My toes tingled into life. Everyone else seemed to have the same problem, because there were groans when they stood up. I looked at my nails and saw that one of them was bitten right down to the half-moon.

Steve drove us home. 'We're going to stay in Harare for a while,' he said.

As we passed through the big iron gates of Cooper Farms, I saw something out of the corner of my eye. A dark mass, like a cloud too heavy for the sky, hovering over the farm. When I turned my head, however, it was gone.

Steve drove us to Harare in the dark. I watched the pools of light from the streetlamps flare and fade.

'Are you going to work tomorrow?' I asked Mum and Steve.

'*Ja.*'

'They won't come back?'

'We'll see what happens tomorrow, hey.'

We drove under the Independence Arch. In the dark it was a white fish leaping over the road.

We stayed in a hotel room in Harare. The air was clean and dry; the weather was mild; the sky thin and pale. I hardly ever saw an ant. My dishes and clothes were cleaned by a machine rather than black hands. It felt like leaving Chinhoyi all over again. Even the sun was not as hot there; by the time it got past all those buildings it was tired out, and we only had a little patch of grass to soak it up. There was no smell of hot earth, manure and cooking fires. Instead, everything smelled of petrol and cut grass.

'How long do we have to stay here?' I asked Mum.

'Agh, not long. Just until this blows over.'

The men at the farm were tall, blond and strong. They came into Mum's office and stood with their legs far apart, pulling their broad-brimmed hats off and wiping their foreheads with them. Whenever there were parties at the farm, everyone got splendidly, spectacularly drunk. It was a point of pride to wake up somewhere incongruous, like face-down in a paddock, or leaning up against a banana tree, or at the wheel of your car. They kept in constant touch by radio. They carried guns in their car. I could not imagine them being beaten by the War Vets. I remembered my uncle as he looked to me when I was young—a man as tall and solid as a baobab, unbreakable. A man who could kill a kudu and a snake, who commanded hundreds of men and could shoot a can clean off the wall with one shot from a BB gun. These men were indestructible. I could not imagine them being cowed.

243

'Bluddy Kaffirs,' said Ian the following night. He had invited the farm managers and their families to drinks at his house. We sat on his verandah looking out over the granite *kopje*, sipping drinks with ice. The maid was clearing plates as he said this. We all flicked our eyes from him to her and back again, but said nothing. Ian looked drunk. He swayed in his seat and his eyes were bloodshot.

'Tell you what I'm going to do,' he said suddenly, sitting up. 'I'm going to pack up everything and leave, and before I go I'm going to stuff this house full of explosives. Then I'm going to hang the Rhodesian flag on the roof and set up a radio to play the Rhodesian national anthem over and over. Then when the bluddy War Vets come to possess the land they'll fire at the house and blow themselves up.' He cackles. 'Bang! Bits of black everywhere.'

'Ian,' murmured his wife.

'I'm not bluddy going to, don't worry.' He sank back into his chair and sighed noisily.

*   *   *

The War Vets did not return. A week later, it felt like nothing had happened at all. I went to the farm with Mum every day—somehow it felt safer to stay together.

It was still day, but the light had the flattened, pastel look of early evening.

'You ready to go?' Mum asked.

'*Ja*.' I started packing up.

There was a crackle on the radio, and a voice. Mum picked it up. '*Ja?*'

She listened. 'Okay. Yes, we'll go now.' She

turned to me. 'Leave that stuff. We've got to head off now.'

'Why?'

'War Vets,' she said briefly.

'Are they coming here?'

'I shouldn't think so.' Mum swung her handbag on to her shoulder, picked up her keys. 'Come on.'

'Why shouldn't you think so?' I did not move.

'We would have heard something.'

'But they just told you.'

Mum sighed. 'Look, they're just on the road. Don't make a big fuss, okay? We'll be fine. We just need to get going.'

She seemed calm. Exasperated, but calm. I followed her out of the door and into the car.

'Here, hold this.' She gave me the radio; a black brick with a long aerial that telescoped in and out.

'What do I do with it?'

'Nothing, just hold it.'

I rested it on my legs as Mum ground the car into gear. We set off down the dirt road.

'Anything from the radio?' Mum asked.

'No.' Just the odd bit of static, like someone tearing open a bag of crisps in the cinema.

The shadows from the blue gum trees lengthened. We were almost at the main road. My head had been hurting since we left the office and intensified until there were little dancing tadpoles in front of my eyes. The sky became purple and warped.

Everything around us blurred, but I saw the pebbles on the road in sharp focus.

'Mum!'

'For Christ's sake, what is it now?'

'Mum, stop. Pull over.'

245

'No. I told you, we need to get moving.'

'Mum!' I tried the door handle. My fingers felt fatter than normal. I could not get it open.

'What the bluddy yell are you doing?' Mum pulls over. 'What's the matter?'

The pain in my head became a throb. When it pulsed, the sky changed colour. 'Please Mum, just stop for a bit.'

'Fine.' Mum switched off the engine, and we sat in silence until my head calmed down.

'Sorry, Mum.'

'You okay now?'

'Yes.'

'All right.' She switched the engine on and pulled out into the road in a cloud of dust. We reached the intersection with the main road and were about to turn right when Mum stopped.

'God. What's that?'

A crowd of fifty or sixty people, men and women, carrying placards and singing. Heading towards the next farm over.

A crackle from the radio. 'War Vets on the airport road.'

'*Ja*, thanks,' said Mum. 'Good timing.'

We watched the crowd move further away. If we had driven out five minutes earlier, we would have been right in the middle of them. My stomach seemed to drop out of my body when I realised this.

'Well,' said Mum, 'that was lucky.'

We turned into the road, and played the radio as loud as we could, all the way back to town.

Mum got a phone call the next morning. Her hand on the receiver was white, and it took her two attempts to replace it. 'I'm not going in to work today,' was all she said.

'Why?'

Mum walked through into the kitchen.

'Why, Mum?'

She leaned on the kitchen counter.

'What happened, Mum?'

She turned around and spoke normally. 'You know the de Bruijns?'

'Yes.' The family on the neighbouring farm. I had not met them, but I knew they were good friends of the Coopers.

'Well, their farm was invaded yesterday.'

I waited. I knew there was more. Mum teetered on the edge of it for a minute, then left the room. I was left with her half-said sentence hanging in the air like a breath.

*   *   *

Mum and Steve talked in their room later, once I had gone to bed. I sneaked down the corridor a little way, just enough to hear.

'Raped . . . kids watched, apparently.'

'And the dogs?'

'They think it was done with a *bhadza*.'

I went back to bed and wriggled my cold feet into a still-warm part of the bedclothes. Pictures hung in my mind like washing on a line. As I started to fall asleep, the washing line became real, and I could hear Saru humming as she lifted each image from the basket and pinned it on to the wire. The farmer's wife with her skirt up around her hips and her thighs laid bare like peeled bananas. The dogs with their throats cut, oozing sluggish blood on to the brown grass.

It was a slow, sick disintegration of a way of life. No one knew what to do. Not my teachers, not my parents. My grandparents called from England every night. Are you okay? Are you hanging in there? I knew they were asking us to come over. I could feel them wanting it down the phone line, but I did not want to go.

Mum and Steve finished a whole bottle of gin that evening. They finished a whole bottle of gin almost every evening those days.

CHAPTER TWENTY-FOUR

When the War Veterans came back, they came officially and without any weapons that we could see. They came without warning, after another week of nothing at all. Smiling, they waved at the workers they passed. Some of the workers waved back. Some of them did not.

Mum and I were on the farm when they arrived. Neither of us told Steve I was still coming to the farm. As far as he knew, I was at school. He left for the farm before sunrise each morning, and so he did not see Mum and I piling into the car at eight o'clock every day. Mum did not want me to leave the office, even just to sit outside, but she had given me my own cellphone now and reminded me to keep it charged and to carry it everywhere I went. Just in case.

'Mum.' I saw the War Vets out of the window.

'It's an official visit,' said Mum. 'There won't be any trouble.'

She carried on with her work. My hands felt cold

and numb. We had seen these men so often on the news. My stomach and bowels seemed to melt into an oily mess, and I ran to the toilet and shut myself in, listening to the crackle of the radio next door.

'Are you all right?' Mum called.

'*Ja.*'

I did not have any control over my body. Everything that was inside rushed out, and left my legs trembling and my teeth chattering. I curled my legs up so I was sitting on the toilet with my arms around my knees and tried to stop my body spasms. Outside the little window I could hear voices, the rumble of tractors and the clank of machinery.

'Are you okay?' Mum called again.

'*Ja*. I said I'm fine.'

I flushed the toilet and watched the water whirlpool down. I knew exactly where it all went, to the septic tank just outside the offices which clogged up every other week. I wished it was that easy to get rid of my fear.

'Come on, man,' said Mum from outside the door. 'They're here.'

I came back into the office and sat next to Mum. She clasped my hand and I could feel her bones underneath papery skin.

One of the War Vets saw us through the window, and waved. His teeth flashed white in his face. I felt my stomach lurch again, shamefully, and something hot rushed out of me.

'Shit.'

Mum let go of my hand. 'What?'

I was too embarrassed to tell her.

A bird flew into our house once. A thrush. It panicked and started banging against the walls and

249

windows, trying to get out, and left a trail of sticky white-and-green behind it. I felt like that bird. But I did not want to admit that I was scared. We were all pretending that we could cope, that we would be fine. If anyone did say they were scared, they were called a bluddy sissy.

'Nothing,' I said, and went back into the toilet. I took my pants off, rinsed them clean and threw them into the bin. I would just have to deal with it. Besides, there could not be anything left to come out.

Mr Cooper called the farm managers together and met the War Vets in one of the offices. He looked relaxed in a white shirt and shorts, the kind of thing he would normally wear for a day on the farm.

We watched the group of men walk in. They were not threatening us—not at the moment—but we knew that they were the most powerful people in the country. One of them nudged another and pointed to a piece of farm equipment, saying something in Shona. The other laughed. They seemed calm, and they were not hopped up on *mbanje* or *dagga*, drugs that fuelled bloodlust. Not yet.

'Mum,' I nudged her. 'Is that Jonah?'

She peered into the crowd. He was standing near the back, laughing with another man.

'*Ja.*'

Jonah looked up at the office window, and Mum and I ducked away. I had a superstitious fear that he had seen us somehow, that he had cursed us.

One of the farm managers described it to us afterwards. The War Veterans reclined on their chairs, taking up as much space as they could.

250

They spread their legs, rested their arms along the backs of the chairs, put their feet up on the tables, and yawned widely and without covering their mouths as if they were going to swallow up thc whole room.

Mr Cooper had a translator who sat beside him and turned the rapid Shona into English, leaving out most of the insults and asides. Mr Cooper kept his face impassive as the War Vet leader talked, spurring him on to even greater obscenities. Then, after a Shona question was left hanging in the air, he opened his mouth and responded in fluent, perfect, colloquial Shona.

After a moment of wide eyes and raised eyebrows, the leading War Vet started to laugh. So did the others. They laughed and smiled and clapped each other on the shoulders as if Mr Cooper were a great friend of theirs who had done some wonderful trick. For a moment the atmosphere in the room was almost warm. You could imagine them buying him a drink. But it dropped away, and the chief leaned across the table with a yellow grin.

'You have ten days,' he said, 'and then we will be coming.'

They left, but they did not go far. They camped in fields on the outskirts of the farm, near the ZANU PF camp that Cephas had joined. I wondered if he would be absorbed into the War Vets, or whether he had already escaped.

'Is Mr Cooper going to leave?' I asked Mum.

Mum shrugged. 'I don't know.'

'What about us?'

'We follow the plan,' said Mum.

There were two photocopied sheets of A4 paper

on the wall of Mum's office. Someone had typed out 'CRISIS SITUATION' in big capital letters, and drawn a picture of a little man with his hands up in surrender.

The first sheet was titled 'Under Siege'. There were steps listed underneath. Phone task force member immediately. Inform the task force member who is in your house. Are they armed? How many are there? What is their attitude? Your task force will call the police. Inform the rest of the farm and call a code. Deploy task force and have other volunteers on stand-by.

The second sheet of paper listed the different codes that could be called out over the radio. Code green meant 'Everything is fine, stay put. Go back to normal. The situation has calmed down.' It was a mint-green digestive tablet, soothing everything. Code yellow meant 'Everyone on alert. Stay near the radio. Not sure of the situation and waiting for confirmation.'

Code red was printed in red. It meant we must evacuate immediately and meet at the airport, because people were injured, a house was under siege, and the situation was life-threatening. There was a list of things to do: find out where the trouble is and take the safest route out; get your family to the airport; wait to find out what has happened and whether you can get back. There was also a note reminding us to take cash for the car park. I could imagine Mum calmly counting out notes from her purse before driving us both there.

When Mum and I got back to Harare, Steve was furious. 'This is what she's missing school for?' he said. 'So she can go get killed by War Vets?'

'We didn't know they were coming today,' said Mum.

'Neither of you should be there.'

'You're there.'

'That's different. I can take care of myself.'

Mum nodded, but her eyes were remote.

'You need to leave. Tell Mark Cooper he can find someone else to do his bluddy books. It's too dangerous.'

'It's fine,' said Mum. 'Everything is under control.'

'These Kaffirs aren't reasonable people,' said Steve. 'These bluddy War Vets don't care about anything but getting the whites off the land. They're high on *dagga*. They won't care if you own the farm or not.' He took a pinch of Mum's skin, near the top of her arm. It went pink under his fingers. 'You're the wrong bluddy colour. That's all that matters.'

'The situation's not bad enough to stop going there.'

'So what do you want to happen? You're waiting for someone to get killed?'

'Of course not, Steve. We have to keep things running. Otherwise they've won, and we might as well give them the farm now.'

'We? It's not our bluddy farm. I'm not having my family killed so that Mark Cooper's farm stays afloat.'

'What about the workers, hey? They live on the farm. They have families to feed.'

'You're not going back there.'

Mum left the room. We all knew she was going back. What's more, we all knew I would go with her.

Steve opened one of his old books. 'Nothing changes, man,' he said. 'It's time you learned that. You and your Mum. Mark Cooper isn't indestructible, you know.'

Neither Mum nor I told him about seeing Jonah in the crowd. We both knew that it would only make things worse.

Another man was killed on a farm near the Coopers'. Several more were beaten. I was not meant to know these things, but I could not help it. The knowledge of what was happening seemed to pass from white to white at impossible speed, as if we were all connected by lines that quivered with each new attack. Every white we talked to seemed to be suffering from headaches those days.

When I got home from school, dropped off by a friend's mother, Mum and Steve were waiting for me. I took my backpack off slowly, unwilling to hear what they had to tell me.

'Do you want a drink?' said Mum.

'Okay.'

She poured me a Diet Coke with ice. I sat down.

'It's about Sean,' Mum says.

'What happened?'

'He's fine.'

'But what happened?'

Sean had been picked up from school by a man he thought was one of his father's drivers. It was an easy mistake. Slipping into that back seat, head full of rugby scores, homework and what-I'm-doing-on-the-weekend, he saw the black face in the rear-view mirror. And if he did not recognise him, well, there were always new workers.

The car seemed to be heading back to the farm, but pulled down a side road unexpectedly. Sean was probably suspicious. He was a farmer's son, a BB-gun killer-of-pigeons, a Shona-speaking, barefoot, Bush-savvy, tough kid. Alarm bells would have gone off.

More men were waiting down the side street. They beat him almost unconscious. Sean was tall and broad for seventeen and had the beginnings of a beard, but he could not hold his own against four or five guys.

'He put up a bluddy good fight,' said Steve. He told us that one of Sean's eyes was completely closed and that he needed stitches on the side of his head. Apparently he also had a broken rib.

'Are the Coopers staying?' I asked Mum.

'*Ja*, for now,' said Mum.

'Why is Sean staying after what happened?'

'He wants to.'

'And Mr Cooper is letting him?'

Mum shrugged. 'Sean will own the farm one day. I suppose Mr Cooper thinks he needs to be here.'

I remembered Mr Cooper coming to pick us up the day we saw the elephant. I remembered him clapping Sean over the ear, and telling him to be more careful, that being the Baas's son would not save him.

I thought of Sean as he was when I first met him. He seemed so much older than me, so grown-up and sophisticated. I remembered riding on the back of his motorbike, breathing in the smell of fresh sweat and cotton washed in Persil.

Lately, I had been amazed at my own ability to take anything that happened and turn it into normality, like skin growing over a scab, and I could already feel this new and horrible event being absorbed into all the others.

I would have told Kurai about this, but she had gone. She left me a knotted bracelet of her old braids, as a joke.

'I'll get a weave in the States,' she said. 'They can do it properly there.'

I wore them on my wrist. They were black and red, with little blobs of glue on the ends to keep them from unravelling. They smelled of Vaseline, and left a scraped, red lesion on my wrist. I did not loosen them, though. I thought I needed that reminder.

*   *   *

Ian, the man who said he would drape Rhodesian flags all over his house and blow it up before the War Vets could take it, left Zimbabwe. On his way back from a neighbouring farm he had been taken by the War Vets and beaten with a fan belt. After six hours, he was released. He came back to the farm with welts on his back, a grim mouth and shaking hands. He packed a couple of suitcases, booked tickets to Australia and told his wife to get the children ready to leave the next day.

'Don't be a bluddy sissy, man,' said Steve. 'Don't be a chicken.'

'Don't you bluddy tell me I'm a chicken,' said Ian. He had welts all over his face and neck. 'Don't you bluddy tell me. It's not worth it, man. I have two kids under five. It's not worth it for a piece of bluddy dirt.'

'*Ja*, well, send the kids to Harare. Stay here and fight the bastards.'

Ian looked old. The stubble on his jaw had

started to come through as grey hairs. 'This isn't a war we can win, man. I'm not watching my kids die at the hands of these Kaffirs. You stay if you want. I'm buggering off. Let them have the land, for all the good it will do them.'

Mum, Steve and I drove them to the airport. The kids played a clapping game in the back.

Ian and his wife were silent.

We drove through farmland and bush on the way to the airport—golden grasses on both sides. Ian had a basket of avocados on his lap.

'You know you won't be able to take that into Australia,' said Mum. 'They'll make you throw it away.'

'*Ja*, I know.'

The car smelled of warm avocado, a sweet, buttery smell like sunlight.

'Now can we go?' Mum asked Steve.

'Don't be stupid,' he said.

I wondered what it would take to persuade us.

CHAPTER TWENTY-FIVE

Again, we heard nothing for almost a week. Then we heard that the War Vets had invaded the Coopers' farm. They were killing the game for food.

'Mr Cooper got some death threats,' said Mum. She said it as if she were saying he got some bread at the supermarket. 'So he asked some of the other guys on the farm to stay at the homestead.'

'Does he have guns?' I asked.

'Don't be stupid,' said Mum. 'That would be

asking for trouble. He probably has them, but he's not going to shoot at these guys and get them angry.'

'Is he going to be okay? Is Sean all right?'

'They're fine so far. The Vets are just camped outside, *toyi-toyi*-ing. Like on Mary and Pieter's farm.'

I imagined Mr Cooper winning the War Vets over, as he won everyone else over. He would go out to them with his smile and outstretched hands, palms up, and talk to them in perfect Shona, complete with swear words and dirty jokes, and they would love him like everyone else seemed to. I wished I could believe my own lies.

Mum did not go to work that week, but kept in touch by phone. She worked on her computer at the hotel, muttering under her breath. If she was scared, she hid it well.

'I have to go back,' she said after a few days.

'Why?' I stared at her.

'Just to get some papers and things,' she said.

'Mum!'

'It's fine.' She seemed calm.

'You can't go.'

'It's no big deal,' said Mum. 'And I have to get that stuff out. I won't stay.'

'You can't go. Something might happen.'

'Nothing will happen.'

'Does Steve know you're going?'

'He doesn't need to know. It's not a big deal.'

Steve would not have let Mum go alone.

'I'm coming with you.'

'Like hell you are.'

'I'm not letting you go by yourself.'

'I'm a big girl,' said Mum. 'I survived the last

258

Bush War, didn't I?'

'Mum!' I could smell her perfume. She looked fragile, bird-boned. She could break with one snap. 'I'm not letting you go by yourself.'

Mum stared at me, and I stared back.

'Do you really need to get that stuff?' I asked.

'*Ja.*'

'Then I'm coming.' I hoped that this strange, superstitious bond our family had created over the last few months would hold true. We did things together.

Mum pressed her lips together. Then, 'All right,' she said. And she went to the kitchen to make us sandwiches to take for lunch. As if we would have time to eat them.

It is strange how invincible we still felt. It would never happen to us. It could never happen to me.

Mum took one of the rifles. 'I told Steve we should have bought a bluddy pistol,' she said, 'Something that would fit in the glove box.'

She laid the rifle along the back seat of the car. It took up the whole seat. 'Do you know how to use it?' she said.

'*Ja*, I think so.'

Mum gave me a quick tutorial. 'Then you just point and shoot. Okay?'

'Okay.'

'Not that we'll need it.'

We pulled out of the driveway.

'Have you heard anything from Mr Cooper?' I asked.

'*Ja*. Apparently things are okay. He took the War Vets out a crate of Castle Lagers, which kept them pretty happy.'

'Okay.'

259

'He says it should be safe enough. We'll go, pick up the stuff and come straight back. And if anything happens we'll just drive right through. We'll be fine.'

'Okay.'

The drive to the farm was just like any other. The heat haze shimmered trees and fences into streaks of colour. I saw a mirage on the road that moved with us, always staying one step ahead. We passed a jeep loaded with young men carrying rifles who laughed and waved at us. I did not know whether to wave back or avoid meeting their eyes, so I lifted my hand slightly and stared above their heads. I remembered the 'Sweet and Sour' game Hennie and I used to play back in Chinhoyi.

Mum played the easy listening station on the radio, and we argued over the channels like we always did. The air conditioning was on, but I wound down the window and gulped in the sweet-grass smell of the air. The sky arched above us, pure and holy and untouched, and it filled me with a strange serenity.

'Here we are,' said Mum when we turned into the farm driveway. There were no *piccanins* playing on the side of the road. There was not even any breeze in the blue gums. We could hear every stone thrown up by the tyres.

'Shit,' said Mum as one hit the windscreen, leaving a tiny cracked star.

When we reached the offices, we saw that there were no other cars in the car park. The roads were deserted, and the farm equipment was still and silent.

Mr Cooper was at the office when we got there. His arms were crossed and he was smiling, squinting into the sun. 'Howzit, girls,' he said as we got out of the car.

Mum had radioed him to tell him we were coming.

'Everything all right, Mark?' she asked.

'*Ja*. They're still saying I need to be out of there by tomorrow, but we haven't had too much trouble.'

Mr Cooper had a black eye and a cut on his head. We did not ask about them.

'Right, I'm going to head back up to the house,' said Mr Cooper. He put his hat back on. It was a broad-brimmed farmer hat and it made him look like a caricature. His eyes crinkled in a smile. 'Cheers.'

Mum looked for the file. I went outside and sat on the step, looking out at the white sandy earth and scrubby grass that passed for a lawn. I saw something moving in the grass and I squinted to make it out.

The snake lifted its broad, blunt head and stared at me. It had a long, tarmac-grey body and a flat, puppet-like line of mouth. We looked at each other. I felt the sun burning my back through my T-shirt.

I opened my mouth to say something to Mum, but no noise came out.

The snake swayed its head to the side, slowly. It gave me one last glance from stone eyes and I felt its cold-blooded spirit reach into my head. We were here before you. We will be here long after you have gone. And we do not much care what happens to you.

It stroked the grass back with its long body, and was gone. The sun was already reddening the back

261

of my neck and arms. I was pale and unsuitable, my feet soft and easily pierced by thorns. The ideas in my head did not work in this place which obeyed older, sterner rules.

'Got it,' said Mum, coming out of the office. 'Let's make a move.'

I did not tell her about the snake. We were about to get into the car—in fact, one of my legs was already half-in—when we heard a voice.

'Medem! Medem!' Lettuce ran up to us, panting and worried.

'Hello, Lettuce,' said Mum. She swung the keys from her finger in an impatient circle.

'Medem, where is the Big Baas?'

'He has gone back to the Big House,' said Mum. She half-turned, as if she were going to jump in the car. She seemed irritated. 'What's the matter?'

'Agh, I need to speak to the Big Baas, Medem.'

'I told you, he is at the house.' Mum wanted him to spit it out. 'What's wrong?'

'They are coming, Medem. The War Vets. There is big big trouble coming.'

Mum stopped jingling the car keys. 'Lettuce, go and find the farm managers and tell them, okay?'

Lettuce shook his head and turned away. He had tried to tell the Big Baas. It was not his fault that the Big Baas was not here.

'Come on.' Mum started the car. 'Get Mark on the radio,' she said.

'Mark?'

'Mr Cooper. Come on, use your brain.'

I fumbled for the buttons. 'I can't do it.'

'Here.' Mum took it, but before she could do anything there was a crackle on the radio.

'Mum, it's Mr Cooper.'

He was sending out a general SOS to all units. Mum turned the car around with a grinding noise and a cloud of sandy soil, and we started driving back.

'Mum!'

'It'll be fine,' she said. She held the wheel of the car in one hand and the radio in the other. She was talking to the farm managers. The car hiccupped over stones in the road.

'Mum, what can we do?' We were two women in an old car with an old rifle. 'Mum, we have to go home.'

'They say they're taking the house now,' said the farm manager on the radio.

'But he had until tomorrow!'

'*Ja*, well, these guys aren't fussed about that. They're hopped up on *mbanje*.'

'We're coming.'

'Hell, no, you guys should get out of here.'

But Mum accelerated up the slope to the farmstead.

'Mum, slow down! We're going to be the first ones there!'

We were almost at the homestead. Mum was still driving fast. We could hear drumbeats.

The electric gate hung off its hinges, and we stopped just outside it. I jerked forward and cracked my head on the windscreen.

'Mum!'

Mum was staring at something outside the window. Shumba was slumped on the ground like a stained rug. His spine was flayed open. There was a stain like oil on the sand of the driveway, but it was not oil.

'Mum?'

We heard shouts; loud voices, speaking in Shona, and laughter; something that might have been a gunshot. We saw the abandoned open-top jeeps parked haphazardly outside the gate; the cigarette butts in the driveway. We saw the broken French windows. The radio spat static, and died.

Mum started to struggle with the keys in the ignition, but her fingers were not working. They looked almost blue with cold. I could not help her, because I could not move.

'The Baas! Medem! The Baas!' Mr Cooper's new maid emerged from the bushes, where she had been crouching, and ran to us. There was blood on her apron. Mum rolled down the window. I was afraid of her, afraid of what she had to say, and I could see that Mum was too.

'Where is Mr Cooper?'

The maid's mouth flapped open, helpless. There was blood on her teeth. She moved her lips, but made no sound.

'Where is Mr Cooper?' asked Mum again. She did not wind down the window any further. She did not open the car door. I wondered if she felt, like I did, that we would be safe as long as we stayed inside the car. I knew it was not true, but I gripped my seatbelt to my chest all the same.

'The War Vets, Medem! They are inside the house!'

'Where is he?'

'He is dead, Medem! The War Vets!'

Blood in the dust. So much of it. Too much to have come from Shumba alone. The War Vets had not spotted us. I could smell urine, and I knew it was coming from me.

'Are you sure?'

'They shot him in the head, Medem!'

Mr Cooper. Dead.

I leaned forward and forced my cold lips to form the words. 'Where is Sean?'

'Sean?' She still seemed dazed.

'The Small Baas.'

'I do not know, Medem.'

'But he is here.'

'I have not seen him.'

Mum and I looked at each other. The maid began to scrabble at the handle of the back door.

'*Voertsek,*' said Mum.

'But Medem, they will find me. Take me to the village.' Her hands were curled into claws.

'We are not going to the village.'

The maid stared at us. Then she turned and ran down the road, clutching her skirts and kicking up the dust with bare feet.

Mum got the car started. Her hands shook so much that the keys rattled together, and she accelerated so hard that I felt my brain pressing back against my skull. We juddered over the gravel, reversed, and narrowly missed hitting the iron gate, which hung off its hinges. Mum could not keep the car steady and we wove across the road, skittering on the stones. We came to rest facing the right way. We sat breathing shallow breaths.

This happened in less than two minutes. I saw the red lights flashing at me from the clock on the car dashboard. As I watched, it clicked over from seven minutes after one to eight minutes.

'We have to go,' said Mum, but made no move to start driving again.

'Mum! Where's Sean?'

'Maybe he got away. I don't know.' She looked

at her hands on the wheel as if they did not belong to her.

'We have to find him.'

Mum looked at me. Her face was whiter than it had ever been. She looked colourless compared to the War Vets, a pale ghost.

'Elise, we can't go back there looking for him. You know that.'

Her mouth was shapeless, like a baby's when it is about to cry.

'But I know where he is.' I did, suddenly, with absolute certainty.

Mum drove around the property to the back fence, where the corrugated iron generator shed leaned up against the wall.

'We can't get in, the back gate is locked.' Her hands were still shaking so hard that they were a blur on the wheel.

'I can climb over.'

'No you bluddy can't.'

But I had opened the door already and climbed out. Mum reached towards me with a whispered scream—'Elise!'—and her face seemed to collapse in on itself. I had never seen her so frightened.

I climbed the wire and lifted my legs carefully over the barbed wire at the top. My jeans were wet with urine, but there was no time to feel embarrassed. I jumped down into the perfectly mowed, squeaky clean grass and ran to the door of the shed. It opened with a clang, loud enough to make my stomach churn.

At first I thought I had made a terrible mistake. The shed looked empty.

'Sean?' I whispered, and the echo gave it back to me. I could see nothing at first, but my vision adjusted and I thought I could make out a shape in the corner.

'Sean?'

I heard a breath, a tiny one, hardly enough to fill anyone's lungs. I moved closer and saw a brief shine of yellow hair. He was sitting with his knees drawn right up and his head resting on them. The bones on the back of his neck stood out like knuckles on a clenched fist.

I touched him on the arm. 'Sean, we've got the car. We need to go.'

He looked up. He hardly seemed to understand what I was saying.

'Come on.' I hauled him up by the elbow and led him outside. In the sun I saw that he had a cut on his head and a sprinkling of blood decorated the shoulders of his white T-shirt like colourful dandruff.

Mum still had the engine running. '*Kurumidzai!*' she said. 'Come on!'

Sean climbed over the fence as if he were sleepwalking. We could hear shouts and the sound of drums coming from the other side of the farmstead.

'Get in, get in,' Mum said over and over. I pushed Sean into the back seat and pulled a seat belt across him. Mum gave me a clumsy, one-armed hug, her wet cheek against mine, and then accelerated again with a lurch. I could hardly see out of the windscreen. Mum hummed under her breath, a mad, high-pitched tune that I did not recognise.

It did not feel like the car was moving. It felt like one of those dreams where you are running away from a monster and your legs do not work. I saw the speedometer, though, and we were driving dangerously fast.

When we left the farm gates Mum swerved off the road on to the long grass of the verge.

We clung to each other. Her cheek felt cold against my face. I did not know how long we stayed there, but we were both shivering and our teeth were chattering as if we were freezing, although the sun beat down and turned the car into an oven.

'Why were you saying the Lord's prayer?' Mum asked me afterwards. I didn't even realise I had been saying it. I asked her why she had been humming.

'I was humming?'

My legs were red and chapped from urine. The car stank. In the back, Sean was white and silent.

And finally, we had found a reason to leave with which not even Steve could argue.

CHAPTER TWENTY-SIX

Shumba was dead, that big floppy Labrador that I took for walks around the farm. Mum tried to hide the pictures in the paper from me, but I knew that his throat was matted with dark liquid and gaping with a pink, vulnerable hole. I remembered the snake we killed all those years ago in Chinhoyi.

And Mr Cooper was dead.

I found these pictures, too. His head had been split open like the mangoes I used to eat naked in the bath, in case I got their sticky juice on my clothes. Mum would cut them in half for me so they were open like wet mouths, and I would suck them and pick their fibres out of my teeth. His head looked just like that, as if a second slobbering mouth was smiling out of his forehead. The blood ran down between his eyes and mingled with the fine red dust that traced the lines on his face. He still wore a faint smile. It was the expression he used to have when he was joking with the workers.

He tapped on the window at night. The wound in his head was black with blood, but his skin was white-green, pale and translucent. There was a faint smile on his face.

He smelled of wet earth after the rains. *Ngozi*. Ghosts of the wrongfully killed, looking for revenge.

'You have the wrong person,' I said to Mr Cooper's ghost. 'We didn't do it. Go and haunt the War Vets.'

He smiled and said something in Shona that I did not understand.

'Go and haunt Sean,' I said. 'He's your son. If you want someone to avenge your death, he's the one to do it.'

The wound in his forehead gaped wider.

'Why us?' I asked, but I knew I was not going to get an answer.

Sean stayed with us for a few days. He did not talk, but drifted around the hotel touching the walls with one hand, as if he would lose his way if he did not hold on to something solid. He smelled of cigarette smoke all the time, but I did not see him smoking.

'Thank you for having me,' he said after a few days. He was very formal. 'I think I'm going to go back now.'

'Are you sure? You can stay here . . .' said Mum.

269

'Don't be stupid, boy,' said Steve. 'Stay here.'

'No.' His fingers looked long and nervous as he fumbled with his cigarette. 'I have to go back. Who else is going to run the farm?'

'But the War Vets are still there.' And the blood, and the memories.

'There are still some farm managers who stayed on.' There was a criticism in his tone.

'We have to go.'

'*Ja*, well.'

'We do. We can't stay now. And you should go, too.'

Sean was scornful. 'Go where, man? You can't just switch this place off. You'll see.'

'Sean, you can't go back there.'

'Not straight away, maybe,' he said. 'But someone has to rebuild it when this is all over.'

His hands were shaking as he lit his cigarette. Mr Cooper's ghost cupped the flame in both hands to keep it from blowing out.

The murder was on the news that night. Seeing it on television made me watch through a different lens. Everything was distorted. Mr Cooper's body was under a tarpaulin, and we could not see it. The thirsty earth had drunk the blood from where he fell and there was only the faintest brown stain on the sand.

I started to shake when I heard the BBC news theme. An English accent told the story of the latest white farmer to be killed.

I thought of all the people around the world who would hear this on the news. I imagined them waking up, yawning, padding through to the kitchen in slippers and pouring a cup of coffee, then switching on the television to see this news item. Another white farmer dead in Zimbabwe. Oh dear. They would watch it the way we watched news from some far-off place. With vague interest, maybe. With indifference. It made me angry to think that someone could watch the news footage, hear a voice saying, 'Mark Cooper was killed on his Mashonaland farm this afternoon,' and just switch it off as if that could make it go away. Or perhaps it would not be on the overseas news at all. Perhaps it would just be another death added to the growing number.

At Mr Cooper's funeral, the church smelled of incense and worn clothes. We sat in the very front pew, next to Sean, staring at the coffin. It was smaller than I thought it would be.

People kept coming up to us and shaking Sean's hand. Their voices were low and they used the same words. Bluddy Tragedy. Murder. Brave. Revenge.

The first hymn started.

> The Lord's my shepherd, I'll not want
> He makes me down to lie
> In pastures green . . .

Mum gave my arm a pinch and I realised I had not been singing. I mouthed the words along with everybody else. Looking to the side, I saw Jonah, Mercy and the two girls. It gave me a shock to see Jonah. What was he doing here? He had joined the War Vets now, the same men who had killed Mr Cooper.

They were in their best clothes—no funereal black. Mercy wore bright orange silk with a frilly skirt and the girls were in white and pink. Some of the congregation gave them disapproving looks, but I did not think it was strange, because I knew that this was what Shona people wore to church, and they were honouring Mr Cooper with the finest clothes they could find.

Jonah did not sing. He stared at the Cross above the altar. At least, that was what I thought he was staring at until I saw the little opening shrouded in curtains, to the left of the Cross.

We sat with a great rustle of skirts and creaking of shoes on the polished floor. We listened to people talk about Mr Cooper.

When they had finished, the priest looked at Sean. There was an expectant pause, but Sean shook his head and sat, white about the mouth, while the congregation craned to see his face.

The priest's voice rose a little. It sounded as if he was building up to something. The curtains to the side of the altar twitched open and the coffin rumbled towards them on little tracks.

'Mum,' I whispered.

'Mmm.' She was staring straight ahead, her eyes red.

'What's happening?'

'He is being cremated.'

'What?'

The curtains opened. The coffin lumbered between them.

I tried not to imagine what was happening, but I could not help it. I had seen meat cooking at a *braai*, and I imagined Mr Cooper scorching and curling up like a piece of *boerewors*. I could not believe we were sitting around nodding gravely and weeping dignified snot into our handkerchiefs while someone burned in front of us.

The Shona believed that burning someone after they had died was wrong. It took a year for a spirit to leave the body and join its ancestors. This way, he was condemned to wander. We were sweeping him out of sight, like Saru swept dirt under the rug.

Jonah got up and walked out. Mercy, looking worried and apologising as she brushed past people, followed him, bringing the girls.

'Typical bluddy *munts*,' whispered someone behind us.

Jonah saw me before he left. He paused at the church door and looked back at me. His eyes were dark and unreadable. And then he left, walking out into the parched and sunlit world.

That night I had dreams about Mr Cooper being trapped in his coffin. I saw him, wide-eyed in the dark, scratching at the lid with his white fingers as the curtains opened and the flames took him.

I knew Jonah would have stopped it if he could.

We saw Sean again before we left. Not in person, but on the television. A woman in a blue suit held a microphone up to his face and nodded as he talked. Her hair did not move, even when she shook her head.

Sean looked thin, all elbows and knees. His hair stuck straight up, like a little boy's. I turned the volume down gradually as he talked, until he was mouthing silently. He looked like a fish swimming in the heat haze, gulping for air. Behind him I saw a gaggle of farm workers. Three of them stared at the cameras, hands hanging uselessly at their sides. One of them smiled and pointed. Look Mum, I'm on television. He made me smile, too, through my tears.

The week before we left, Mum and I both got

dysentery. We threw up every few minutes, so often that sometimes we had only just finished flushing the toilet when the next spew of vomit rumbled up and out. We could hardly walk. We clung with both arms to the porcelain as if we were drowning in the bathroom tiles. As soon as we had finished vomiting we drank as much water as we could, so that there was something in our stomachs to throw up and it was not just foul-tasting nothing, shuddering out of us in humourless Ha-Ha-Has.

It got so bad that Steve had to drive us both to the hospital. We took a bucket each in the car, the green ones that Saru used to soak the dirty cloths in. It was embarrassing, lugging our puke-filled buckets into the waiting room. I was still throwing up, even though there were people staring at me. I could not help it. The room filled with the humid smell of vomit, and the other people in the waiting room went green. The doctor hurried us through to his room before we made everyone sick.

'Pull down your *broekies*,' he told me. I was too weak and sick to care if he saw my bum or my privates, so I did as he told me. He jabbed a needle into my bum.

'Move your legs like you're riding a bicycle,' he told me.

The injection stopped the vomiting for a while, and when it came back it was not as violent.

We spent that week lying in bed drinking water and eating boiled rice. I stared at the ceiling while Mr Cooper's ghost tried to attract my attention from the bedside. He mouthed things at me that I could not hear, but I understood what he was trying to say. You do not build houses for them to be stolen and defiled. You do not raise children to die in the dust with an axe in their skull, unwanted, in a country that hates them.

Mum asked me what jacket I was going to wear on the plane.

'I don't know yet.'

'Well, decide.'

'Why do I have to decide now?'

'You just do.'

'Fine.' I chose one, and Mum took it away. She returned with it the next day.

'Here, put it on.'

The jacket crackled as I put my arms into it.

'Mum!'

'What?'

'My jacket's making a weird noise.'

'Put it back on.'

'But I'm hot.'

'Put the bluddy thing back on.'

'Why?' I was suspicious. I crunched a corner of the fabric in my hand, and heard that rustling again.

Mum sighed. 'I sewed US dollars into our clothes last night.'

'What?'

'You heard me.'

'But we're not allowed to take it out!'

'Why else do you think I'd sew it into the lining?' said Mum. 'Look, we'll be fine. Just act normally.'

Normally. I could not remember how.

My grandparents were excited. They called us every night to ask if we were still coming, if everything was ready, if we were sending boxes over yet. They did not talk about what happened on the farm, or what was happening on the other

275

farms.

There was no time to feel sad. We saved everything for the other side, when we would be miles away. We needed to get away from this place where there had been so much death.

Steve went back to the farm, taking a gang of friends and a stack of rifles in case of trouble, and collected our things. When he got back, he drove us out to a remote well and threw in his weapons. His old bayonets, his rifles. They juddered along the sides and fell into the water with a muffled splash and clang.

'Worth a fortune, some of them,' said Steve, but we both knew that was not the point. We could not take the guns with us, and we certainly could not leave them in the house to be found.

We said goodbye to Saru and Tatenda for the last time. Saru cried, not so much because she was going to miss us, but rather because it was hard to find a job when so many whites were fleeing. Mum promised to send some money. We gave them our address in England. We were lucky, to be able to leave. They were stuck here. I was relieved to be going, and guilty to be relieved.

We sat on the verandah for our last dinner, cobbled together from the odds and ends that were left in the fridge. I heard ice clinking in the glasses and the whine of the evening's first mosquito.

'Won't miss these buggers,' said Steve, slapping his arm.

Mum reached out and stroked Steve's shoulder. Her eyes were red and puffy.

A bird cried from one of the trees.

'Listen,' said Mum. 'The loerie.'

We heard the loerie every day. It was a

nondescript grey thing, with a haunting, high-pitched shout. 'Go 'way, go 'way!'

I had known ever since I could remember that the loerie was the Go-Away Bird. It only just occurred to me that its song could be any number of things—it depended on how you listened.

'Why is it called the Go-Away Bird?' I asked Mum.

'Because it says Go Away.'

'But . . .' I thought about it for a second, then remained silent. I thought it was significant that we had always heard it as 'Go Away', every day, all these years.

EPILOGUE

Madam Elise

Come see Beauty. She is very sick.

Rudo

And an address. The letter arrived just a few days before we were due to leave.

I had always meant to write to Beauty again. I kept her neatly written letters in a drawer. I saw wistfulness in them now, and I noticed the way the words sloped backwards like sad pairs of eyebrows. The shaky handwriting seemed brave, the exclamation marks little waving flags.

Mum drove me to the village where Beauty was living.

'Are you sure you're all right to go in?'

'*Ja.*'

'All right. I'll be waiting here.'

Beauty's niece met me at the door of the hut. She was tall, with fierce, dark good looks. I could tell she did not like me.

'Come inside.'

I followed her into the semi-darkness of the hut and through to a tiny bedroom. There were no curtains on the windows; instead, a batik was pinned up to block the angry sun.

Beauty was in bed. Thin, with skin like a pecan nut, brown and pockmarked.

'Beauty.'

She frowned and rolled her eyes. She did not seem to recognise the name.

'Her name is Rufaro,' said her niece. 'Rufaro Bvumbe.'

I never knew.

'Rufaro.' That seemed disrespectful, in a way Beauty never did. Or, at least, in a way I never thought it did. '*Mai*Bvumbe.'

She turned her head on the pillow. It was yellowed where her head had rested.

'Do you remember me?'

She licked her lips with a dry tongue.

'It's Elise,' I said. 'From the farm.'

She smiled and held out her arms.

Later, when we had cried and talked, Rudo gave me a bowl of *sadza*.

'Thank you, but I am really fine.'

She glared at me. 'Please, eat.'

She was insulted. Chastised, I dipped my fingers into the stodge and put it into my mouth. It was difficult to chew. Suddenly the whole idea of eating seemed impossible. I felt a moment of panic as the *sadza* lodged itself in my throat, but managed to force it down somehow.

Beauty had a plate of *sadza* and relish as well. She exclaimed loudly at how delicious it was and how Rudo had become so good at cooking meat lately and making it tasty. She dipped the same piece of *sadza* in the relish over and over, nibbling at it and making noises of appreciation. It was hard to watch her eating, or pretending to eat. When she finally stopped, Rudo took the full plate away quickly so we would not have to look at it any longer.

'That was very good,' said Beauty.

'Yes.'

We sat there for over an hour. Beauty slept for

most of that time. I think I slept too, for a few minutes, because I brought my head up with a jerk and felt frightened, for a second, at the time I had lost.

Beauty rolled her head towards me, and smiled.

'Do you remember my aunt?' she said. 'The one who was cursed?'

'*Ja.*'

'I think I have been cursed.'

'No.' I rested my hand on hers. 'You could not be.'

'The *N'anga* said you were cursed too,' she said.

I nodded. I did not know what to say.

'Our ancestors always bring justice,' she said and closed her eyes.

'Do you forgive me?' I said after a while.

'For what?'

And I did not know what I was apologising for. But I knew from the ache in my stomach that there was something, something unforgivable, that was my fault.

The night before we left, I dreamed that I hunted a *tokoloshe* one more time. I was back on the farm. I climbed out of bed and walked barefoot through our empty house.

The house was empty, but that was because the ghosts were all outside, under the pockmarked moon. I saw Sean sitting on the back doorstep, small and hunched. I saw my uncle wandering at the end of the garden, eternally lost, tapping his compass. I heard Mr Cooper's voice saying something in Shona that I could not understand. I saw Jonah stooping to tend the flowerbeds, Susan and Jane playing Catch around the vegetable patch, Mercy hanging out the clothes on a washing

281

line which glinted silver in the dark, Beauty kneeling to scrub the front steps. I saw Archie chasing phantom flying ants and the ghosts of moths. I smelled cigarette smoke.

We left so much behind. But the ghosts came with us.

I heard crickets. An owl. A faint crackle of wind in the top branches of the flamboyant tree. Sleepy clucking from the henhouse, where something had obviously disturbed them. Something running in the thick hedges. The rubbery flap of a bat above my head. The ground was dew-wet already, and I knew that thousands of insects were beneath my toes in the grass and in the earth. The air was full of night; of the shrilling of crickets, the sharp, tinny taste of blood, the sense that something is watching you.

I walked to the bottom of the garden, by the compost heap where the shrews and mongooses lived, under the tallest avocado tree. I stood on the overripe fruit that had fallen to the ground and I felt it squish between my toes. As I walked I knew the avocado meat was picking up bark, leaves, dirt and grass, coating my feet, and I was glad.

I stopped right at the end of the garden. This was where a *tokoloshe* would live. Quiet. Away from people. Near water. I wanted to see one before we left. I wanted to tell it why I was going, why I didn't have a choice. I knew it would not care or understand, that it lived in a different, older time with different, older rules that were as inescapable as gravity. It would not care what this white, maggoty creature thought. This interloper. This outsider. But I wanted to tell it anyway.

I wanted to tell it all the things I knew.

How I was exchanging the harsh, blood-red real world for something safer.

How, although I was white and bred for cold, I was as African as the chittering mongoose that lives in a world of snakes.

How I did not think I could live anywhere else.

I sat under the avocado tree and stared into its branches. I felt the world slow down and the air thicken. I heard the mosquitoes stop their shrill whine. I could hear the *tokoloshe* breathing, and I knew it was coming.

ACKNOWLEDGEMENTS

A book is a collaborative effort, really—I may have written it, but it would not be in this solid and bookish form without the help and support of many other people, to whom I am hugely grateful.

Vivien Green of Sheil Land Associates, my wonderful agent, for taking a chance on me and being an invaluable source of support and encouragement.

The team at Harvill Secker, particularly Liz Foley and Ellie Steel.

Professor Patrick Evans and the MFA programme at the University of Canterbury in Christchurch, New Zealand, who read the book as I wrote it and encouraged me along the way.

Rachael King, who has been my mentor and guide through the thick undergrowth of the publishing process.

Readers of my blog and 'real-life' friends for ongoing support online and off.

My parents, family and Zimbabwean friends (especially my darling Caroline!) for being so generous with their memories.

My husband David, who kept me sane.